NORDIC NIGHTMARES

The Best of Nordic Horror

Also Edited by
Margrét Helgadóttir
from Solaris

Nordic Visions:
The Best of Nordic
Speculative Fiction

NORDIC NIGHTMARES

The Best of Nordic Horror

Edited by
Margrét Helgadóttir

SOLARIS

First published in Great Britain in 2026 by Solaris,
an imprint of Profile Books Ltd
29 Cloth Fair
London
EC1A 7JQ

www.profilebooks.com

1 3 5 7 9 10 8 6 4 2

Printed and bound in Great Britain by
CPI Group (UK) Ltd, Croydon, CR0 4YY

A CIP catalogue record for this book is available from the British Library.

Our product safety representative in the EU is
BGC Sustainability & Compliance,
7 avenue du Général Leclerc, Paris, 75014, France
baldwinglobalconsulting.com

ISBN: 978 1 83786 857 5
eISBN: 978 1 80649 342 5

MIX
Paper | Supporting responsible forestry
FSC® C013604

CONTENTS

INTRODUCTION

As a child, I would often look under my bed and into my wardrobe before I dared to turn off the light for the night. The fear of the dark, or more precisely, the fear of the unknown dangers that might lurk in the dark, kept me awake for hours. An innocent pile of clothes on the floor could send me into spirals of anxiety because it resembled a hulking monster that, if I stared at it long enough, seemed to be moving towards me.

As an adult I can analyse and understand where this fear came from. I have learned that the dangers that aren't hidden, and the ones you encounter in bright sunlight are probably scarier. Nevertheless, the fear of the potential dangers that darkness might hide is something I haven't outgrown. I have learned to live with it. I've even written scary stories myself. But I know that if I read a really disturbing horror story before bedtime, the kind that sits in my subconscious for a long time, I might not be able to sleep that night.

And bless it, that is exactly what horror fiction does so well. Using frightening images, it pushes the boundaries of comfort and pokes at our deep-seated anxieties. But I wouldn't have it any other way. As Werner Herzog said, "What would an ocean be without a monster lurking in the dark? It would be like sleep without dreams." How dull life would be without the darkness balancing the light, or the chance to conquer your fears and grow.

What I learned when I edited the seven volumes in the anthology series *Fox Spirit Books of Monsters* (Fox Spirit Books, 2014-2020), was that people across all time, all over the world, have told scary stories. You can find traces of monsters and frightening creatures in ancient texts, architecture, art, in legends and myths, and even in old sea maps. Scary stories have served not only as entertainment and fun, or as a tool to keep children from dangerous situations, but they have also taught us how to listen to our instincts in situations when we feel something is wrong, when we need to make a crucial choice of fighting or fleeing.

In addition, we learn that no matter how critical the circumstances are, it's possible to survive, to escape, if we use our brains and willpower. Researchers also think that horror stories have a therapeutic function, that they could help reduce the anxiety we feel about events in the real world.[1]

So, in short, horror fiction matters. You should start reading it!

Beyond the fear of monsters, predators, and murderers, however, I think what sets off our adrenaline is a little bit different. It can be facing a lion on the savannah or

---

[1]David Robson: "'The paradox of horror': How scary films can soothe your anxiety'. Article in BBC 26 October 2025.

a serial killer in the car park. But it can also be a case of being trapped in an inescapable work situation or a marriage. And sometimes the true horror is finding out that there are things we can't explain, or escape—surely our biggest nightmare.

Your home base matters too. If you live on the coast, you might be more afraid of the storms out at sea or the great monsters of the ocean. If you live in a big city, you might be more afraid of crowds or of meeting people with evil intentions, maybe even fearing that they are possessed by malicious spirits. And of course, different horrors and fears will emerge from living in a war zone compared to a more sheltered region of the world.

What is frustrating is that even though we know about this multitude of cultures and ways of living, we have only been served a fraction of the world's stories for many years, with Hollywood as the major dominating channel for distribution. Which is sad. We love a good classical vampire story, but there are so many excellent tales from all over the world about terrifying creatures who hunt us solely for our blood. I would like to read those too! And yes, I know there are many authors who write excellent stories that build on cultures other than their own. But the risk of misunderstanding is high, and people might feel that their cultural heritage is being exploited or appropriated, and that their own version will never be heard or even known.

So, I am a strong believer that *who* tells the story is important. The choice of authors influences the stories that are told and how they are told. Anthologies are an excellent tool in this way: they are a wonderful opportunity to showcase many writers within the framework of one book. Anthologies will never be perfect, of course. Finding authors can be demanding. Sometimes they are simply not there; sometimes they may not have the time or even any interest in contributing. Not all authors like to write short stories either. Yet I feel very lucky as an editor. I've always been able to put together the anthologies I have envisioned.

Nordic Visions (Solaris, 2023) helped me get more speculative short fiction from my own region—the Nordic countries—out to the English-speaking world; *Nordic Nightmares* has provided an opportunity to narrow my focus on one of the genres presented in that first volume. It has been illuminating to investigate the murkier side of Nordic fiction and see how its typically dark humour and concerns about nature and wilderness are also reflected in the horror landscape of the region. In this volume I have collected a lovely sample of dark and scary stories from the Nordic countries of Finland, Denmark, Greenland, Iceland, The Faroe Islands, Norway, and Sweden. The majority of the stories are presented in translation, and I am forever grateful for the work the translators do, helping to bring our stories to the world.

The stories in this book are different in length, theme, and tone. Some are classical horror stories that will hopefully put terror in your heart. Others are perhaps not creepy in a "traditional" sense, yet they portray nightmarish situations that are horror stories in themselves, whether it is being in the middle of an inescapable volcano eruption, being trapped in a terrible marriage, or suddenly finding yourself in a confusing world where everyone seems to know you, but all you see are strangers. These stories may not provide the scares you expect, but they will hopefully make you reflect on the characters' horrifying situations.

* * *

WHILE WORKING ON this anthology, I have pondered the status of horror fiction in the Nordic countries, which is not easy to categorise with certainty. Suspense thrillers for children and young adults appear to be quite common in the region; thrillers and crime novels for adults too. Many readers are familiar with authors such as John Ajvide Lindqvist or Yrsa Sigurðardóttir. The Nordic region does indeed have lots of unsettling, scary, and disturbing literature. It looks like it often leans towards darker psychological dramas, horror that rises from being isolated, or from trying to survive in the harsh winters and the winter darkness, or stories portraying the terror that roams the mountains or dwells in the deep oceans.

In general, the horror genre appears to me to be more on the fringes. Maybe pure horror is a harder sell for Nordic publishers, like it often is for the other speculative genres. Sometimes it's marketed as a thriller or literary novel, despite containing several distinct elements of horror, even supernatural components. It might not be a conscious choice either, but related to the Nordic style of writing; I find that—in addition to their play with the weird and surreal—many Nordic authors mix elements from different genres into their work, making it difficult to place their writing strictly within specific genre boundaries.

That said, things are gradually moving to bring horror out from the cold in the Nordic publishing landscape. The genre seems to be blossoming in Finland, Sweden, and Denmark, countries where you'll also find several short story authors working within the speculative genres. In Greenland there is an attempt to engage more young people in writing, but it hasn't quite stretched to genre literature yet, which is why I am especially chuffed to have two stories by Greenlandic authors in this book.

* * *

Finally, I wish to use this opportunity to pay my respect to Tor Åge Bringsværd, one of the contributing Norwegian authors in this anthology. Bringsværd passed away late in the summer of 2025, only days after accepting the translation of his story for this book.

Bringsværd was a giant in Norwegian speculative fiction and wrote numerous books, novels, short stories, and television scripts. He was the recipient of many awards and prizes, and was, for his outstanding writing, appointed Commander of The Royal Norwegian Order of Saint Olav in 2024. His last novel, *Magnoliadamen*, was published only days after his death.

I only knew Bringsværd for the last five years of his life, but I still feel that he is one of the few people who has truly influenced my self-confidence as a writer and editor. I thank him for the encouragement he gave me as an author. I knew him as a positive soul with a warm personality, who sometimes looked on with amusement at the world, someone who was genuinely curious and interested in others. I thank him for all the stories he gave us, for all his quirky and wonderful worlds, and for writing stories that were not afraid of asking big questions. I am so grateful to be able to include one of them in this anthology, to be able to show English-speaking readers some of his amazing work.

I hope you will enjoy reading this and all the other stories in the book!

Margrét

EDITORIAL NOTE

Where the stories in this anthology are reprinted from a previous publication, the original spelling has been preserved at the author's request. You can also find story-specific author notes in the individual biographies at the end of the book.

FINLAND

THE SILENCE OF THE HOST

by Marko Hautala
Translated by Jenni Salmi

"Dirty diapers turn me on," said the caller.

He lowered his voice, as if worried that someone might overhear him. Which was funny, considering he was on live radio.

The show's host, Pekka Sauri, sighed.

"Well, does it harm you in any way?" he asked, sounding slightly bored, as if the caller had confessed to nothing more than binging on sausages.

"I work in a nursing home," the young man on the line continued.

Silence.

"Okay," Sauri nudged.

"My coworkers do not appreciate it when I take the patients' dirty diapers with me into the bathrooms."

The caller's tone was stilted, overly formal; an attempt at dressing his issue in a tuxedo.

Sauri began to probe into the caller's life. Eemil listened to the conversation in disbelief. He twirled the corkscrew cord of his headphones around his thumb and stared out the window into the late August darkness, trying to comprehend that somewhere right at this moment there was a man who was turned on by adult diapers covered in shit.

How disgusting. How hilarious.

The story would be perfect material for school the next morning. Toni and Vesku would be impressed. Maybe he should save the story for their lunch break. Vesku had a sensitive stomach and would start gagging for sure. Maybe that would convince Toni and Vesku to go with him to the Sugar Wine Factory one more time. They might laugh together again like they used to, leaning against the walls with tears in their eyes.

Eemil caught himself looking at his own smirking reflection in the window. The outlines were blurry, like in a soundless earthquake. He unraveled the cord around his thumb and took the headphones off. His ears welcomed the fresh air.

Eemil quietly cracked open the door to his room, until he remembered that Mom and Dad were not at home. He had forgotten this small detail while listening to *Night Line*. The whole apartment was brightly lit, although it was half past one in the morning and there was no one else around. Eemil had simply forgotten to turn the lights off. Nothing more to it. He would have been fine in the darkness, too.

In the kitchen, Eemil drank a glass of lukewarm water. On his way back to his room, he paused in the living room.

When Mom and Dad were gone, home became inexplicably foreign. The rooms weren't just empty. They were super empty. Hollow.

Eemil used to be happy if Mom and Dad spent the night

away. He could finally do whatever he pleased. Lately, though, a shade of discomfort had marred the nights his parents had left him alone. The empty home no longer meant freedom. Mom and Dad took off much too often, and without warning. Toni and Vesku were doing their own thing. They didn't call Eemil, and they didn't come by, even when he invited them.

The empty apartment hummed like the cargo hold of a spaceship. Lamps whirred and light washed over the walls, exposing them like the ocean floor, uncovered by drought. When Eemil looked slightly to the left, he could see a sliver of Mom and Dad's room. The lumpy duvet on the bed; its corner touching the floor.

Usually Mom made sure that the bed was made properly, but apparently, they had been in a rush. Eemil had woken up to the front door banging shut, so he had no idea what had gone down while his parents were getting ready. He had gotten out of bed and watched from the rain-speckled window how Mom and Dad had carried their luggage toward the parking lot. Mom had fumbled. Dad had grabbed her shoulders. Not to support her, but to drag her along faster. Eemil had watched until the familiar figures had transformed into mere blots of color among the water running down the glass. They'd be back, he had told himself. Parents always did. They had no choice.

Eemil went back to his room. Placing headphones over his ears created enough pressure to keep unpleasant thoughts and the spaceship's hum away. Much better.

He caught the end theme to the news. *Night Line* was about to continue.

The next caller was a drunk woman, who complained about how other women withheld sex from their husbands. Most of the calls were about sex, one way or another, which kept things interesting. Eemil was thankful for Toni who had recommended *Night Line*. The show was on air at one in the morning, when Sunday turned into Monday. Listening to it was like being part of a secret society.

"These airheads call the show and share totally embarrassing things, and the psychologist helps them fuck all," Toni had said.

Eemil agreed. He'd already found Pekka Sauri's silence odd from the first time he had listened to the show. A host like that would never be let on air anywhere other than in Finland.

Callers would blab about their mortifying secrets, and most of the time the psychologist remained completely quiet. At most, he might sigh heavily and dish out some bullshit like "well what do you think you should do about it?" Being a psychologist must be the world's cushiest job if you were paid to do that. Eemil, Toni, and Vesku had all decided to become psychologists. And if some loon were to complain to them about hearing voices, they would only sigh and ask, in their best Clint Eastwood voices, "Well what do you think you should do about it, punk?"

After the drunk woman, a man called and told Sauri how he was keeping a three-eared hare hidden from the hunters in his village. Eemil tried to memorize every little detail so that he could repeat them to Toni and Vesku right after the diaper story. At some point, the calls became boring. Eemil felt compelled to listen, even though sleep was weighing on him.

"Eemil," Sauri said suddenly.

A whisper, right in Eemil's ear. Like a secret not meant for the other listeners.

Eemil startled himself awake right as he was about to fall off his chair. The bright light in the room invaded his eyes and made him lean on his desk.

It took him a moment to make any sense of the situation. Sauri had never whispered his name. Of course not.

Eemil rubbed his face and sat up straight. There was no way he could fall asleep now, although he also didn't know why he had to keep himself awake. It just was a part of his plan. Eemil slapped himself on the cheeks and focused on listening.

The next caller was an elderly woman who lived alone in a large house and was afraid of the dark.

"I keep the lights on at night," she said.

Hearing this made Eemil abandon his last hopes of sleeping.

"Does it harm you in any way, though?" Sauri asked.

"Well, me being so old and all," the caller responded, "I don't want to keep the lights on like some baby. The electric bill's through the roof, too."

Then, that painfully long silence.

"What's so scary about darkness?" Sauri finally asked.

"I don't know," the woman said. "Nothing, I suppose."

"But you said there was something scary about it. I just wonder what that might be."

Eemil twisted the headphone cord tighter and tighter around his thumb.

"I just…" the caller said. "I just worry that…"

The pause was too much even for Sauri to bear.

"What?" he asked.

"I just worry that…" the caller continued, "that someone… that in the darkness…"

"Yes?"

"That someone will jump me."

The woman started to laugh. Her voice cracked and rattled in Eemil's eardrum. His hands jerked toward the headphones, but just as Eemil was about to pull them off his ears, the caller hung up.

An unusually long silence followed. The white noise went on. And on. Icy, tickling waves traveled along Eemil's back.

Come on, say something, Eemil prayed. *Anything.*

"Well, well," Sauri continued, and cleared his throat. "Let's listen to some music then, shall we?"

Listen to some music? Eemil couldn't believe what he was hearing. Didn't Sauri feel the need to remark on that laughter?

Apparently not, because now he heard music. Some calming classical crap. Eemil cursed and yanked the headphones off. He looked toward the window.

That was a mistake.

The blurry reflection looked off. Where Eemil's mouth and eyes were supposed to be, he saw only a dark gray smudge. His brain was telling him he was looking at his own reflection. Who else would it be, looking back at him?

Eemil chuckled, a bit forcefully, but chuckled, nevertheless. He liked the way it sounded in the darkness. It sounded like the laughter of someone who wasn't scared of anything. He refused to look away from the reflection until it looked normal again. And he stood by his decision. When he turned his head, so did the reflection. When he raised his hand, the reflection obeyed him. All was well.

Except that his thoughts returned to the Sugar Wine Factory. To the face in the window.

* * *

The ramshackle abandoned house in the forest by the shore had been their private paradise at first: it was a place where they didn't need to worry about some snooping adult smelling their sugar wine pots or finding their weed stash. For whatever reason, even the addicts and hobos didn't like hanging out there.

There were downsides, too. In the winter you had to wade through waist-deep snow to get to the house, and it felt much colder inside than outside. In all other seasons, the piquant aroma of the place was a challenge, especially for Vesku, with his sensitive nose and all. "A medieval battle ground three days later," Toni had described the stench.

One windowless room downstairs felt so oppressive that none of them wanted to set their foot in there. Its floor was lined with about five centimeters of candle wax and in the middle of the room there was a dark splotch that had seeped deep into the floorboards. The boys could only guess at its origin. Mold? Motor oil? Blood? The imagination was the limit.

These were minor issues, though. The house also had its charm.

Upstairs, a fascinating black-and-white photo hung on the wall. In it, a cloaked man wore a turban on his head and sported a pointy mustache. Although faded by time, his gaze was still so piercing that it seemed as if he could hypnotize you into giving away all your money and joining his sex cult. In one hand he held a dark staff, in another a thick book.

Their first night at the house, Vesku had dubbed the black-and-white guy Count von Scrotumsniff. They had all agreed that the Count was the founding father of the

Sugar Wine Factory, as well as its protector. They had to bow to his image every time they entered the room, like samurais in *Shōgun*.

The protective glass over the image had shattered, allowing moisture and mold to bleach its edges. That's why it had taken a while to even notice the print at the bottom edge. After taking turns peering at it, they figured out what it said.

Jag kallar fram anden från det svarta djupet. It was Swedish.

The sentence was in quotes, which Toni took to mean that the Count's most effective pickup line had been preserved for future generations. He translated the sentence as *I summon the spirit from where the sun don't shine,* which the boys deemed as an apt description for both the stench of the house, and the ghastly smell of the sugar wine they brewed within it.

THEY USED TO go to the Sugar Wine Factory together, but that night, Eemil had promised Toni and Vesku that he would go alone after school to pick up two bottles that they could drink later in the evening. It would have been an easy task during the day, but he set off much later than he had planned. By the time he got to the house, the sun was already setting behind the forest.

Eemil had braced himself, stepped over the threshold, grabbed the bottles, and taken off without looking back. As he ran across the yard, he heard a faint sound from behind. It could've been a bird, but for some reason a thought popped into Eemil's head: a child. A child who didn't want Eemil to leave. What a strange thought. Eemil had stopped. And turned to look.

An utter, about-to-shit-his-pants shock.

Someone looked back at him through the window. A featureless, pale face. Crude in a way, reminding Eemil of a small child's drawing that had come to life, and was now looking him straight in the eye. Just a scribbled mess where its eyes and mouth should've been. Eemil was certain that a smile had spread across that face. A smile that looked a bit too eager. The classroom loser rejoicing when he finally managed to make eye contact with someone.

Eemil had probably screamed. His memory was hazy. Either way, he had run back to the road and dropped one of the bottles in the forest.

Only later, the possibility occurred to him: maybe it was his own reflection in the old window's warped glass.

Eemil had told Toni and Vesku this the very same evening. He could not pass on such a good story, not even if it humiliated him. The missing bottle needed an excuse, anyway. Toni and Vesku had mocked him all evening; even more so when they ran out of booze. But one thing was crystal clear: neither of them had volunteered to fetch the missing bottle from the forest. Nor did they ever go back to the Sugar Wine Factory. They hadn't explicitly made a pact on the matter. The place just fell off their weekend plans.

Later Eemil realized that their visits to the house had always been hasty. And maybe the smell wasn't solely to blame for that. The rooms in the Sugar Wine Factory were empty in a particular way. Lonely. Abandoned.

Hollow.

* * *

EEMIL TURNED HIS gaze away from the window.

He got off his chair and walked out of his room in exaggerated, determined strides. "You must stamp your feet hard," Dad had said years ago on a hike. "It scares the adders away." Suddenly, the memory made Eemil sad, because it reminded him of a time when Mom and Dad had still noticed him and hadn't taken off every week to different hotels or spas to "get away" and to "sort things out". Coded adult language.

Eemil walked to the bathroom as if he were on a hiking path covered in adders. He closed the door behind him, dropped his pants to his ankles, and sat on the toilet. Only then did he realize that he didn't need to go. As he washed his hands, he thought he heard someone speak. Eemil turned the faucet off and held his breath.

A muffled, choppy whisper continued for a moment, then blended into the hum of the silence around it.

Eemil dried his hands, opened the door, and waited a beat before stepping over the threshold.

Nothing to see here. Only the brightly lit spaceship hum.

Eemil came back to his room, without giving a single glance at Mom and Dad's room, where the lumpy duvet was still slowly slipping toward the floor.

Once the adrenaline spike started to come down, his desire to sleep returned even stronger. Eemil lay on his back on the bed. He closed his eyes.

The voice came immediately. That quiet whispering. It sounded like a sarcastic voice commenting on his pathetic attempt to fall asleep.

Eemil opened his eyes and bolted upright. The whispering continued. He turned his gaze toward the headphones on his desk.

Elementary, dear Watson. *Night Line* was still on, and

the voice came from the headphones. Eemil's relieved sigh turned into laughter. He got off the bed, sat in his chair, and put the headphones over his ears.

It was probably for the best to stay up all night, just as he had originally planned. A few hours after *Night Line* ended, he would start hearing his neighbors get ready for their day. The stairwell would echo with doors opening and closing, along with the whining of children who had been woken up too early.

Eemil concentrated on the show.

As always, the calls turned more boring toward the end. The callers were increasingly drunk and incoherent. It was difficult to keep up.

Still, Eemil listened to them, and tried to ignore the gnawing feeling that someone was staring at him. He knew why he felt this way. Every now and then his reflection in the window flashed in the corner of his eye, making him imagine all sorts of silly things. Eemil looked intently at the cord coiled around his thumb. When the temptation to glance at the window became too much to bear, he squeezed his eyes shut.

That's when sleep returned to his body, like a numbing blanket. Eemil struggled to stay awake. Eventually, his mind drifted into a peculiar in-between state. Sentences, even single words uttered by the callers, created images in his head; images that began to live their own lives.

"Actually, I'm calling about my kid," a slurring woman's voice said.

Eemil was only half-aware of what he was hearing. He imagined he was standing on the roof of the apartment building, watching an enormous flock of jackdaws flap against sunset. It formed a gigantic vortex that began to turn counter-clockwise.

"And?" Sauri sighed.

"My kid has something…" the woman tried but didn't finish the thought.

Eemil realized he was no longer watching the flock of jackdaws; he had turned into a bird among them. He was flying and watching a vast herd of animals on a savanna below him.

"This is so difficult to talk about," the caller sniffled.

Antelopes and gazelles and who knows what comprised the herd. The beasts moved in massive, ever-evolving formations, suddenly changing direction, as if manipulated by an invisible puppeteer. Gradually, the whorls split into two. Then into three. Eemil floated above them and wondered whether it was he who made it all happen.

"I'm afraid of my own child," the caller sobbed. "We're afraid of our kid."

Eemil was still observing the savannah and the three whorls formed by the herds of animals.

"How old is your child?" Sauri asked.

Eemil realized that the whorls had formed two eyes and a mouth. They were unfocused and constantly moving. Scribbles. Like a small child's drawing.

"Thirteen," the caller replied, suddenly sounding much less drunk. "Our child is thirteen."

Eemil opened his eyes. The light in his room chafed his eyes, as if the air was full of fine, whirling sand.

"All right," Sauri sighed. "Is your child somehow violent toward you?"

The caller blew her nose and let out a wavering sigh.

"Not exactly, no," the woman said. "But the things the kid says… they're terrible. We just can't handle it anymore. We had to run away again. Run away from our own home. Do you understand? We had to leave our child alone in our home."

Her voice broke when she said *home*.

Sauri remained quiet for a long while. The white noise on the line grew louder. Eemil caught himself looking directly at the window. At his own reflection. At a figure who wore oversized headphones. A mouthless, eyeless stranger.

"Well, teenagers can be challenging to their parents," Sauri said. "They push their boundaries and sometimes it gets hard to deal with."

"That's not what this is about," the woman said. "I know what teenagers are like. Normal teenagers. This is… different."

Silence. White noise. It made Eemil think about another dimension, where it was constantly dark, even when all the lights were on.

Det svarta djupet.

"So, what do you think this is all about, then?"

The caller searched for an answer for a long time. Among the white noise, Eemil heard another sniffle and a stifled sound, when the tears she had been holding in broke through their barrier.

"I just think that…" the caller began.

"Yes?"

"I just think that something has gotten into our child," the woman said.

"I'm sorry?" Sauri said.

Suddenly he sounded alert.

"I don't know," the caller groaned. "Something… evil."

This time, her voice remained steady. She was in complete control now that she had given up all hope.

The white noise on the line grew louder; a drizzle turned into a torrential downpour.

Say something, Eemil shouted at Sauri in his mind. *Just fucking say something!*

But the hissing on the line went on, growing stronger. Eemil couldn't turn away from his reflection.

Finally, the familiar sigh.

"Listen here," Sauri said. "I think it would be best if we forgot about evils and things like that. Otherwise we'll never move forward."

The caller said nothing.

"Teenagers can be real… chameleons," Sauri continued. "They provoke; they try on different roles. But I think you two should be responsible parents and go back to your child, right now. A thirteen-year-old may seem like an independent person, but honestly, that child still needs an adult, and badly. The child needs you."

The woman let out an empty laugh.

"I'm not going back there," she said.

Now Sauri's trademark sigh sounded more like a moan.

"Well, what were you thinking about doing, then?" he coaxed. "Taking off and leaving your kid alone, huh?"

"It's not my child," the caller said.

"But it is," Sauri laughed, annoyed. "Just a moment ago you said you were worried about your child."

"It's not our child," the woman said. "It's something else. It has polluted our home. All the rooms are…"

Eemil twirled the headphone cord around his thumb and waited for the word to drop.

Hollow, he thought.

"Hollow," the woman said.

Like an echo.

Eemil's skin crawled. He noticed he was humming some idiotic hit song he'd heard on the radio as if everything was fine and dandy. No problems here. Everything was under control. Eemil imagined how tomorrow he, Toni, and Vesku would laugh at the diaper guy, and the three-eared rabbit, and the woman who believed her child was possessed by some fucking evil spirit.

A completely strange woman. From another planet. From the deepest craters of Mars.

Eemil convinced himself of this, but his skin continued to crawl as if it wanted to furl in, doing its best to escape this room. This empty

hollow

room.

Eemil tore the headphones off his head, yanked the plug out of the player, and shot up so quickly he sent his chair flying. He grabbed Slayer's *Reign in Blood* from the shelf and dropped it on the turntable. The player's needle screeched as it settled in the vinyl's groove. The opening song began to flood in from the speakers. The noise might wake the neighbors and make them come ring the doorbell, but in a funny way, that's what Eemil was hoping for. Anything would be better than waiting for the dawn in these quiet and empty

hollow

rooms.

But nobody came to the door. Finally, Eemil took the needle off the record and didn't know what to do with himself. He was too scared to look toward the window. He was too scared to leave the room. He was too scared to listen to the silence. He had only one option. Like a convict serving his time, Eemil lifted the headphones back onto his ears.

The last few notes in a classical tune were fading out. Eemil hoped that the next call would be something truly bonkers, and something that would make him forget about his troubles.

"We have fifteen minutes left of *Night Line*," Sauri said. "And we have our last caller on the line. Who am I talking to?"

Among the phone line's buzzing, just muffled whines and hissing.

"Hello?" Sauri said. "You're on the air. Who is this?"

"I have no name," a voice suddenly rasped.

A strange response. Usually people would give a pseudonym unless they were too drunk to worry about it. But the voice was even stranger than what it had said. It sounded like an electrical current was trying to form words.

"Sounds like we're getting some interference," Sauri said. "If you have your radio on, can you turn it off, please?"

"No radio."

"All right, then. Let's just try to muddle through. So, what's on your mind?"

The muffled, whiny voice hissed and rumbled. It sounded like a leaky pressure cooker.

"I was left alone," it responded.

The voice didn't reveal whether the speaker was a man or a woman. Or whether it was an adult or a child.

Sauri digested this answer for a moment. He was probably wondering whether it was a prank call.

"Alone in what way?" he finally asked.

"All alone."

The speech rhythm was jerky. The caller must've been altering the voice on purpose. Maybe they were using a speech synthesizer or a similar contraption.

"May I ask you, how old are you?" Sauri said.

"I'm a child."

The response was instant, as if the caller had predicted the question.

"How old a child?" Sauri asked.

"A child."

Eemil twisted the headphone cord.

"All right. And you're saying you were left alone?"

"Left alone. The man went away."

Sauri was obviously confused. He held a long pause before going on.

"What man?"

"The one who invited me."

The electrical whining and static grew louder.

"Invited you?"

Sauri pronounced the words slowly, as if practicing a new language.

"Invited me out of the darkness," the caller said.

Eemil's thumb had gone numb. The cord had twisted around his finger in a thick black coil.

"I don't think I quite understand you," Sauri sighed. "Do you mean you're completely alone right now?"

"No."

"Okay... So you do have company?"

"My friend found me."

"I see," Sauri said. "Is this friend an adult?"

"A child."

"So there's two of you there."

"Yes. My friend found me. Brought me along."

Long, long silence.

"You mentioned that you were invited out of the darkness," Sauri said. "What did you mean by that?"

"The man invited me out of the darkness."

"But… that doesn't make any sense. Where's that man now?"

"He didn't want to be a friend," the voice said. "He broke. He sleeps under the floor now."

The static in the line increased for a second. Then it went away completely.

"I'm sorry, I didn't hear what you said," Sauri said.

Eemil was sure that Sauri had heard. They both had heard.

"The man is asleep," the voice stated. "Under the floor."

Eemil had never heard Sauri stammer. But now, the psychologist took his time to search for the right words. It wasn't entirely because of what the caller was saying, but because the background static in the line had disappeared so suddenly. Sauri, too, must have noticed it. It felt like being plunged under water, into some depths where the only sound was the caller's voice.

"Listen now, anonymous caller," Sauri sighed. "We need to cut to the three o'clock news soon."

The whiny hiss returned on the line so fast that it startled Eemil. His heart pounded, but he was relieved. The caller must've hung up. Good, good. It would be great to hear the news for a change. Some boring adult stuff about Ronald Reagan and Mikhail Gorbachev and Pope John Paul and Finnish politicians who would explain to him how all past decisions had always been good. Eemil could have listened to the news until the morning.

"My friend doesn't want to see me," the caller said.

It took Eemil a moment to grasp that the caller was still on the line. He prayed that the call would be dropped.

"I see," Sauri sighed. "How about we make a deal? You call me again later if you still feel like it, but we're going to cut to the news right now. Does that work for you?"

No reply. The whining and hissing silence dominated.

"Does that work for you?"

Eemil stopped twirling the cord around his thumb. He wanted to continue performing this mindless movement, but it was no longer possible: he'd coiled the cord all the way to the end. Its metallic plug reflected the ceiling lamp's light.

"Should we go to the news?" Sauri repeated.

Eemil didn't know who he was asking, exactly. Maybe some sound technician or whoever was around during radio broadcasts.

"What do you say?" Sauri asked.

The voice was closer than before. It sounded like Sauri had pressed his lips into the microphone.

"Do you want to hear the news?"

Eemil heard the words, although it shouldn't have been possible. He had unplugged the headphones from the stereo. He had listened to *Reign in Blood* for minutes. At no point had he plugged the headphones back in. And yet Sauri went on.

"What do you say?" he asked.

The familiar, monotone voice. Not in his ears, but in his ear canal. In the hollows of his skull.

"Do you want to hear the news?"

Eemil stared at the shiny, silver plug and wouldn't look up. For once, he hoped that Sauri would stay quiet. He wanted complete silence. Eternal silence.

"Do you want to see your friend?"

Eemil knew he had no other choice. He raised his chin and looked at the window.

It reflected his room back, blurry. And the room wasn't empty.

It was hollow, yes. But not empty.

My friend doesn't want to see me.

The figure standing behind him didn't have any defined features.

"Do you see it?" Sauri asked.

Eemil nodded slowly. Quiet laughter emanated from the headphones. A darkness purred at him.

The creature's hand landed on Eemil's shoulder. Its face was pale, nearly white, like drawing paper or puffy, absorbent diaper fabric. Its eyes mere dirty stains. Instead of a mouth, it had a messy coil, barely recognizable as a smile.

'Friend,' the creature said.

Eemil tried to scream but couldn't.

He tried to escape into a memory, to a moment where his lungs and mouth still obeyed him. To a memory where he pressed his palms against a cold glass. The figures carrying their luggage halted for a second, as if they had heard his voice despite its distance and the roaring rain. But no. Eemil saw how the two blotches of color turned into bright sparks, then they were extinguished by the rain.

'Friend,' the creature behind him repeated.

Eemil realized that it wasn't a question, but a statement. A plea by the one invited out of the darkness.

"Friend," Eemil replied, because neither of them had much choice.

THE JOYS OF THE TABLE

by Johanna Sinisalo
Translated by Sarianna Silvonen

I LOVED HER.

I fell in love with her among the glow of linen tablecloths and the tinkle of crystal glasses, among candlelight and the aromas of rare delicacies. Who wouldn't have?

I am old and experienced. I have seen and met with plenty. But she was my one and only, and she was taken from me. Torn from my side. Banished from me.

That, I could not bear.

I have had many owners. I have always been valued. My legs have beautiful, ingenious curves and the sides of my back are bordered by delicate but all the more elaborate grooves.

But she was the first in many decades who bothered to sand the flaking, exhausted, overly dense and tacky surface from my sides, legs, and back. Then she restored me to health by brushing me all over with sweet new life that permeated down to my pores. I reacquired my colour, my selfhood, my slow breath. I grew younger. My every seam radiated a deep, wooden gratitude.

And she, my beloved—she gasped passionately upon seeing my handsome state of readiness; she caressed me and sighed in satisfaction, and I shivered down to my deepest grain at the touch of her gentle hand.

Our relationship was perfect from the moment I came to her.

Every day she dressed me several times, dressed me and undressed me. She always did it in a tasteful manner suitable for the occasion. I was covered with soft fabrics in matching shades and decorated with flowers as well as seasonal colours and items. Every now and then, at regular intervals, she garbed me in royal linen and laid stately candelabras and clinking silverware on my back.

She waxed my surface regularly. I remember the gentle sweeping, curved caresses of her hand as she stretched over me radiating appreciation and love.

Yes, it was love.

But there was also the Other.

IT ALL STARTED gradually.

Of course, he, the Other, would sometimes pat my back, or more precisely smack it when he had stern words to say. Even more often he would set his glass on me with a clank when the drinking song was over or when there had been some other important reason for him to quickly knock back his drink, accompanied by a grunt.

But soon he would pound his fist upon me even in situations where I did not understand why it was necessary. Increasingly often the Other would rush away from my side in the middle of an ordinary mealtime, leaving his chair to clatter against my legs or sides, and I could hear my beloved gasp sharply, sometimes even cry out faintly in fright.

Then there were evenings and nights when he, the Other, sat beside me for ages after my beloved had already gone to sleep, his loin weighty, his hand heavy, banging his glass on top of me time after time, spilling sticky, corrosive substances on me. He sucked and held reeking sticks that sprinkled grey, foul-smelling filth on my surface. Sometimes he would set these sticks down, and they would roll from their glass cradles onto my back. Once one of them was forgotten smouldering on my skin and left me with a deep, ugly, black burn, a scar beyond repair.

I remember when my beloved came downstairs, how she first screamed and then wept upon seeing the mark. Oh, how she pitied me!

Occasions when my beloved oiled, dressed, and decorated me became less frequent, and more and more often the Other would force himself by my side, increasingly regularly setting not only his heavy glass but an even heavier bottle on my back.

In the morning, my beloved would shed tears upon my skin.

I LEARNED: ESPECIALLY when the others get intoxicated, I have a chance at revenge. Like all of us, I know how to extend myself, I can stir in my immobility, for a brief moment I can take up a space other than that which I usually inhabit. I expand my being for a fraction of a second, shift myself just slightly in time and space, and the object of my revenge, following his customary routes, not knowing to expect my trap, walks right into my corner.

His hip bumps into me painfully, leaving a bruise, and he lets out a curse. He is cursing his own seeming stupidity and clumsiness; that piece of furniture has always been there, in exactly that spot, and he has no idea of my part in the incident.

Even though these bruisings gave me a momentary satisfaction, it was not enough. And finally something happened from which there was no return.

It was night, and the Other came home, but he was accompanied by an even more otherly other emitting an unfamiliar, piercing stench of heavy perfume, and soon an undressed, writhing body was slammed on top of me, and the Other crashed down on top of it, and they started to shake me in their sweaty, sticky frenzy.

As they were grunting like animals and spilling their repulsive fluids all over me, I heard the door bang and recognised the footsteps of my beloved. The steps stopped, the jerking movements on my back paused, and my beloved's voice sounded like the core had been ripped out of her.

After that, I never again felt the touch of her hand, the sweet wax and flowing linen, but I did not yet know it then. Glasses and kegs and corrosive substances and burning sticks and humiliating secretions just rolled over me at an accelerating pace, and then the shrill-voiced and stinky others waned and were replaced by a steady stream of growly-voiced others who abused me even more gravely, who would ravage and soak me day and night with their bottles—even glasses were no longer necessary.

I MISSED MY beloved, and naturally I understood at some point that she would never come back. And I was racked with anger and loss at the same time as I was scratched and battered by the barbarians gathered around me. Filth and muck collected on my surface, my back was covered in gunge and ash, and my once so handsome hide was pockmarked with black scars.

It was time.

It was well and truly time.

I waited until the Other was sitting down at my side by himself. It took a long time. Some kind of change had taken place, as he no longer invited more others to hang around for nights on end. Once he had even feebly tried to wipe my back with a moistened rag. He had sat down next to me, but only to eat something quickly heated, and nothing pungent had sloshed out of the glasses he had set down lately.

But then the moment occurred. The Other came to me once more, and the sound of his footsteps echoed with nervous expectation. I heard the clanking of dishes and the shrill signal of the heating device, and then he placed his plate and glass upon my back, and finally I felt also the weight of a bottle that had become familiar to me.

The Other poured out a glass first, without touching his meal yet, and drank, and his sigh of relief told me everything.

The Other ate, and all along I could sense his battle with and against the bottle. I could feel him stretching his hand towards the bottle many times but pulling it back. He moved the bottle further from himself in annoyance.

He was stronger than I had thought.

I had to step in.

I arched my back just slightly. I gave my surface an infinitesimal slant. I tightened my grain in some places and loosened it in others so that the Other noticed nothing when the bottle glided towards him lightly as a feather. Soon he noticed it standing right by his forearm again.

I felt the bottle staring at him. I felt him staring at the bottle like an apparition.

The Other cursed in amazement and something else, maybe relief, maybe the fact that destiny seemed to be spurring him on in this way. And so the bottle was lifted off my back and a great portion of its weight poured into the glass.

When the glass had been filled and emptied twice and filled yet again, I carefully lifted one of my legs, just a smidgen. When the Other put his glass on my back, I let myself rock, and the glass shook, almost toppling over.

He cursed again.

He rested his palm on my edge and tested me. As I was still holding one of my legs a bit shorter than the others, his push made me sway.

The Other swore yet again but did nothing. That would not do. He was already almost trapped. When he reached for his drink again, I shifted myself so that the bottle lurched, and he thought he had almost spilled it himself by accident.

This was enough.

To make sure, he lifted the bottle off my back and set it down next to my other leg. I understood him well. That seemed a safer place for it.

The Other rocked me again to find the shorter leg, which he deemed the cause of the near accidents. He found what he sought, took a wad of paper that had served as a napkin, and arose from his chair. He crawled under me, lifted my leg, and started to cram the wad under my sole. Just as I had envisioned.

Now I concentrated on my other leg, the one where the bottle was, and moved it, just a teeny bit, but it was sufficient: the bottle started to fall over, and he made a panicky crawling movement towards it, towards the most important thing in his life. And as he reached out for his precious from beneath my belly, I gathered all my strength, and with a fierce, overwhelming exertion, I allowed my centre of gravity to rise and change, and thus, with elemental inevitability, the edge of my oh so heavy back began to fall.

When my edge hit the back of his neck and he was flung onto the stained carpet, the crunching sound alone told me that he would never rise again.

I KNOW THAT I will not have to wait long for new owners. The scars and stains will be sanded away from my surface and my new skin will glow again.

But now I am conscious of my power and rejoice in it. I will never forget my beloved but neither will I forget my moments of degradation.

I am calm and tranquil on the surface, but I will have you know that if you sit down by my side, my grain is flowing with sweet passion. And I will never, ever hesitate to rise up—should the need ever present itself—against those who treat me cruelly.

ANGELA'S ARTWORKS

by Pasi Ilmari Jääskeläinen

Translated by Sarianna Silvonen

A PANDEMIC HAS ravaged the land. Because of the stringent restrictions, Angela Prosper, 57, has not met her dear artist friends face to face for almost a year. She has also been unable to visit the beds of her three lovers to sweeten her busy working days. Not long ago, one of them lay dying in intensive care, hooked up to all sorts of machines, but Angela was not allowed in even to say goodbye.

The artistic circle of friends exchanges news every day by means of electronic messages. They find comfort, sometimes even hope, in their shared misery.

But gallery doors remain closed one week after another. The masterworks created by Angela's friends in their lonely studios no longer reach collectors shut in their homes. Some of her friends can no longer afford food. Angela has long enjoyed great popularity among both critics and the buying public, thanks to which she is able to donate to charity and help her less fortunate friends under the prevailing circumstances, and she is grateful for this.

Angela herself is thus not threatened by hunger or deprivation, but now that her paintings cannot be shown to the public either, she no longer feels like painting. Her sleep is fitful, her days are restless, and she cannot be bothered to take care of herself other than by dyeing her greying hair red once a week. Even though she never meets anybody, keeping up her original hair colour seems important to Angela for some reason.

"For me, art is the only way to struggle towards the truth about myself and the world! Art is the ultimate challenge! I know that one day I will have said everything I am ever capable of saying, and my brush will no longer reach the canvas. On that day, may death redeem me!" This pompous and defiant declaration was made by Angela Prosper in an interview given slightly before the start of the pandemic. These words haunt her now that her creativity is flagging.

Without a public, there is no art, only meaningless dabbling.

Angela stares at the wall and squeezes her fingers.

Then she receives a surprising commission that changes everything.

ANGELA SITS IN the dark living room scrolling through her friends' messages on her phone and yawns. She should probably get to bed.

Then a strange voice addresses her, and the phone falls to the floor as she loses her grip.

The voice belongs to a child.

Angela discovers a pallid boy standing by the door. That is odd, because she distinctly remembers carefully locking the front door after returning from her solitary walk earlier that day.

The boy enquires whether Angela is 'the famous artist who paints pictures that are about childhood but never have any children in them'.

'ANGELA PROSPER'S WORKS are executed with a dazzlingly masterful technique and regularly feature seemingly empty scenes that nevertheless vibrate with drama left just outside the frame. Little hints—forgotten toys; caps, hats, and mittens lying on the ground; a backpack left in a bottom corner—indicate that children were present just a moment ago. The charged atmosphere forces the viewer to wonder what might have happened. Prosper has never depicted actual children in any of her works because according to her own words, she thinks they are "ugly and rather insignificant little creatures".' (Art critic in a daily newspaper.)

WHEN ANGELA ADMITS to being the person sought by the child, there is an uncomfortably long pause before the little after-hours intruder states that he has spent 'a lifetime' looking for Prosper the artist.

Angela is annoyed by the child's melodramatic words. Yes, she does live far from the nearest neighbours, sheltered by the green wall of the forest. She knows very well that outsiders have difficulties finding their way to her address. But the night-time visitor's way of emphasising his efforts still seems like the kind of exaggeration and begging for pity that is typical of children.

Angela thinks that children are noisy, self-satisfied, and trivially uninteresting creatures, surprisingly often also unpleasant to look at, 'in many ways caricatures of rational and well-formed adults', as she explained when discussing her artistic choices in one particular interview. Angela has never enjoyed spending time around children. Her friends are amused by her questionable reputation for slapping, pinching, and pulling the hair of children who stray too close to her.

However, the child who has now turned up at Angela's house has the good sense to stay far enough away that Angela can't even make out his facial features in the dim room.

The child announces that he is bringing Angela a commission from his master and rattles off a litany memorised by heart: "You have seven days to create seven new paintings. At the end of this period, I will come to collect the paintings, introduce myself to you, and pay the rest of the fee, which, as you will note, will make you gasp for breath." (At this point, the child places an envelope containing the advance payment on the corner of the table.) "The paintings should continue your famous series of scenes with the exception that this time you will also include the children."

The precocious child enquires whether he may return to inform the sender of the offer that Prosper the artist would care to accept the commission.

"But won't it ruin the whole idea of this series of works?" Angela wonders. "Adding children to them?"

Of course, the simple creature has no answer to this.

When Angela finally gets up and walks towards the envelope left on the table, the child runs out of the room. The front door opens and closes. Angela peeks into the envelope, sees the banknotes, is convinced that the offer is genuine, opens the window, and yells out into the dark woods: "Your master can come pick up his seven paintings in seven days!"

Then she notices that the boy has tracked muddy water all over the floor, and her joy is mixed with anger: the little nuisance had not even bothered to wipe his feet before intruding into someone's home! And now she has to start mopping the floor at this time of night...

Angela sleeps for three hours.

She dreams of her dead lover, who looks at her with dark, worried eyes and bends down to whisper something to her.

Then the black wooden clock strikes midnight and Angela wakes up. She gets dressed, climbs the stairs up to her studio, and begins the first of her seven new paintings.

I begin with the colour blue, Angela reports in a message to her friends after an hour. *Surely you know my summer scene (*Blue Swing 1*) that shows a meadow with a big maple and an empty swing hanging from a maple branch? The sky in the background is blue, with cottony clouds drifting across it. Even though there are no people in sight, the scene radiates joy, and it is clear that something so pleasant and happy has just taken place here that the feeling is preserved even though the people have left. I have never wanted to ruin this atmosphere by adding snotty-nosed children with odd bodily proportions (unlike many of you) but now I must finally do so to satisfy my mysterious client. Wish me luck, friends!*

Her friends' encouraging comments provide Angela with the strength to add the first child to this scene that she has so often repeated. The form of a girl takes shape in the swing that has thus far stayed empty.

Then it is time for the second child: the blurred figure of a smiling boy pushes the girl on the swing.

When the girl's hair acquires a glowing red colour, Angela realises that she has just painted herself.

I FINISHED THE *first painting tonight, and now I'm going to sleep for a couple of hours before starting on the next one,* Angela messages an update to her friends.

Her friends—those who are still awake—wish her sweet dreams and urge her to occasionally nourish herself with something other than cucumber sandwiches and black coffee, *otherwise you'll run out of steam in the middle of the job, you fabulous old gal.*

THE KNELLING AT *midnight woke me up again (that damned clock is really still for sale—cheap—if any of you darling doodlers would care to ruin your good night's sleep with an antique clock that my silly father claimed once belonged to an American writer named Poe) and I started to work on the second painting. It is now three in the morning (or is it still night?) and I note that I am working in shades of purple. A remote, wooded lake shore is taking shape on the canvas, familiar from my earlier works (*Purple River 1–7*). The red-headed lass is frolicking in deep waters and urging the boy to follow her into the lake. The cap forgotten on the shore, which in the earlier version of the scene was the only sign of anyone having been present, in addition to a hair ribbon hanging from a branch, is in this painting still on the boy's head, even though the girl has already persuaded the boy to take off the rest of his clothes and his skinny* *rump shines in the sun. The boy is already stepping into the water, as he fully trusts the girl, which the girl seems to know all too well...*

One of her friends comments: *Angela, it's wonderful to hear that you're so inspired, but won't you please send us pictures of your new works soon?*

Angela replies: *Sweetie, I will as soon as I can, but I managed to break the camera on my phone and will have to take the pictures with that cheap ancient camera that I bought when our gang was visiting Berlin—if only I can find an unused roll of film somewhere...*

THE THIRD PAINTING is filled with a penetrating greenness. Black-and-yellow-striped wasps and horseflies are patrolling above the lawn. The heat has made them angry. Deciduous trees stand in the background, motionless. The wind has died. The air stands heavy as a stone wall.

Angela takes a break, drinks black coffee, and writes to her friends: *I always considered my* Meadow 1–4 *paintings so extraordinarily oppressive that I never thought anyone would want to hang them on their wall, and I didn't understand where the atmosphere really came from, but now I realise that there was a third child present—the one whose wind spinner has been flung to the ground, broken, and whom I now see fleeing outside the frame to escape the wrath of the red-headed girl.*

The boy familiar from the two earlier paintings stands stiffly behind his furious friend. Inviting a new friend to this encounter was a bad mistake. An affront to the girl. Now the boy understands it too.

Angela messages her friends in agitation: *The red-headed girl does not want to share the boy with anyone.*

This green painting is so charged that my hair is standing on end as I work on it, the colours are hissing and sizzling and searing with the girl's terrible possessiveness.

Her friends comment: *Hah, Angela! Looks like that cranky little redhead you painted doesn't support free love and open relationships like yourself!*

DURING THE FOURTH day Angela naps for a few minutes every now and then and continues her work by conjuring up a field of yellow dandelions on the canvas. However, the colours do not glow with a summery light; if anything, the painting gives a sallow impression. The original versions of *Dandelions Screaming (1–5)* were interpreted by a daily newspaper critic in this way: 'Dandelions are supposed to be bursting with yellow energy, but in all its skilful expressiveness, Angela Prosper's dandelion field is rancid, downright repugnant, and the summer has lost all its glory.'

Angela writes to her friends: *Now I'm regretting having accepted the commission. I'm cold and I don't feel well. (But don't worry about me, darlings, this shall pass.) Did I already mention that U.R. visited me in my dream and probably tried to warn me?*

Her friends encourage her: *Only three more paintings left, you delightful rogue. Get some sleep and finish the job—we're rooting for you out here!*

So Angela summons up her strength and paints a red-headed girl in the dandelion field. The girl is sitting on a rock and her face is too shadowed to properly make out. In the background behind the girl, the boy can be seen sitting in a swing. A black-haired girl is pushing the boy. She radiates a sense of triumph.

No.

Angela adjusts the expression so that the black-haired girl only looks happy, after all.

The boy looks relieved. He likes his new black-haired friend a lot more than that bossy and possessive redhead.

THE FIFTH PAINTING is filled with cold white shades. All colours have died. The original works (*Winter 1–8*) featured nothing but a small snowman in a snowy landscape.

Now Angela understands that the snowman is a clumsy portrait of the boy.

Made by the red-headed girl.

The girl's hand touches the snow-boy's cheek. Her face is filled with such horrifying loneliness that Angela collapses into her chair and weeps.

ANGELA'S ARTIST FRIENDS write: *Angie, sweetie, where are you, what's going on? Shame on you for not reporting on your progress! We're expecting a full account of the fifth day's painting. (Just joking, dear Angela. Of course you'll write to us when you have time, you must be incredibly busy! Tons of kisses and a shitload of hearts!)*

WHEN THERE ARE only two paintings left, Angela decides to give up on the whole shebang but knows it's not really possible.

When she falls asleep for a while, her dead lover strokes her hair but says nothing.

* * *

The sixth painting: blue and red. A thin crust of ice covers the pond in the forest. It is early spring. Maybe April.

The critic's review of *An Altogether Ordinary Pond (1–6)*: 'The children, who in Prosper's other works have left the scene only moments earlier, appear to be just on their way here, each of them from their own direction. The upcoming dramatic encounter casts the long and strangely scary shadow of heavy emotions over the meeting site.'

Now the children are finally here.

Angela paints with cold fingers that no longer seem to belong to her.

Her brush is guided by something that she knows deep inside.

The girl is standing on the shore, her hair, red as blood, spilling out from under her hat.

The boy is standing on the other side of the pond, hesitant.

The girl's hand is stretched out, beckoning the boy to cross the thin ice.

"It will hold," Angela says out loud in the studio, "I walked across too!"

A message from her friends: *Angela, we've tried calling you (yes, we know you're busy, but you could still pick up at least), we're a bit worried here in our own small burrows. You haven't been infected, have you?*

The last day begins. Angela has toiled away to the dark side of exhaustion and no longer needs sleep. Her fervent brush strokes red and black paint on the canvas. In fact, the painting seems to be creating itself, and Angela can do nothing but look on helplessly as her last artwork is completed.

At first, it seems like the girl isn't present after all even in this new version of *Farewell (1–3)*.

Then it becomes obvious that the red colour churning all over the painting represents the girl's spiritual presence at its purest. The white ice in the middle of the pond has cracked, revealing a sliver of night-dark water.

The critic wrote of the original works: 'The cold water of the pond is not water, of course, but represents everything that we allow to remain hidden from ourselves under the icy crust of oblivion so that we can get on with our lives.'

The boy, however, has disappeared from sight. He has probably gone home. Good. Angela feels relieved.

But then her brush dips in and adds a little white hand sticking out of the black water.

ANGELA OPENS THE advance fee envelope again. She is too tired to feel any surprise at seeing it filled not with banknotes but small pieces of paper.

The topmost note is hard to read because the text has been smudged by water.

So you decided to stop talking to me in the schoolyard. I've got something super important to tell you. I'll be waiting for you by the pond at 6 p.m. tonight! Your friend forever, A.

ANGELA DOES NOT need to turn around to know that the boy is back.

Once again, he has slipped in like a thief in the night.

"Who dares," Angela poses a pointless question to nobody at all. "Who dares to offend an artist with such an insulting joke?"

A NERVOUS BURST of laughter fills the studio. When the sound dies out, Angela can hear water dripping from the boy's ghost to the floor. The child has brought with him the coldness of the wintry pond and now waits together with Angela.

The black wooden clock strikes midnight. Footsteps, incredibly light yet leaden, begin to rise up the stairs.

Her friends: *Seriously, Angela, what on earth is going on?*

Angela has time to send a brief reply: *All done now, the client is here too*.

DENMARK

NEITHER HEAVEN NOR HELL

by Martin Schjönning
Translated by Olivia Lasky

THE BOG TOOK my father.

At least, that's what the evidence seemed to suggest. He was gone, in any case—gone from bankruptcy court, from the financial crimes unit, from the tax authorities, from the local protest groups, from the creditors and the death threats. Gone.

A local hunter's wirehaired pointer found his slippers. One was lying in the untamed raspberry bushes that formed the border between the backyard and the wilderness, the other a kilometre further into the forest. The dog also tracked down his glasses in a willow thicket at the edge of the bog where the undergrowth imperceptibly, capriciously morphs from solid ground into treacherous mire.

Patrick and I moved in that November. The house by the forest was, to my surprise, in my name. I suppose that must have happened when I signed one of the numerous tear-stained documents in the days following my mother's death. After ten years of living in cramped city flats, all of our belongings fit into a load.

Although the house by the forest was only sparsely furnished in the most restrained Scandinavian style, our belongings were hardly even noticeable. It was as though they withdrew into the outer rooms, found their way into hidden corners, were piled up and kept secret in the anonymity of the annexes, disappeared into the darkness of the crawlspaces.

Dad's barristers fought a bloody war around us that they lost miserably, and with each battle they retreated from, they appeared—each time more battered and more pitiful—at the house by the forest; the only refuge.

But I didn't offer the wounded warriors much comfort or encouragement. They could bicker and brandish obscure legal paragraphs all they wanted while Dad's poisoned Grand Design crumbled between their lily-white fingers. It was no concern of mine, and it certainly wasn't any concern of Patrick's. We hid from the peasants' revolt, from the journalists, the wolves, and the authorities behind the walls of the forest—where they couldn't reach us. Guarded by the latticework of alder and oak, we abided where defrauded investors, misled tenants, and swindled contractors couldn't enter.

The autumn darkness concealed the house's grandeur. When we arrived with the rented moving van, the house barely rose above the ground—or so it seemed, at least. It looked like the burial mound of a mighty chieftain, now disgracefully sunken with age. But inside, it was comfortable. Dad's housekeeper had removed the police tape and any traces of the forensic technicians' fruitless tests and measurements. She hadn't touched anything else. The bottle of single malt and the lone glass still stood on the kitchen table. In the enormous, meticulously furnished room, those two small objects appeared much larger and more important than they had any right to. My father's last meal—before the bog took him.

The housekeeper showed me the clothes she'd laid out for him, still hanging untouched on the dressing chair in the bedroom. A single-breasted navy-blue suit with a modestly trimmed lapel, practical double vents, three buttons on the front, three more on the sleeves. A dove's egg-blue shirt with a breast pocket. A tie, conservatively striped in navy and bottle green, grenadine-woven.

A carefully considered courtroom ensemble for the unquestionably guilty, yet outwardly contrite, businessman. A man of initiative and action, but at the same time deeply serious and above all practical, a man whose transgressions might be excused by an uncontainable drive, an unwavering vigour, an energy that could not, or perhaps *should* not, be bound by the petty regulations and zeal of perfidious bureaucrats. A suit that signalled success but restraint, youthfulness but respectability; a complete self-portrait of masculine civil courage.

He was wearing his bathrobe when the bog took him. Who knows—perhaps there was a handwritten letter in its pocket, one he'd forgotten to leave behind, tucked beneath the whisky like a message in a bottle flung blindly into the choppy waves of the future. Who knows? Maybe he'd tried to explain himself; an actual apology was out of the question. Who knows? Maybe, as the solicitors put it, he was in a 'depressed state of mind' and had no real sense of what he was doing. Those who knew my father wouldn't find that explanation particularly likely.

THAT FIRST EVENING, Patrick took two clean glasses from the china cabinet. Dad's glass was still standing on the table between ours as we emptied the bottle in silence. The next morning, Patrick had cleared the table before I woke up.

"Can you handle it?" he asked. "Being here, I mean?"

The panoramic window facing the forest had been recently cleaned and the pane was cold beneath my fingertips.

"Here? What would be wrong with that?"

He handed me an espresso.

"All the bad memories. Your dad, your mum, that time we were—"

"None of that's the house's fault. I *want* to be here. Here, with you." The coffee was bitter; he had, as always, made it just a tad too strong.

"Aren't you going to miss the city?"

The moon was just visible, like an old scar on the bluing sky. The sun rose up from the bog, surrounded by flitting waxwings migrating south.

"No."

A FOX CROSSED the lawn. It was between morning and noon, some day in December, and the sun had yet to creep above the treetops. It was cold, but nowhere near cold enough. I remembered how frost clung to every blade of grass when I was a child. I recalled the snow—fine as spun silk—that adorned each twig on the old trees in the garden, precise and delicate, as if applied with a goat-hair paintbrush. I thought back to the winter sun that used to bathe the forest in a godlike golden-white light. Now, it hid behind a permanent film of grey clouds. Grey clouds over a grey earth covered in grey buildings, inhabited by grey people staring out of grey windows through a veil of grey rain. The fox trotted off, provocatively fearless, likely pleased with the changes that kept the birch mice from hibernating.

"During the Bronze Age, it was even warmer than it is now." Patrick read my mind, entering the conversation in medias res. To people who didn't know us, it seemed like a magic trick. Or like Patrick suffered from Tourette's.

"So there weren't any seasons back then either?" A memory floated through the air and landed on my hand. A snowflake. Mum and I sitting at the kitchen table in the house by the forest. The scent of freshly baked butter cookies, unbearably, almost nauseatingly sweet—but only almost. In front of me, a wooden puzzle with the seasons laid out in succession—spring, summer, autumn, winter—trees, flowers, people, houses—systematic, karmic, harmonious, universal. Would that puzzle make any sense at all to children who are born now? Would they recognise anything beyond autumn's eternally overcast, melancholic dampness? The snowflake melted.

"They were there, they were just different. Like the landscape."

"Tell me about it."

Patrick was a landscape architect, and it was more than just a job title to him. On more than one occasion, he'd come home axed from a project, proudly recounting how *they* had called him a 'fanatic'. Patrick was turning his profession upside down, *they* had said. Instead of forcing nature into human paradigms, he was trying to push humans to the edge of nature. He took my hand.

"Come with me."

He pointed out a lone linden tree in the forest, squeezed between hazel and wild blackberry bushes.

"There were still primaeval forests. Lindens were more

widespread than beeches are now and there were a lot more large oaks. Entire forests of them that the farmers hadn't cut down yet."

The terrain he painted for me was still untamed. The fragile seedlings of civilisation cowered behind wattle fences and stone walls along windswept coasts. Narrow paths trodden by merchants and warriors skirted respectfully around densely wooded ridges and the vast marshes that separated the villages. Torchlight couldn't penetrate this place. What lived here could see, smell, and hear its way through the darkness that left humans blind. Only the thinnest of threads connected one settlement to another across a vast, spongy morass whose inner geography was known only to outlaws.

We stopped at the edge of the bog. Thirsty alder trees with exposed roots rose above us, trapped in the mire, their thin arms stretching up towards freedom. Grey sallows had forced their way in between. Fallen, rotting trunks jutted out of water and soil, pale yellow wood bulging from open wounds, overgrown with ground ivy and long tufts of verdigris moss, attacked by fiery orange clusters of velvet shank mushrooms. The bog water reflected it all: the tangle of lifeless reeds and self-important cattails, the ragged treetops, the eternally grey sky, the warty birches' glistening bodies covered in boils of fungi.

"They made sacrifices here. Jewellery, weapons, food. Tossed it into the lakes and bogs. Livestock, ships… people."

The bog, which had been the very edge of the world to the people of the past. The opposite of life. Everything here was in the process of decaying, being consumed, sinking, and disappearing; everything here was constantly, actively dying. It was here that our glorious, illiterate ancestors came closest to the gods. In this endless entropy, this unceasing saprophytic, cannibal orgy.

What kind of gods would ever choose to live here? And who would choose to offer sacrifices to them?

As we made our way back towards the house, its walls emerged between the trees like a mirage, like something I'd simply imagined.

PATRICK RECREATED THE evening it happened, in his own image.

"It's important, Adrian. We have to recapture it. Make it ours. Make it us."

The fox darted after a few wrens. The crowns of the alders swayed softly in the wind. It was New Year's Eve.

I nodded, because, as always, he was right.

The guest bathroom upstairs wasn't the nicest in the house, but that's where it happened. Patrick had placed a few scented candles on the shelf above the sink. A mild, tonic aroma of cedar and orange mint mingled with the steam from the shower. The mirror had fogged up, and the figures behind the glass were only vague outlines. He stood behind me, his arms wrapped around me. The heat from his body seared against my skin. His hands were strong and rough from converting ornamental gardens into animism, but also soft and supple from hours spent at the drawing board. With his left hand, he gently lifted my scrotum, with his right, he tenderly, carefully guided the razor over my skin, removing the stubble. He turned the instrument in his hand, and with a few measured strokes, shaved the very top of my inner thigh before switching sides.

It was at that moment that Dad had opened the door, completely unannounced. And it was from this point that we had to reclaim history, to rewrite an entire decade.

I'd gotten hard. I could feel him. Pressed up against me. Patrick's fingertips spread the shaving gel along newly emerged areas of nervous, expectant skin. The tip of his nose nuzzled me behind my ear. The blades of the razor licked their way from the base towards the head, the hairs they encountered along the way submitting without resistance. He harvested me. My blood pumped hard just beneath the rice-paper-thin layer of skin, purple, ready to spurt out with unruly force if Patrick cut even a millimetre wrong.

Dad didn't get angry when he found us. That wouldn't be like him at all. But I had nonetheless always imagined that he would be, all the times I had cowardly envisioned this inevitable, worst possible moment. He didn't shout, though. He didn't scold us; he didn't turn on his heel and stomp away. He just looked at us. Two teenagers, one clumsily embracing the other in an attempt to teach him how to shave his most intimate parts. My stiff cock, pointing at the spectral figures in the mirror, and—in seething hormonal assertiveness—not shrinking, not even under Dad's reptilian gaze. His face took on the same creases as when he was considering buying a contaminated plot, ripe for development, as when the choice was between toast or cornflakes in the morning, as when he decided to allow the press access to Mum's funeral.

Now, Patrick washed me with a cloth and dried me off. We sat down at the table in our kimonos and continued the re-enactment as he swapped out the props of that time with others that were sublimely superior.

That New Year's Eve, Dad had gone into town, to a party for wealthy men and young women at a hotel so expensive the staff could be trusted to hold their tongues—no matter what they might bear witness to. Patrick and I ate dinner in silence, prepared by the housekeeper and reheated in the microwave by Patrick, who was still in shock. Beef cuvette, roasted potatoes, red wine sauce, steamed green beans. Soulless, shackled by tradition, the culinary equivalent of a suburban cul-de-sac. We skipped dessert and got drunk on wine and spirits chosen by Dad—a man with more capital than culture, more ego than taste. We snorted questionable cocaine laced with unknown additives and rambled manically about everything besides what had happened, what Dad had seen, what we had done. It wasn't even midnight when we sought senseless solace in each other's bodies in my single bed. Sought so brutally—an illegal dogfight, a grave robbery, a Gestapo raid—that it would have torn us apart if we could have remembered all the details afterwards.

Now, I often dream of bog bodies.

Of people whose soul-deprived, butchered, disposable bodies were left at the water's edge, among snails and beetles, on a living sheet of composting leaves. Accompanied by the bleating roars of crumhorns and lurs, by animalistic throat-singing from chanting shamans, and—surely—grief-stricken cries from the deceased's loved ones, they slowly sank into the mire, down into the unknown, the abominable divine, the non-place between worlds. They sank and bitter water invaded every orifice, both the natural ones and the manmade. Frigid, acidic, airless, life-denying water seeped in, attempting to drown the already hanged and mutilated. And as an extra punishment, a further refined humiliation, the acid tanned their tissue, the cold preserved them like vegetables in a root cellar, and the lack of oxygen delayed the decay of their flesh.

Now, they dwell silently behind display glass smudged with children's fingerprints, on exhibit for their descendants, blackened by age, twisted like old rags, bent and flattened by the pressure of millennia—but still invariably, unforgivingly humanlike. Resurrected, they are displayed obscenely among us, hideous and mocked. They triumphantly show off their mortal wounds and broken, deformed limbs, peddling their suffering, their trauma, their meaninglessness. They ended up in neither heaven nor hell. The gods did not accept them. They were only worthy of haunting us.

We point at them. We shudder as we parade past them in the museum halls. Even their fingerprints are preserved. If we were blindfolded and they reached out and gently brushed a fingertip across the hairs on our arms, could we tell the difference between them and us? If we ran our own fingers through their thin red hair, over the leather on their fermented skulls, who would it feel like? An acquaintance? A friend? A beloved?

Are their lips soft?

I WAS ENTHRALLED by Patrick's mouth. Two peach pit-coloured mountain peaks, joined by a Hochtal depression, rising above a horizon of pink clay soil. He smiled and the mountains lifted from the earth. He smiled and revealed nature's perfection. He smiled and I crumbled.

The champagne fizzed. He placed the first courses in front of me: grilled oysters drizzled with mezcal. Scallop ceviche dusted with crushed, dried black trumpet mushrooms he'd foraged himself in September. Cod tail steamed in vermouth, bathed in browned butter. Warm sourdough rolls spread with pesto made from wild garlic we'd picked and frozen in the spring—another time, another world.

"While you wait." He poured me a glass of Silvaner and continued plating.

"Are you trying to get me drunk?"

"Of course."

It was a meal full of conflicting desires. Each new sensation was overwhelming in its own way, and the enjoyment had to be drawn out so not a single detail risked being lost. At the same time, one's eyes had already spotted the next bite, spurring the brain to imagine its scent, its texture, its taste, urging one's fingers to reach out and grab it.

Poached duck egg resting in a nest of raw hop shoots, Romanesco, raspberries, and slices of dried Nonnetit apple. In our glasses, a salty, electric Gamay grown in volcanic soil. Carpaccio with shaved North Sea Cheese, nettle crumble, love, elderflower vinaigrette, tender chickweed. Butter-fried zwieback shaped like spoons rendered cutlery unnecessary when Patrick served piping-hot marrow bones with a potpourri of horseradish cream, chopped yarrow, fried beet cubes, crisped parsley, and charred fennel.

"I love you."

"I love you."

I watched his hands as he garnished the first dessert with casual, provocative dexterity. The hands that had massaged me in the bathroom, the fingers that had combed through the hair on my chest. A pink water lily opening in the sunlight, a chameleon changing colours, a grasshopper jumping off a blade of grass.

Matcha ice cream on pale nut brittle, dusted with finely chopped white chocolate, dehydrated cherries, and fresh basil. A glass of Gewürztraminer. Butternut squash cake with chilli flakes, dripping with a ginger-honey glaze. A glass of Oloroso. Goat cheese on toasted malt bread, brushed with balsamic, topped with a pickled walnut. A glass of Chartreuse Noix.

Midnight loomed, full of promise. In the city, they would be preparing for the annual firefight in the streets: fireworks, broken glass, vomit, dancing, ambulances, boxed wine and supermarket champagne, exhilaration, disappointment, small-town types eager to be deceived, the countdown, the apocalypse, the climax. The fox trotted out of the forest with a small animal between its teeth, an owl hooted, the moon painted the trees as a sharp-toothed grin. Patrick knew me so well that he could read the future in my entrails, through my skin. I trembled, relaxed my muscles, blocked the entrances to the corrupted inner chambers of my mind, sensed that I was sensing less sharply, my blood alcohol planned just as precisely as everything else Patrick's hands had created that evening.

"And finally..." he whispered, placing the last course in front of me.

I reached for the silvered straw. Two lines of glittering, pulverised crystalline ketamine, framed by candied violets, accompanied by a glass of absinthe laced with ice-cold sugar water.

"Finally."

* * *

Silane (SiH_4) is a colourless gas with a boiling point of -112°C. It is a silicon-based chemical analogue to the more commonly known methane. Silane emerges under anoxic conditions, when dead organic matter dissolves and ferments underground. In marshlands, an upper layer of porous, likewise decaying vegetation forms a barrier that prevents the silane from escaping. When the gas nonetheless finds a labyrinthine escape route—threading its way between twigs, bone splinters, stems, and stalks, through the densely packed porridge of crumbling plant matter—it releases, for the briefest flicker of a moment, a sharp, intensely unpleasant, caustic stench akin to that of acetic acid.

Several conditions, including the wetland's inherent permeability and viscosity, influence how and when silane is released. The flux of gases, however, is consistently governed by fluctuations in atmospheric temperature. As the upper layers of water cool, they sink, displacing the warmer water closer to the bottom. As a result of these hydrodynamic movements, the sediment is disturbed and fragmented, stirring up pockets of trapped gas.

Since such drops in temperature most often occur at dusk, this release happens predominantly after nightfall. Upon contact with the oxygen-rich surface water, silane instantly demonstrates its pyrophoric talents and spontaneously ignites. The sudden jet flames that consequently sprout and surge upward, ravenous for oxygen atoms, are characteristically bluish-white and could arguably, from a phenomenological standpoint, be said to interweave all the classical alchemical elements: earth, water, air, and fire.

When, under the right circumstances, multiple such gas pockets are expelled in what appears to be chaotic, poly-rhythmic series, it might, in the misty darkness of night, appear to the feeble human eye as a single point of light, moving erratically. Accounts of these nocturnal tongues of flame—and folkloric 'explanations' for their existence—can be found across the globe, particularly in damp, thermally volatile regions such as Scandinavia and the British Isles.

Curiously enough, the occult connotations associated with these swamp flames are, across cultures, overwhelmingly negative, described in dramatic terms as ghost lights, satanic apparitions, omens of death, or malevolent spirits. In the 17th century, on the threshold between dark mysticism and potentially darker, legitimate science, the phenomenon (quite fittingly, given Dad's life story) came to be called *Ignis Fatuus*—foolish flames.

Forgive me.

THE ORGANIC LUBE smelled like olive trees. Millimetre by millimetre, Patrick gently pressed his middle finger deeper inside me, quietly, quietly humming along to a Portishead song. He kept humming even as he withdrew his finger and spread my buttocks and entered me with his tongue, engrossed, concentrated, captivated. The ketamine had already taken hold of my consciousness and was slowly tightening its grip, perfectly synchronised with Patrick's manoeuvres to loosen me up. I buried my face in the sheet.

I sank into myself and let my imagination take control. How much did I love Patrick? How deep inside me was he already? Torturously slowly, two fingers penetrated me up to the middle knuckle.

(Serial killers who kill in pairs are rare, but by no means unknown. For some of them, the ultimately profane yet sublime act of murdering another human being is too monumental not to share the experience with someone else. Most of these duos are brothers or cousins who have been shaped from a young age by the same environment, the same culture—or rather the lack thereof—and who have consequently developed a kind of 'folie à deux', a shared madness that only the two of them can understand. Others belong to the more plebeian caste of murderers who, while potentially enjoying their calling, predominantly kill for vulgar profit and form pairs purely for practical reasons.)

"You're ready for three fingers now," he breathed into my ear, and through blood-red, cottony membranes of narcotic resonance, the weight of his words (there is *no* way to explain it to an outsider) vibrated into my brain, signalling to my already feebleminded sphincter that…

(And finally, a third variant of this peculiar predatory species appears: the 'infatuated' serial killers, one might call them, as their actions seem to be driven by equal parts fascination and delusion. Such an infatuated killer duo almost always consists of a dominant partner who sets the criminal and creative, and especially sexually pathological, parameters for their joint activities, and a passive, submissive partner—an accomplice with hybristophilia—who assists, complements, and supports the object of their desire, often unconditionally.)

My nether regions were one enormous, boiling, convulsing heart muscle contracting and expanding according to Patrick's plan, utterly beyond my control.

Numb, yet seismographically sensitive. Every single nerve absorbed and relayed every impression, crushing me beneath the burden of information. Patrick eased his cockhead with brutal finesse into the epicentre of my destruction.

(It is often the job of the follower to act as a decoy. To track down, ensnare, and disarm the individual victims, to prepare them for the chosen one's use. The dominant is also often explicitly sadistic and wants to act out intricate scenarios. Here, the submissive must predict the other's needs and be prepared with chains, duct tape, cattle prod, hunting knife, sledgehammer, and whatever is needed to sanitise the scene. Voyeuristic, obliging, bewitched, and self-destructively loyal. Many would do it, but only out of fear of reprisal. Not me!)

His grip on my neck and my lower back. My rock-hard erection against the petal-soft sheets, sticky with pre-cum. Our rhythmic, rapturous sighs. The steam on the inside of the windows. The condensation droplets formed unpronounceable words in a supernatural language. Bodies so hot they melted into one. The fox pottering about. Volcanic sperm formed channels in my flesh.

(*I* would do it out of *love*. I would throw myself at his feet and beg him to wield all his cunning, inventiveness, fastidiousness, and savagery—all that energy I now know he spent on shame and secret self-torment. He should shine like a merciless, all-consuming sun and burn the universe to ash, victim after helpless victim, if only so I could kneel beside him and ecstatically watch his light cast my shadow. I would do it the very second he asked me to. I would cherish every drop of blood and bile he commanded me to wipe away. I would press the barrel of a pistol to the glistening forehead of some nameless beast of a man and pull the trigger without blinking. I would kiss every blister that blossomed on my palms as I buried a corpse. I would do anything, *anything at all*, if only he were here to command it.)

THERE ARE TWO foxes.

My urban gaze has rendered me nearsighted to nature. I can barely distinguish between the species of birds, the types of trees, or the differences between male and female foxes. I don't hear the same divine music from the forest and the bog that my ancestors danced to beneath the harvest moon. It's already February, and winter still hasn't come. It's only February, and life has already awakened from hibernation, almost before it even began. The male fox darts back and forth between its den at the bottom of the garden and the main road a few kilometres away, where he collects roadkill snacks for his little nuclear family underground. Too early. Far too early. Too late?

I sit in the kitchen where Patrick and I once shared Dad's whiskey. The housekeeper has quit. I am completely alone—apart from my foxes. It probably smells less feral down in their den than it does in here, in the house by the forest. I watch the rain through the wall of bottles before me, as it lazily yet persistently transforms the lawn into something closer to a fen.

The light plays through the still-bare treetops and reflects in the puddles. Blades of grass and twigs sway in the wind. It reminds me of flashing emergency lights. Of neon signs, scrolling marquees, traffic lights, and the thousands of headlights and taillights we used to look out over from Patrick's bachelor pad up on the tenth floor, filled with potted plants and dried herbs, so long ago. The light came in, but the sounds stayed below amongst the masses, torn to shreds by the wind before they reached us. The air was heavy with the scent of Patrick's bitter coffee, potting soil, and gasoline fumes sneaking in through the ventilation system.

Patrick's gaze was arresting. He was no coward when it came down to it. He looked me straight in the eye. He met his shame head-on.

"You'll forgive me?" he asked, almost accusatory.

"I *have* forgiven you."

"I left you."

"You left me. And now you'll have to take me back."

"Adrian… You don't understand. I… He… This place…"

"I get it. I get it, Patrick. I've known him my whole life."

"He…"

"What did he say? What did he ask for?"

And I *did* understand, because I had known Dad my whole life. It didn't surprise me that he'd arranged a meeting with Patrick, the pimply, somewhat insecure, yet unmistakably ambitious, inventive, diligent, talented, aspirational—and thus transparently self-seeking—young man he'd caught *in flagrante delicto* in the guest bathroom, my budding manhood in his hands. Nor did it startle me that he'd been polite, even gracious, when he made his offer, as if it were perfectly reasonable. It didn't astonish me in the slightest that Dad had been quite generous, offering to cover Patrick's rent, finance a study trip to France, secure him an internship at the country's leading landscape architecture firm, and even pay a monthly fee—all in exchange for Patrick's noninvolvement with me. The only thing that struck me as odd was Dad's need to explain himself. How he'd told Patrick that he didn't *really* oppose what we were doing. It just wasn't something I, the heir, should be engaged in. It didn't fit the image. He ran a masculine enterprise. And that was all there was to it.

"He didn't even ask me to do anything. Just… disappear from your life."

"And now I've found you."

"Adrian, how can you… After what I did." His eyes wandered, pausing momentarily on the bandages around my wrists.

I took his hand—strong, soft, supple, his, mine again. "How could I not?"

The house by the forest shifts, the way old houses do, when the temperature changes. The woodwork warps, the foundation burrows invisibly into the gullet of the dark earth. I woke up that New Year's night, despite the ketamine and alcohol in my veins, despite the long dinner, the hot bath, the subsequent tangle of bodies and the flood of oxytocin they had stirred up. The house woke me, but only just in time for me to bear witness to the unravelling of my microcosm, helpless to stop it.

Patrick was gone. The heat from his body still clung to the sheets. The bathroom door was ajar, revealing only darkness. I sat up. Too quickly. Precious seconds bled away while my senses struggled to catch up with my body. Dizziness prickled at my throat.

"Patrick?" The name tasted strangely obscene in my mouth, as if I were a heathen mockingly calling out to God. Nobody answered.

Rising to my feet and finding my way through the house I'd known since childhood gave me what I suppose is an uncomfortably vivid glimpse into how those disabled by dementia must experience the world. Unfamiliar constellations drifted past outside the windows. The hallway runners sent out invisible tendrils that coiled around my legs. The walls shifted whenever I reached for them to steady myself. The garden door, which connected the kitchen to the foxes' domain, stood wide open, inviting the cold inside.

"Patrick?" I could hear the confusion in my own voice. It sounded exactly like my mother's when she was tottering about the house in the anaesthetic disarray of her final months, calling out for pets put down long ago.

For ten years, I had always known where he was. For ten years, he had never gone anywhere without telling me first. Now, I was stumbling over the precipice he'd left me on without a word.

The grass was damp and flicked against my bare thighs. Only now I realised I was naked. Still, I let the house and its promises of warmth and safety fall away behind me. The soles of my feet split open on sharp stones and thorny fallen branches hidden amongst the weeds, but the cold soon blessed them so I could no longer feel the pain. One of the foxes barked shrilly, the sound heartbreakingly human. The dense undergrowth scored red lines across my face and torso as I crossed into the forest. Twigs got tangled in my hair. The darkness enveloped me, thickening, crystallising, trying to hold me captive, but I fought my way even through that, out of myself, out of control, unable to stop and think—because I knew what my thoughts would tell me.

"Patrick?" My cry rang out hoarsely through the

forest. A flock of wood pigeons took off in a panicked frenzy, thrashing through the treetops above me. Like me, they knew where they were going, and they knew the way there, but something—a fundamental flaw in their nature—kept them from taking the most direct route.

He could be anywhere. He could have called a taxi and gone to meet it, headed down towards the country road where the fox-father foraged. He could be in the workshop behind the garage where he often busied himself when sleeplessness took hold. He could, for that matter, still be in the house itself—perhaps in the basement, searching for a particular book in a still-packed moving box because he'd woken with a new idea and simply couldn't find peace again until he'd checked something or other, and where on earth was the box we'd shoved the books on mycology or viticulture or Ottoman garden design into, we really should have labelled the boxes better, and when he'd finally found the book, he would open it at once, but before he'd leafed to the right page something else would have caught his attention, and the next morning, on the first day of the new year, I would find him asleep on the floor, the book open beside him, perfectly banal, perfectly harmless, just as I'd done so many times before… but no. Patrick was in the forest, and I knew where he was headed.

My shin collided with a moss-covered stone. Everything vanished in a flash of transcendent pain. The forest floor forced its way into my mouth and smothered my howl. Damp, half-rotted leaves plastered themselves to my torso and thighs. I tumbled down a short slope, got to my feet again, and staggered on, breathless and sobbing, between the moonlit trunks that looked like set pieces from a 1920s German Expressionist film.

I was about to call out again when I caught sight of them. Patrick's kimono, with its vivid swirl of green and yellow patterns, was unmistakable, even though the bottom half had soaked up the dark brown bog water, making him almost blend into the landscape. I recognised the figure leading him as well.

It was Dad. Or rather, what was left of him. He floated above tussocks and roots clad in decapitated reeds. His body was hunched over, his neck bent forward, and his feet hung like raptor claws beneath his belly, a grotesque caricature of an unborn fetus in a mother's womb. His skin, stretched taut over his bones, was cracked and weathered, making him—even though he glistened with moisture slowly dripping from hairline fissures—still appear desiccated. He emitted a pulsating, bluish, ghostly light that illuminated the swamp a few paces around him. Patrick's shadow reached out towards me.

I stopped running. Battered and gasping for air, I approached the phantasm, momentarily convinced it would shatter like a devil's mirror if I got too close. The two of them were out among the alders, where the ground turns foul and treacherous, but they didn't stop. They continued deeper into the trap, further out into the bog.

I shoved my way through a cluster of withered teasels. Their dry stalks snapped and their bristly, spiny seeds clung to the hairs on my legs. Ice-cold, oil-black water bubbled up between my toes. My ankles disappeared and I groped for solid ground with my feet. A sucking, drawn-out sigh escaped the sodden earth with every step. By pure chance, I found a narrow strip that rose slightly above the water's surface—nothing more than a winding trail of fern-covered hummocks and slimy tree stumps, but it led me closer to my goal.

I had now gotten so close to Patrick and the Dad-creature that I could hear it rasping out an unbroken, blasphemous litany of horrors, spewing a tendril of words that coiled around Patrick's neck and held him in a stranglehold.

Dad's words stabbed needles through Patrick. The message slid through his flesh like a scalpel, loosening the skin so it peeled back, revealing the network of nerve fibres. Spirals of smoke rose where the denotations melted neurons into mercury with soldering-iron precision, shimmering enticingly, iridescent blue in the glow of Dad's aura. The water now reached Patrick's waist. His great shame was leading him to the scaffold. The memory of the betrayal he'd committed, the humiliation he'd consented to, the vile barter he'd entered into, the transaction he'd reduced us to—it was all pulling him towards the endpoint. Treacherous promises of finally finding peace banished the last doubts from his mind, chased away the last hopes of making amends, of finding salvation, of receiving the forgiveness I had long since granted him.

I screamed. My lips could no longer shape his name. I screamed only to drown out the poison being poured into Patrick's ears. And the forest screamed with me. But it was too late. He took one last laboured step and vanished abruptly into the mud as if one of the ancient demon gods, roused from millennia of slumber, had caught scent of his sacrificial flesh and swallowed him whole.

And so the bog in seconds took what life had taken decades to create. The Dad-creature lingered for a long moment, its body stripped bare, swollen with light, hovering above the water, salivating, hollow lust in its eyes. Then it sank as well. The hatred within it set the bog to a boil. I crawled naked through the veil of mist for hours before I finally found my way home.

I HAVEN'T SEEN the fox in days. February has slipped into March, but the cubs still haven't left the den. Where is he?

When will Patrick come?

I picture the fox. He's been struck by a car. His hip is shattered; he drags his hind legs behind him. He curls up, whimpering, in the roadside ditch. His gaze freezes in the moment of death, fixed on the mangled young hare he'd skulked onto the road to pick up.

I can wait as long as it takes. I'm not in any hurry.

The mother fox pokes her snout out. She's hungry. Her cubs are hungry. Without meat, she can't give them milk. The sun is rising. She squints and steps forward cautiously.

The house by the forest. My childhood home. When we arrived in autumn, it already reminded me of a sunken burial mound, a place where memories have gathered, layer upon layer, on the ridge of the roof, weighing the walls and rafters down into the embrace of oblivion with geological patience. I can hear the tiles splitting.

The mother fox slips out through the thicket, where fresh, dewy buds have appeared. I put the bottle to my mouth and imagine her finding her mate's carcass. I picture her tearing the meat from his bones, transforming his proteins into milk. I imagine the cubs sucking him from her teats.

I long for the bog, but I wait for my shining guide, my lantern carrier, the person I so naively believed I had saved by forgiving him—but who had never forgiven himself. The man I am profoundly ashamed to love so fiercely, even after he sold me.

Day breaks. I know that when Patrick comes, it will be at night. I know the curse is nearly burned out. I know that I am the last link in the chain.

I know that the bog is waiting for me.

A PRETTY PARCEL FOR A PRETTY PRICE

by AR Frederiksen

THE PARCEL IS wrapped like a gift, but I know better.

It sits on my doorstep, with my name on it, and I want to kick it.

White spots scatter across my vision, like snow in summer. I grab the doorframe with both hands and lock my knees in place. Easier said than done.

A parcel means only one thing these days.

The national postal service stopped delivering packages a long time ago. To avoid lawsuits, that is, from citizens who suffered heart attacks and post-traumatic stress disorder when they received parcels they'd forgotten they'd ordered.

"I'm sorry." Maryam's voice startles me. Her fingers brush my back. "I'm so sorry."

I manage to wheeze, "Next in line, I guess."

Maryam's hand falls from my back. "Renee, I don't…"

I finally let go of the doorframe. The distress in Maryam's voice helps me focus. Turning to her, I drop my hand on her shoulder. "It's okay. You can be relieved it's not you."

She bites her lip, drawing my attention to her mouth despite the damning parcel by my feet, which is the effect she's always had on me. "I don't want to be relieved," she says, shuffling beneath the weight of my hand on her shoulder. "It'll happen to me eventually."

I pat her shoulder once. "But not yet." A wan smile. "You're still in the clear."

When I turn back to the parcel, I notice an elderly couple across the road. They're walking their dog. Or they were, at least, before they stopped to watch me with my parcel.

I try not to cower. Instead, I hold my head high.

I knew this was coming. We all know. Maybe not that elderly couple and their dog, though. They look like they might be denying it all. All my luck to them.

Maryam pushes up beside me in the doorway until we're both staring at the parcel, wrapped in shimmery foil that looks like it belongs on a catwalk rather than a USPS office. It belongs to neither place, really, and I'm just trying to distract myself from what comes next. The knowledge slithers along my spine, lying flat, pressing gently inwards.

"If they're rounding you up…" Maryam trails off. She's doing that a lot.

I shake my head. "Nobody says they're going by age."

Maryam sighs. "No, they go by social circle."

I finally kneel by the parcel. The elderly couple with their dog are still staring, spectating, from across the road. I have the perverse urge to unveil the parcel here, out in the open, and give them a taste of what nobody in their right mind should want to witness until it's their turn. But I remember having done the same before. I have been a spectator before. I am no better than them. We're all preparing ourselves for our parcels, only in different ways.

"Social circle?" Craning my neck, I look up at Maryam, her face haloed by her curls against the winking sun. "That's what you think they go by?"

She shrugs, biting her lip once again. "Acclimation and proximity seem the most natural selection process." She jerks her chin forward, at the parcel. "What's the deadline?"

The foil of my parcel shimmers like something unreal because it *is* something unreal.

Rubbing my clammy hand across my mouth, I say, "I need to open it to see the deadline, I think. There's only my name on the outside. Look there."

Maryam's fingers thread through my hair where she stands behind me. I'm still kneeling on my own doorstep. "Open it," she says. "Rip it off like a Band-Aid."

We broke up months ago, back when the parcels first started showing up, and people began to understand. It could be worse. A lot of people divorced and got abortions, but we never got that far. Whole families jumped off bridges together, and the government legalized assisted suicide. Most people chose to simply wait for their parcel delivery, though.

I stand and nudge the parcel inside with my foot. "Let's go inside. Mr. and Mrs. Smith have too good a view over there. They'll keel over if I open it here. They know better."

Popular movies always portray alien technology as something flinty and silver-black. Blue. Or a pulsating purple, like a discolored artery. They mimic the palette of the galaxy, the void of space. But alien technology isn't like that. Not the kind that came here, anyway.

That kind is organic. Soft. Malleable. It has to be. That's another thing the movies get wrong; they always portray aliens as wanting the planet instead of the people.

Once inside, I put my pretty parcel on the kitchen table.

Then, pulling at the shimmery foil, I open it, unveiling the ugly stuffing.

"It looks like an overgrown pimple," Maryam says, breaking the silence.

I inhale through my nose, but it has no smell. "I sure as fuck won't be popping it."

The flesh-colored sphere rests on its nest of foil, swaying gently to an unheard tune. If I stare at it for too long, I fear I'll see eyes popping open between fleshy folds. My own eyes. It sets my heart racing and my neck prickling. The back of my tongue tastes bitter, spit pooling, and I swallow that bitterness alongside the equally bitter truth of this moment.

"The deadline is today," I announce. "So. There is no deadline. Basically."

Maryam glances at me. Her eyes are wide, her mouth ajar. "Where do you read that?"

I don't read it. I don't even see it. I feel it. A pinprick in my side like I've run for too long without a break. To her credit, Maryam doesn't ask again when I stay silent. She wraps an arm around my waist and presses her nose against my shoulder.

I put my hand on top of hers where it rests on my hip. "You don't have to stay. If they truly select based on proximity..." I pause and then reroute entirely. "And you don't have to see it happening. I don't want you to see it happening. I don't want—"

Maryam kisses me. It's sweet and soft. And then it isn't.

"One last time?" she breathes against my mouth, salty and feverish at the same time. I nod, my knee knocking against the chair. The motion jars the table where two eyes pop open between fleshy folds, one at a time. I don't see it, but I feel it.

Pop. I curl myself tighter around Maryam. *Pop*.

BY THE SECOND hour, it begins to look like me.

It's no longer a pair of eyes on top of a kitchen table, but has morphed to the right height, the right weight, and even the way that I hunch over my phone when Maryam texts me immediately after she exits my house for the last time.

I go to the park, leaving my phone behind.

We sit on a bench, my doppelganger and me.

It has accurately copied my facial features, but they're blurry around the edges. Like a memory gone stale. A painting left in a humid basement. I'm enough of a scientist to look at my doppelganger and appreciate the way it has even included the scar on my chin that I got from a drunken fallout with my sister before she got her parcel half a year ago.

A child runs up to me, pigtails bopping in her wake.

"Mommy says I give good hugs," she whistles, folding her arms behind her back. She's missing one of her front teeth. I smile faintly. That explains the whistle. "I can give you a good hug. Do you want a good hug?"

I'd take a bad one, honestly, but the child's mother is approaching. Her face looks like it's two seconds from caving in on itself. I take pity on her and shake my head at the child.

"Take care, kid," I say just as the mother reaches us.

She grabs the girl by the shoulders, her knuckles going white, a gold band wrapped around one finger, and then hauls the girl away. She doesn't look at me. At us. Not even a flutter of her lashes. Looking might make it real, after all. It's a different approach than the elderly couple with their dog. I smile wryly and look at my hands in my lap, open palms facing upwards.

"Children get special parcels," my doppelganger says. "They're simpler creatures."

A shiver curls around my neck like a choker, a key turning in a lock with a quiet click.

"So," I say, "that's what my voice sounds like to others, is it?"

My doppelganger smiles at me. "We're right on schedule."

Fear and fascination pull the skin on my scalp tight. "Fantastic."

"Fantastic," my doppelganger repeats, modulating the tone to match mine.

I level my voice before asking, "And what happens when the schedule ends?"

My doppelganger blinks at me and something slots into place on her face. A muscle. A joint. Sinew. A pair of teeth aligning, the angle of her jaw flattening out. I'm staring into a mirror, no blurry edges in sight, and I want that hug now. Good or bad. I almost stand up to walk down the path where the mother and child left, but my doppelganger stops me.

She pats the bench, head cocked. "Sit, please."

I realize I'm standing. "I'd rather go home."

She smiles. "Sure. Let's go home."

Anger takes root in me, but it doesn't fully sprout until we return home. At that point, it has sprouted and curled along my spine, throbbing gently at the base of my neck. Months ago, my job gave us counseling on grief management. That was when people still thought the parcels would be a temporary thing. More localized, at least. Reality has caught up by now.

When we return home, my doppelganger enters the house first.

I stay outside, just for a moment, to watch a blackbird flop about in the bushes. Birds don't receive parcels. No animal does. Some people inject themselves with animal blood to put off their parcel delivery, but I'm more the type to face my problems than avoid them.

That's why I nearly lose my shit when I walk inside the house.

Maryam is perched on the kitchen table, my doppelganger standing in between her spread legs. Maryam rips away from their kiss. At first, she's startled by my appearance. Then her face shifts to shock. The temperature in the room has dropped below freezing. Or maybe that's my anger talking; it's no longer a dull ache at my neck, but a full-blown fire-hot rash across all of my body, from toe to scalp.

My doppelganger steps away from Maryam and beams at me.

Maryam stumbles off the table. "I thought—fuck—I thought it was you."

I say nothing. She wasn't supposed to come back here. And if she did, she could at least have used her shit for brains. My anger coalesces in the tips of my fingers.

They itch.

Smiling tightly, I stride past both of them to grab the oyster knife I've never used before now. I hate oysters. I hate all shellfish. The knife is lodged deep in one of the bottom drawers. By the time I finally get it jostled free, my smile is in rigor mortis on my face. The knife is a solid weight in my palm, and it will land a solid blow.

I will pry myself open like a clam.

Maryam is there, halo of hair blocking my view. "Stop. Renee. Don't forget Loulie."

I wave the knife at her. "Don't fucking pretend you don't want me to do this. You want it just as much as I do. Be lucky I'm the first one of us."

Her mouth snaps shut. She steps aside and curls in on herself. The truth hurts.

My doppelganger awaits me. She doesn't move away when I approach. She doesn't even raise her arms. Her smile stays on her face even when the first slash of the oyster knife splits her cheek in two. *Slash*. Then her chin. *Slash*. Then her throat.

The ripest of red mists, sweet and tannic, *swoosh*.

It shimmers in the air, caught by the lamplight, and then it lands flat on the carpet.

My doppelganger stares back at me, one eye filmy. A gutted fish. She crumples by my feet in a soft squirt, a heap of meat no different than what was once in a parcel labeled with my name. I let my anger lift me up, knowing I'll fall deep otherwise.

Maryam's hands are gentle when they wrestle the oyster knife free from my grip. Those same hands are cool as they encircle my face. She stares at me. I stare back at her. When she releases me and steps back, her chin trembling, I know she's seen her future self reflected on my own face. The future of us all. She'll have to cope with that.

There's blood on my forehead. Cooling. Like glue.

I'm about to wipe it off, but then the doorbell rings.

I make it to the door without my legs giving way beneath me. The ground doesn't swallow me up, but I think maybe it should. Maryam follows me, but it's not as if she has a choice. None of us has a choice. I can deal with that. I know as much now.

I open the door.

The parcel is wrapped like a gift.

I clear the gravel from my throat, asking, "How many times did Loulie do it?"

Maryam isn't threading her fingers through my hair this time but stands far away from me. Her voice is small when she answers, and I know it has nothing to do with the literal distance between us. I find that I don't care. Maybe I will later. When the shock is gone. That is, if I am ever allowed to feel any shock. If this is the speed I'll have to work at, I wager the shock will simply never come, but stay buried, and perhaps that's good.

"Ten times," Maryam answers. "Loulie did it ten times before she couldn't do it anymore. It gets worse, Ree. They become more and more like you. And then they start to fight you. Properly." She drops the oyster knife to the floor. "It learns from you."

I clench my hands into fists by my sides. "Then I'll keep learning, too."

I can kill myself over and over again; that's fine. *Pop, pop. Slash, slash. Swoosh.* Anything so I won't die. Anything to outlast this. A pretty parcel for a pretty price.

I grab my gift and bring it inside.

MR SCHADAY

by Mikkel Harris Carlsen
Translated by Olivia Lasky

What is the knocking at the door in the night?
It is somebody wants to do us harm.

As far as I'm concerned, it all began in the widow Schumann's guest house on the edge of town. The room I rented was cold and miserable, with a threadbare carpet and mouldy stains on the reddish-brown wallpaper. But it was what I could afford. The furniture—none of which was mine—bore traces of the previous tenants, one of whom had apparently had the unfortunate habit of scratching their unclipped nails on the armrest of the easy chair. It always caused a certain discomfort within me when I caught myself rubbing my fingers against the scratches that had been left behind. It could even occur to me that by repeating another's compulsive ritual, I was somehow diligently working to erase my own frayed self; after the dark years, there was evidently nothing left of that once so promising 'I' but that which might be absent-mindedly rubbed off against an armrest.

To all appearances, the house was the only inhabited dwelling in the area. It was a rare occasion when others appeared on the street, and then usually a vendor hawking soap and other household goods, or a cripple dragging himself along on crutches or else perched atop a cart, rowing himself forward with his arms to beg in town. Behind Mrs Schumann's kitchen garden, vast fields stretched out, long since overtaken by thistles and various other weeds. From the window of my attic room, I could just make out the spire of the bombed-out cathedral in the city centre.

Mrs Schumann shared the ground floor with her invalid brother, Emil, who, in addition to being paralysed from the waist down, had also lost the power of speech. He still proved himself to be a rather capable chess player, however, and after dinner, we would often spend many a pleasant hour hunched over the pieces, with victories and defeats distributed more or less evenly between us. When he expressed delight over winning a game, a wet gurgle rose from his scarred throat, which always made me look away. His sister occasionally reproached him for the fact that, besides the two rooms upstairs, she couldn't rent out one more, but she always spent a long time apologising after such an outburst, assuring him that, of course, he wasn't a burden—or whatever else she might have called him in her fit of anger.

Despite these complaints, the room next to mine hadn't been rented out in the six months I'd been living in the house, which gave me the luxury of being the only one who used the toilet in the attic corridor. This convenience came to an abrupt end, however, when Mrs Schumann announced one morning that she'd finally found a tenant for the vacant room.

I was sipping my morning coffee before heading to work when she shared the good news in a manner that was both joyful and dignified. I myself was less enthusiastic and left the house feeling dejected. Not only would I now have to share the toilet with someone else, I would also have to live with the sounds of their daily tasks and routines. I thrived best in silence and was easily irritated by the smallest disturbance; even the slightest rattling or the mere clearing of a throat from the next room could be enough to unsettle my peace of mind.

The new tenant had already moved in when I got back that evening. During dinner, Mrs Schumann—with an air of great importance—whispered that Mr Schaday, who wanted his meal to be served in his room, seemed to be a highly learned and respectable gentleman. She was convinced he must be a professor or something to that effect, but hadn't yet had the opportunity to question him, as he had disappeared into his room immediately after moving in with strict instructions that he was not to be disturbed. When I asked about his age and appearance, she fell silent and simply stared at me with a look of perplexion. She hesitantly raised her hands as if to trace his outline in the air, then gave up and murmured that he was difficult to describe. But he seemed "highly learned and respectable," she repeated, clearly bewildered by her inability to provide a clear description of her new tenant.

After a game of chess with Emil, which I won, I went up to my room to read a bit. Standing before my door, I considered knocking on the one beside it to get the introduction over with but decided to put it off until breakfast—unless he preferred having *that* served in his room as well.

Once inside my little cubbyhole, I lit the reading lamp

and stood in front of the bare wall, listening. The wind whistled in the window frame. Down in the parlour, Mrs Schumann burst into laughter; Emil had presumably made some sort of blunder.

Just as I was sitting down in the corner with a book, I heard the sound of a typewriter from the other side of the wall. Already irritated at this first disturbance—which would hardly be the last—I bit the inside of my cheek, struck by the clumsiness with which he seemed to be operating the machine. The keystrokes were so hesitant and uncertain that I thought of a child laboriously spelling its way through a difficult text. He could scarcely be so 'learned' if he typed in such a manner. Or perhaps he, too, was an invalid, though less conspicuously than the poor fellow downstairs. Annoyed, I gave up reading and reluctantly went to bed.

As a result of the increasing autumn storms that rattled the evenings, I had been plagued by sleeplessness for some time. That night, I slept even more fitfully than usual. Each time I awoke, I thought I could hear the clattering of the typewriter on the other side of the wall, but when I held my breath and listened, all I could hear was the wind whistling in the window frame.

I felt the urge to use the toilet just as dawn began to break. As I staggered into the corridor, I saw the light on in the frosted window of the bathroom door and returned to my room. Luckily, I fell straight back asleep and thereby secured a couple of unbroken hours of rest until Mrs Schumann rang the bell.

I didn't have the chance to greet my new neighbour at the breakfast table either, as it turned out he had already left the house. I could have sworn I heard him pottering about in there while I was getting dressed, but to be fair, a mouse scurrying in the walls could just as easily have produced a similar sound.

Mrs Schumann, who—most unusually for her—still had her nightcap on, seemed strikingly absent-minded that morning, as though she, too, had slept poorly.

During my lunch break, I ran into an acquaintance at my favourite café, Max Beckmann, who worked with the municipal registry at the city hall. I asked him if he knew anything about Mrs Schumann's new tenant, a Mr Schaday. Beckmann replied in the negative, adding that he wasn't aware of any reported moves, either in or out of the city, during the past month. Perhaps even longer.

We ate in silence that evening. Emil, naturally, was excused, while Mrs Schumann seemed even more preoccupied than she'd been that morning, which wasn't at all like my otherwise lively and talkative landlady. I was exhausted after a long day at work and went straight to my room after dinner, though not without a pang in my heart as I chose to ignore Emil's rattling of the chess pieces behind me.

Once again, Mr Schaday sat next door, hammering away at the machine, and once again, I had to give up on reading. I thought it might be a good opportunity to introduce myself—and at the same time hint at how sound carried through the house.

But just as I rose to act on my resolve, I was overcome by a violent resistance in my body and practically fell back into the chair. A sudden feeling of dread welled up inside my chest like a suffocating growth, making my throat tighten. The light from the reading lamp seemed to grow dimmer, a shadow fell across the room and made it appear larger, deeper; the colours had darkened or almost seemed drained from the furniture. On top of it all, I became aware that the typing next door had ceased—and then, at that very moment, there was a knock at the door.

I didn't dare move, let alone breathe, and simply stared at it. It still seemed to be getting darker around me. And colder. Downstairs, I could hear Mrs Schumann scolding poor Emil and—for one futile moment—I considered crying out for help with every ounce of strength I had. But the horror had settled on my chest like a wax seal.

Another knock came at the door, this time quite slowly, as though no one besides me was meant to hear it. I still didn't dare move a muscle and marvelled at this paralysing fear that was preventing me from reacting. Nothing on this earth could make me open the door. I would rather throw myself out the window!

My nails pressed into the armrests, deepening the scratches already etched there, and it occurred to me that a previous tenant might have once sat in this very same predicament.

A whispered prayer to the God I no longer believed in threatened to escape my godless mouth. I was now gripping the armrests so tightly I feared my fingers would snap like dry twigs. Just then, the lamp began to shine more brightly, the shadows dispersed, and Mr Schaday resumed his typing in the room next door.

I felt utterly foolish once the terror had released its hold and scarcely recognised myself. What on earth had driven me to react in such a way? And what would my neighbour think if he knew I'd been sitting here, trembling at the prospect of meeting him?

So as not to betray my presence, I chose to go to bed early, though I struggled to rid myself of the thought that he must have heard me come upstairs. Still, I undressed as quietly as I could and crept into bed. The bedsprings tattled and forced me to lie motionless in a rather unfortunate position until, little by little, one slight shift at a time, I managed to get comfortable. If I met him the next day, I would somehow communicate that I hadn't been at home, and that the wind was responsible for many strange sounds in the old house.

In the morning, I heard him bustling about next door. Last night's fear still clung to me, but determined not to postpone the meeting any longer, I left my room and walked down the corridor.

At that moment, Mrs Schumann stepped out of the neighbour's door with a mop and bucket in hand. Mr Schaday had already left the house.

I LINGERED OUT on the dark street when I came home from work, rust-coloured leaves rasping past in the wind, and looked up at the windows of my neighbour's room. It was impossible to tell whether there was a light on inside or not. For a moment, I considered turning back to the city and spending the night at an inn but dismissed the thought. After all, I couldn't be certain that he had, in fact, heard me.

However, it wasn't only the memory of yesterday's embarrassing episode that plagued me, but also the concern that it—or something similar—might happen again. Perhaps I should simply take the initiative and get it over with, I thought, and strode resolutely through the front door. Mrs Schumann immediately scurried over to take my coat and inform me that my neighbour had gone out of town for a few days. I was once again spared from meeting him.

In the meantime, dear Mrs Schumann had returned to her former self, and together with Emil, we sat down for an exquisite meal that she had evidently spent most of the day preparing.

That evening, I stayed downstairs and played three long games with Emil. He won them all, but it was well deserved, and for once, I didn't avert my gaze when his outbursts of joy bubbled up in his throat. In the days that followed, I relished the return of the old order—if only for a fleeting moment—and the once familiar, homely atmosphere settled over the little guest house again.

Later that week, I was woken in the wee hours of the night by creaking footsteps in the corridor, and it was not without a certain disheartenment that I concluded that Schaday must have returned from his journey.

But as I lay my head on the pillow, I heard a sound that jolted me upright. It was the sound of a key being placed in my keyhole.

I stared dumbstruck at the door. In all the time I'd been lodging at Mrs Schumann's, I had never once locked my door at night, fully trusting that the front door on the ground floor afforded me sufficient protection.

While the key continued rattling in the lock, I tried to decide whether I could reach the door before he grasped the handle and discovered it was unlocked but had to admit that—yet again—I was far too terrified to act. The notion that it might only be my neighbour, who, in the dim light of the corridor, had mistaken our doors, was of no comfort. On the contrary, I huddled wretchedly in the bed and awaited the unbearable moment when he would step in and I would find myself alone with him in the dark.

The sounds soon ceased, thank God, and I heard the door being unlocked and opened in Schaday's room shortly thereafter.

A long, wheezing breath escaped my chest. When I was finally able to think clearly again, I resolved that I would not let the coming day pass without meeting him. By doing so, I would undoubtedly learn that he possessed none of the demonic powers my imagination had bestowed upon him, and the fear would forever be driven from our house.

This resolve, however, was already met with resistance the next morning, since Mr Schaday had left the house by the time I came down to the dining room for breakfast. Thus, the meeting had to be postponed until the evening, and if that too should end in failure, I would compose a letter of welcome and slip it under his door.

I was stirring sugar into my coffee when a knock came at the door, and as Mrs Schumann was busy in the kitchen, I took it upon myself to open it. A man in a ragged uniform stood outside, two crutches pressed tight beneath his armpits, one trouser leg tied in a knot beneath his stump of a leg. The cripple nodded silently and handed me a brown envelope, which I accepted with the suspicion that he had been holding it between his wet lips while knocking. Back at the table, I read the following typewritten message:

> *Have important information reg. your neighbour, Schaday. Please meet me at the shopping arcade at 1 p.m.*
>
> *Yours faithfully, Max Beckmann*

I read these words over and over again, finding it remarkably peculiar that my acquaintance had written me such a message. What could it possibly mean? Excited, yet also ill at ease, I hurried off to work and awaited the lunch break with mounting nervousness.

When at last the town hall clock struck its single chime, I positioned myself in the bustling shopping arcade where Beckmann had asked to meet me. He came scurrying towards me a minute later, visibly agitated.

"Good, you got my message," he mumbled, hustling me into a corner. "I don't have much time but listen: it is of the utmost importance—a matter of life and death, in fact—that you and your neighbour, this Schaday, never be in the same place at the same time. Do you hear me?"

I caught myself staring at him in astonishment.

"What do you mean? We're next-door neighbours!"

"Yes, yes! But you must never find yourselves in the same room. It's of the utmost importance!" he insisted, blinking anxiously behind his foggy spectacles.

When he met my sceptical gaze, a moment's self-control seemed to descend upon him.

"Yes, I know it sounds absurd," he said, smiling tensely, "but you must believe me; it is not only a matter of your own safety, but also of mine. Of everyone's!"

With this cryptic warning, he looked around nervously and disappeared from the shopping arcade at a jog while I was left standing there, frozen like a pillar of salt.

Though Beckmann's words sounded utterly insane, they somehow still made perfect sense given my present circumstances. Had I not felt this all along—that we shouldn't meet, Schaday and I? It was like a state decree, unavoidable and beyond dispute. Was that not precisely the explanation for the icy terror I had felt when he knocked at my door?

On the walk back, my previous plans for meeting Mr

Schaday that day gave way to a firm resolve to avoid him at all costs.

I was, however, soon forced to admit that while evading him had previously been effortless, it now proved to be a veritable challenge. Already the next morning, I heard Mrs Schumann speaking with someone downstairs in the dining room, and from her overly deferential tone, I had to conclude that it certainly wasn't Emil. Although I couldn't hear the other voice, I didn't dare go down, fearing it was my neighbour, who until then had always left the house before me. Instead, I slipped back into my room, waiting with the uneasy sense that this game of hide-and-seek was destined to become a fixture of my daily life. And in that, I was not mistaken.

My everyday existence turned into one long, evasive manoeuvre. If I heard Schaday on the stairs, I immediately darted into my room to hide. By arrangement with my superior, I had, most graciously, been allowed to start work half an hour later on the condition that I remained at the office a full hour longer. I was therefore the last to leave and bore the responsibility of locking up the building, which at times tempted me to stay there for the night, when my fear of Schaday was at its worst.

Naturally, I considered moving but didn't have the means. My meagre income allowed me to maintain only the most basic existence, without any chance of saving, and I could hardly hope to find rent as reasonable as Mrs Schumann's. I tried to seek out Beckmann several times to get him to elaborate on his warning, but he seemed to make a point of avoiding me and was always in a hurry should I happen to run into him.

Fortunately, my evenings with Mrs Schumann and Emil were left in peace, though I was always on edge if a sound from upstairs reached us. Mr Schaday continued to request his dinner be served in his room, where, according to Mrs Schumann, he was working on a manuscript. My overwrought nerves naturally impaired my chess-playing abilities, and I soon became easy prey for Emil.

My greatest source of vexation was this: it seemed to me that Schaday was always using the toilet whenever I had the same need. The light was always on in there when I crept into the corridor, and I had to wait patiently in my room until I heard him close his door. Only in the mornings and late at night did I have the toilet to myself.

There was one late night, however, when I got a terrible fright while sitting in there. Without any warning whatsoever, someone suddenly tried the door handle. I nearly screamed. The little latch danced in its socket in rhythm with my panicked pulse, and a shadow slid slowly across the frosted pane.

I held my breath and listened. Schaday's room was directly opposite the bathroom door, so I surely would have heard if he had gone back inside and now had to assume he was standing out there, waiting. I was therefore not only forced to carry out my business with an audience, but I would also no longer be able to avoid finding myself in the same room with him when I stepped out into the corridor shortly thereafter.

For a moment, I sat in silence, hoping the house might miraculously be struck by one of those bombs that had, only a few years earlier, turned the city into a heap of ruins. Then I swallowed my shame, finished my errand, and flushed.

No one was waiting outside, the corridor was empty, and I slipped back into my room. Only when I lay my head on the pillow and exhaled did I realise that I quite possibly hadn't drawn a breath since Schaday tried the bathroom door.

THE NEXT MORNING, I again heard Mrs Schumann conversing with Schaday downstairs and hurried back to my room. I was already running late and checked my watch impatiently. Luckily, I heard the slam of the door shortly thereafter and drew the curtains. Now I could get a glimpse of my tormentor at last!

But to my great astonishment, I saw that it was none other than Max Beckmann bustling down the garden path, his attaché case tucked under his arm!

What could this mean? Was he the one living next door under the name Schaday—and for some reason wanting to keep this from me?

When I came down to the sitting room, I could scarcely contain my agitation and no doubt frightened my poor landlady out of her wits. My voice trembling, I demanded an explanation.

Wailing and wringing her hands, Mrs Schumann confessed that she had promised her guest not to reveal his visit, but one look at my face quickly made her decide that her loyalty to her tenant bore greater weight.

Beckmann had presented himself as a representative of the state on an important errand that was a matter of public safety. No, more than that, even. But before he could reveal any more, Mrs Schumann had to swear not to reveal anything about the matters she was now to be entrusted with.

But what he had told her was nothing more than a repetition of what he had previously shared with me:

that her two tenants must, on no account, meet one another, and that she must promise to do whatever she could to prevent such a thing from occurring.

Once I'd comforted a visibly shaken Mrs Schumann, I had to rush to catch the tram. I breathlessly flung myself into a vacant seat, my thoughts in disarray.

So the scoundrel had tried to enlist my unsuspecting landlady in order to lend weight to his request. But what could his motive be? On what grounds did this so-called 'representative of the state'—I almost laughed aloud at his conceit—wish to keep me and Schaday apart? My earlier suspicion that Schaday and Beckmann were one and the same no longer held, since, unlike me, Mrs Schumann had seen Mr Schaday with her own eyes.

My thoughts grew unruly in my agitated state, but although I would have loved to defy Beckmann and prove that his demand was utter nonsense, I was nevertheless unable to ignore the dread I felt at the thought of meeting the enigmatic Schaday, the shadow on the glass pane.

Perhaps, on the contrary, I ought to be grateful that he had involved Mrs Schumann in the matter. *He* wasn't the only one who'd gained a new ally.

I slept at the office that night and was thus forced to endure the following workday weary and unkempt.

I DIDN'T HEAR anything from Schaday for the next couple of days, and Mrs Schumann was tactful enough not to mention him. While we hadn't spoken of it further, it was evident that she was determined to do whatever she could to keep us apart. When I sat down at the breakfast table, she would signal with an almost imperceptible nod or a discreet motion of the hand that Schaday had left, and in the evenings, she was nearly as tense as I was whenever there was a sound from upstairs. I sensed that, should he unexpectedly come down into the sitting room, she would intercept him, thereby giving me the chance to escape through the front door.

Emil, blissfully unaware of all this, seemed not to notice these small signals we exchanged with one another.

On the third day, however, I felt the need to be alone and went up to my room. I hadn't heard the typewriter in some time, but that evening, he was pounding away at the keys in there, faster and more assuredly than before.

I carefully dragged the easy chair over to the wall and sat down. There was something at once soothing and unsettling about the monotonous typing and the little jolt at each line shift. I tried to focus on the fact that, just on the other side of the thin wall, sat a man—a 'learned and respectable gentleman', as Mrs Schumann had described him—writing on a perfectly ordinary typewriter. For a brief moment, my unnatural anxiety gave way to a mawkish urge to excuse my behaviour, but just as I considered leaving all that nervousness behind and stepping out to knock on his door, my heart began to flutter in my chest.

I feared that he had had the same idea, and if the typing had stopped at that moment, I would likely have fainted from fright. Fortunately, Schaday continued to type merrily away.

I awoke in the easy chair later that night. The wind made the rafters creak. He was still working at the machine next door, but the keystrokes were now as slow and hesitant as the first time I had heard them. It sounded as though each key was being held down for quite some time before he released it, and I immediately got the impression that he was writing in his sleep or some kind of trance.

There was something soporific about the sound, something hypnotic, which lulled me into dreams of fairground jugglers, sawdust, and horses that could add and subtract on command. For the rest of the night, I slept more heavily and deeply than I had in a very long time.

Although he still terrified me, I could not deny that he roused a particular curiosity. I therefore allowed myself the habit of settling down each evening to listen to his work. It was a nerve-wracking situation that nonetheless felt safe, like studying a python through the glass pane of a terrarium. I thought that I might be able to rid myself of my fear in this way.

If nothing else, the sounds did in fact help me to fall asleep—at least at first. Before long, however, the typing took on a new, ominous tone. Each evening, he seemed to be typing faster and faster, until it no longer sounded as though he were typing at all, but rather hammering away at the same key at an impossibly frenzied pace.

I had no idea how I was supposed to respond to this sinister, orgiastic maelstrom and simply sat mute, paralysed, staring wide-eyed into the reddish-brown wallpaper. Could they really not hear it downstairs, and should we not do something—as the poor man was clearly stark raving mad? Was that why I was not allowed to meet him? Because he was of a sick mind? Perhaps once a learned and respectable gentleman, but now an outcast who might infect others with his insanity? Plagued by morbid and depraved thoughts, a threat to public safety?

Hadn't we all only just been in the grip of madness?

Now, it was time to forget and to move forward, towards healing and rebuilding.

One evening, in the midst of such a turmoil of typing, it suddenly fell silent.

For some reason, I reacted to this unexpected interruption with a horror more intense and overwhelming than anything I had previously experienced with regard to my peculiar neighbour.

I instinctively rushed out of my room and down into the corridor, snatched up my hat and coat in passing, and left the house. I caught a glimpse of Mrs Schumann in the sitting room, who looked up from her knitting in alarm.

Out on the street, I dodged a dark figure hobbling along with a crutch and caught a tram. That night, the office would once again serve as my lodgings.

THE FOLLOWING DAY was a Sunday. An incandescent fog had wrapped itself tightly around the city. I spent the morning walking around the lakes and had a light lunch at a modest eatery in the city centre. Afterwards, I settled on an ashlar by the ruins of the old monastery—yet another cultural treasure the dark times had devoured.

Faith had been a natural foundation of existence when I was younger, and the rubble around me somehow reflected my later break with the worldview instilled by a religious upbringing. Where was the Lord—without whom not even the tiniest sparrow falls to the ground—when the cities were burning and chimneys were raising their accusations up towards the sky?

Behind these soot-blackened walls, rising so admonishingly from the dark earth, men had once sought His grace through repetition and renunciation, *ora et labora*. Repetition upon repetition, bell toll after bell toll. And as the brothers of the order had submitted to the closed circuit of repetition, so too did the factory workers, the street sweepers, the cobblers, the schoolteachers—everyone. Repetition, routine, security. Wasn't all culture and civilisation simply an endless warding-off ritual, meant to keep something unbearable at bay? And when that *something* came knocking late one evening, what could one do but cling to the familiar, claw one's nails bloody on the repetition, and hope that it would pass by?

Paradoxically enough, these and other thoughts gave me a certain kind of comfort, and I was therefore in reasonably good spirits when at last I set out for home. Naturally, it was still necessary to avoid Mr Schaday, but I had a strong feeling that today, this wouldn't pose a problem. At least not in the light of day.

As I made my way up the garden path, everything seemed to be radiating peace and calm. Shrouded in a quilt of fog, the house appeared to be the safe and inviting refuge it had once been. I removed my hat and coat in the corridor, hung them on the stand, and stepped into the sitting room.

I'd scarcely had time to get my bearings before it happened: a vast shadow flickered before my sight; a darkness so dense it blinded me, as though I were staring into the sun. I felt tears streaming down my cheeks and feared that my eyes were melting like pats of butter on Mrs Schumann's frying pan.

He's here! seared through me. But when I regained my vision, I saw only Emil sitting in his wheelchair in the corner, a woollen blanket draped over his lap.

"Oh, Emil," I gasped. "For a moment, I thought Schaday was here."

"He was," he answered in a quivering voice. "He touched me."

Before I could even grasp the fact that Emil had spoken—clearly and distinctly—he threw the blanket aside and rose to his feet. He took a single step forward on stiff, uncertain legs, spread his arms wide, and stared at me with a dazed, maniacal gaze.

"He touched me!" he shrieked. "Schaday!"

Terrified, I backed out of the room, found the front door behind me, and stumbled out into the mist. The fog bank parted like sheets hung out to dry as I ran headlong down the street. I glimpsed the outlines of crippled figures dragging themselves past me in the opposite direction—hobbling, limping, crawling.

I burst onto the boulevard at the end of the street, unable to make out anything but the tram tracks and skeletal silhouettes of the chestnut trees. I had to get to the city, where I could disappear into the crowd.

I barely managed to remember that my coat was still hanging in the entrance, and that I therefore had no money, when two bright lights pierced the fog ahead of me.

I THOUGHT I heard the monotonous murmur of a large gathering, all talking over one another. I woke up and remembered the collision with the tram. When I opened my eyes, I did not, as I had expected, see a hospital room, but rather my own.

Mrs Schumann sat at my side with her knitting in her lap, studying me closely.

"You're awake," she observed, and patted me on my arm reassuringly.

When I tried to sit up, a sharp pain in my leg hindered me. At the same time, a pounding headache drove my hand to my brow, where I found my head swathed in gauze.

"Yes, you've taken a few knocks." Mrs Schumann lifted her hand from my arm.

I had to swallow a few times to clear my dry throat.

"Shouldn't I be in the hospital?"

"Oh no, that isn't necessary. You saw for yourself what he did to Emil."

At that moment, a cry sounded from the sitting room that made me freeze.

"Schaday!"

"Schaday!" Mrs Schumann repeated, chirping melodically as she clapped her hands. "He's finally finished his book. Emil is reading it aloud right now to all who will listen. You should see it! The sitting room is full of those who have been called, and more are coming all the time!"

I stared at my hostess in disbelief, not knowing how to respond. During my unconsciousness, she had apparently been seized by the same sanctimonious madness as Emil.

"He's been waiting for you to wake up. I'll fetch him at once. Now you will finally meet. He will lay his hand upon you, and you will become one. The blind shall see, the lame shall walk!"

Mrs Schumann rose, set her knitting aside, and left the room. Her tapping little footsteps faded down the corridor. Downstairs, the voices grew louder. I wouldn't be able to escape that way. I glanced at the rain-soaked windowpane but doubted I had the strength in my current state to climb out onto the roof and down the gutter pipe. When I tentatively attempted to prop myself on one elbow, I had to give up at once and fell back into the bed with a groan.

"Schaday!"

I could hobble over and lock the door, but it would hardly do more than postpone the inevitable. Mrs Schumann had her own key. Should I try to block it with the chest of drawers or the wardrobe? No, that would be of no use; it might buy me a little time at best. My deranged hostess could quickly rouse the crowd downstairs to break in.

A moment later, I heard Mrs Schumann's voice in the corridor, but the raindrops on the window and the ever-rising cries of jubilation from the sitting room made it impossible for me to make out the words. A deeper voice joined hers.

Now it was really happening!

I squeezed my eyes shut and pressed myself down into the mattress, as if I might dissolve by sheer force of will, leaving nothing behind but a strip of gauze and a faint impression in the clammy sheets.

There was a single knock at the door, and without waiting for an answer, Mrs Schumann entered, speaking softly to someone else.

"Here he is," she said. "He's still a little groggy after the accident."

I opened my eyes, fixed my gaze on the doorway, and knew that the world would never be the same. Everything stood on the brink of a profound transformation; new souls and new bodies, splendid and unfamiliar.

No, no, it is the three strange angels.
Admit them, admit them.

—D.H. Lawrence

GREENLAND

THE QIVITTOQ

by Gertrud-Marie Kreutzmann

On that day, the 19th of August 2016, I went on a weekend trip with my now-husband, Inuk, to his family's off-grid cabin, deep within the fjord. The weather was perfect for August—neither too warm nor too cold—and the female mosquitoes had already perished, so we could finally be outside in peace. Inuk and I had only been together a few months, and I was thrilled to spend an entire weekend alone with him, away from everything and everyone.

On the way to the cabin we passed several boats heavy with rifles and equipment. This wasn't unusual; the caribou hunting season had just begun. Inuk had promised I'd kill my first animal that weekend, and the thought filled me with unbridled childish excitement.

The cabin stood not far from shore, at the foot of a slope that opened up to the fjord. The view was like something out of a dream: the deep blue sea stretching out endlessly, dark mountains rising on either side, and thin streams of meltwater running down the slopes. I remember breathing in and feeling my whole body loosen up. My shoulders relaxed, the line between my eyebrows softened, and the only sound was nature itself: the distant crack of ice from the icebergs, the soft murmur of water, the hush of the wind. It was the kind of silence that presses against your ears and reminds you of how much noise you are surrounded by in your everyday life.

When Inuk finished storing our food, he glanced at me. "Want to take a walk uphill?" He sounded eager, but that wasn't surprising. I knew that it had been a while since he had been here.

I was already lacing my boots. Without answering, I grabbed my pocketknife—the one with my name engraved on the handle. "In case we catch a caribou," I said, almost proudly.

"You think we'll find one in the first hour?" Inuk said, a teasing glint in his eyes.

"Optimism never hurt anyone."

We set out, our boots sinking into the soft moss, the air smelling of salt and damp earth. As we climbed, the temperature dropped just enough for our breath to fog. We talked about everything—what we wanted, who we hoped to be, how our paths might fit together. He spoke with such calm certainty about his future, while mine still felt like a question being written. It was easy to love him out there, where the world was stripped of everything unnecessary.

Halfway up, we stopped on a flat rock overlooking the fjord. The ocean below was still as glass, a perfect reflection of the sky. I took out an apple, sliced it in half, and handed him a piece.

"See?" I said, smiling. "Already useful."

He laughed, his booming mirth echoing off the rocks.

Then he brushed his thumb over my chin and kissed my cheek. The warmth of his lips felt hot against the chill air.

We continued towards the lake where his family usually hunted. Inuk looked around.

"He was last seen walking towards the lake," he said, his voice suddenly cracking with bitterness.

JUST BEFORE WE left for this weekend trip, Inuk had told me about his uncle's best friend who'd disappeared during a hunting trip a few years back. He was last seen walking away from the cabin at dawn, with nothing but the clothes on him. They'd all searched for him: Inuk's uncle and the hunting team, even the police came. When he didn't show up, the police investigated his disappearance. They had even arrested Inuk's uncle—they'd suspected him of murder, but due to the lack of evidence, he was soon free to go.

After the disappearance of his best friend, Inuk's uncle had never been the same. He'd become strangely remote and withdrawn. And Inuk was left alone.

It was Inuk's uncle who'd spent time with him when he was a teenager, giving him the care and attention he needed. Inuk's parents worked and travelled a lot, so he'd often been home alone. But his uncle had stepped up and spent time with him, teaching him about hunting and tracking animals. With his uncle gone from his life, Inuk found himself alone. Again.

WHEN WE REACHED the lake at the mountain top, the sun had dipped low, tinting the melted glacier water a deep orange. But no caribou was in sight. Disappointed, we decided to head back before nightfall.

But as we descended, the air changed. The light faded faster than it should have, and an odd heaviness settled over the valley. I kept glancing around, half-expecting to see someone standing among the rocks. Of course, there was no one. There couldn't be. We were alone in the area.

Then I heard it: a long, low howl from somewhere on the ridge. It didn't sound quite like an animal; it sounded almost human, drawn out until it broke into something raw.

"Did you hear that?" I whispered.

"Probably a fox," Inuk said. "Plenty around here."

But his eyes flicked towards the ridge, and he said nothing more.

By the time we reached the cabin, the cold had deepened. There was no heat on inside, so Inuk went out again to fetch firewood from the small outhouse. I turned on the battery-powered lamps and tried to shake off the unease that was creeping under my skin. Through the window, I watched him closely, trying not to lose sight of him. But he was moving slowly and unbothered. He belonged there in a way I didn't.

When he came back inside, he lit the fire.

I emptied my pockets. Everything was there except my knife. I searched again, even checked Inuk's jacket, but it was gone. "Did you take my knife when you went outside?"

He frowned. "No. You must've dropped it."

I tried to laugh it off, but the thought of losing it made me strangely uneasy. Not only had my grandfather given it to me for my 20th birthday, so it held a lot of sentimental value, but no one would feel safe with a knife that was missing—who knows whose hands it could end up in. And no one wished to meet a *qivittoq*.

As darkness fell, we ate dinner by the fire. Inuk was quiet, his eyelids heavy. While I couldn't stop thinking. Maybe it was the fire and memories of other long nights around the flames, and all the legends told there. The tales about the qivittoq began to crawl back into my head.

A QIVITTOQ WAS once a person. Someone who had turned their back on society—out of shame, sorrow, anger, or something darker. They'd left their families and walked into the wilderness, never to return.

But leaving was not just exile. It was a kind of becoming. The elders said that these persons would no longer be human. They became part of the land itself, able to run like the wind, vanish into thin air, or take the shape of animals. Yet, they were alive. Just changed.

INUK YAWNED. "WE should go to sleep early. The caribou come to the shore in the morning."

We added more firewood and climbed into bed. He fell asleep instantly. I couldn't close my eyes. The wind outside grew louder, the cabin creaking softly with each gust. Every sound was amplified—I could even hear his heartbeat and mine.

Sometime after midnight I heard it: three distinct knocks on the window. One. Two. Three. I sat up, heart pounding.

"Inuk?" I squeaked, shaking his shoulder. No reaction.

The knocks came again, this time on the opposite wall. Then a scraping, like something dragging along the outer boards.

The noise moved slowly around the cabin, circling.

Then came the smell—thick and sweet and rotten, like spoiled meat left too long in the sun. It filled my nose, clinging to the back of my throat. I pressed my face into Inuk's shoulder, trying to wake him. He only mumbled in his sleep. The scratching outside stopped. Silence.

I must have drifted into sleep, because when I opened my eyes again, it was dawn. Pale light spilled in through the small window. The fire had burned down to embers. I got up and peered outside. The ground around the cabin was disturbed; the moss was torn up and I spotted shallow footprints in the mud.

When Inuk woke up, I told him what I'd heard.

He stared at me for a moment, then shrugged. "Probably someone hunting nearby."

"No one's this far in," I said. "You know that."

He didn't reply. He just began packing for our morning hunt.

THE SKY WAS clear when we set out, the light bouncing off the water in the fjord. Everything looked normal again, but I couldn't shake the feeling that we were being followed. Every time I turned, something shifted at the edge of my vision, like a shadow ducking behind a rock.

We reached the lake before noon. The air was completely still. Not even the gulls called. Inuk scanned the hills with his rifle. I stood a few paces behind him, clutching his spare knife, pulse hammering.

That was when I saw it—a shape further away on the ridge, too tall and too still to be human. Its outline shimmered faintly, even though the air was cold. I blinked, and it was gone.

"Inuk," I whispered. "Look."

He followed my gaze, squinting. "There's nothing there."

Then a low growl rolled across the mountain top. We froze. A rock tumbled, splashing into the lake. Inuk raised his rifle. Another sound followed, higher this time—a scream that twisted through the air. It wasn't an animal's.

The figure appeared, moving with unnatural high speed. Its limbs were long, and its head was sharply tilted, revealing its long and tangled hair. I saw pale skin stretched tight over bone, dark stains around its mouth, and dark circles under its eyes. It was holding something in its right hand, something metal.

My knife.

I couldn't move.

"Suersaq!" Inuk shouted, his voice breaking with fear.

The creature halted at the edge of the lake and stared at us. Its eyes were sunken but alive, gleaming with something between rage and sorrow. For a moment, it oddly seemed to know—no, recognise—him: Inuk.

Slowly it revealed the knife in its palm and held it out for us to see. It stood there, not moving, and seemed to accept that we'd seen each other. All of sudden I had the overwhelming feeling of loneliness—did I somehow feel what the creature felt?

It let out another cry, deeper this time, and the air shook. Inuk fired. The loud shot echoed, but the gaunt figure didn't fall. Instead it turned its head towards him and screamed again—a sound so raw it moved me deeply. Then, just as suddenly as it had appeared, it stepped backwards and vanished into the ground.

The silence was thick and absolute. My ears rang from

the shot. I could still feel its gaze on us, even though there was nothing there. We turned to leave, and I didn't dare look back.

THAT DAY WE packed and left before the sun touched the horizon. Neither of us spoke on the way back. The fjord was calm. Too calm.

As if nothing had happened.

When we reached the other cabins and boats, I glanced towards the mountains one last time. For a brief second, I saw it standing high on the ridge—motionless. Even from that distance, I could see the faint glint of my knife in its hand.

It didn't move. It only watched us, head cocked to the side, as the boat took us further away. And I knew then, without a doubt, that it was no coincidence we had crossed it, and that the stories were true, that it was a qivittoq. It looked at us from afar—warning us, in its silent, unblinking way, to never return. And we respected that: we never came back to the cabin.

LATER, WE HEARD stories of people who'd also met the slender figure with a knife in its hand. It plagued me: my knife—being used to torment other people, who were only trying to enjoy nature as it is meant to be.

Inuk finally seemed at peace with his grief. His family never used the cabin again. The place has now been haunted for several years. No one hunts there anymore—that area belongs to *it,* the qivittoq, whom they used to know as *Suersaq*.

THE TUPILAK

by Pivinnguaq Mørch
Translated by AneMarie Ottosen

WHEN I SAW what the witch had sent, I blacked out.

I don't even remember how I ended up there, but I found myself on top of the stairs, looking down.

I turned up the light of my oil lamp, then stretched it out to see what was below me. I waited for something to come into view, but since it was completely quiet, I started to walk down the stairs. The only sound came from my steps on the creaking stairs, and my gut told me to slow down.

At the bottom I immediately spotted melting footprints of snow. I started to wander through the rooms, still waiting for something to happen. In the beam of the only light source, the one I carried, I saw how the shadows from my furniture danced in different shapes and sizes. My uneasiness did not help at all, because my imagination transformed the shadows into frightening things.

I felt chills and sweats at the same time.

I realised that I had been in every room since I had come down the stairs. When I looked back up, I detected new footprints of snow, starting to melt.

Trembling, I tried to listen again.

My lifeless home was dead quiet but all of a sudden I heard a gasp. It startled me so much, I almost dropped the lamp.

I glanced up. I couldn't see anything in the dark, but then the darkness turned into outlines. The outlines became edges, so distinct that they looked like a human about to crawl down the stairs.

I heard heavy breathing; I wanted to direct the light towards it.

But suddenly I felt that my arm was unable to extend. I stood frozen, and for a moment it felt like I was having a night terror because my whole body was completely rigid, unable to escape.

Something was holding onto the rail of the staircase.

The creature that had scared me senseless was about to show itself, and all I could do was watch, helpless. Entering the light, the creature looked pale, as if it had emerged from the depths of darkness.

The foreleg came first into the open as it stepped down. The leg held still, while the other foreleg followed the same pattern. What I thought were legs just grew longer and longer, so far-reaching that they covered two thirds of the stairs. The legs stretched and stood next to each other, and the creature was holding on with its paws.

Then it gusted air out of its mouth, making me lose my breath, while what I thought were its legs began to bend like arms.

Regrettably I lingered to catch a glimpse of its face. It sounded like it was having a hard time breathing. It all made me anxious, and my head was spinning with thoughts. I wanted to close both my eyes and my ears.

I couldn't predict what was going to happen next.

When all my hope was lost, its jaw of bone emerged from the darkness, and the creature seemed to be creeping downwards. The oil lamp's light flickered and the creature looked like it had shapeshifted. As it came closer, I could see its head move from side to side. It looked unnatural.

The long arms began to extend again, and since it had no eyes, the creature seemed to use its nose to locate me. Its body had human skin all the way up to the top of its head, but not a single hair on its body. It was so thin you could see the rib bones on its chest.

The arms began to twist again, and they started to shake. With the arms bent all the way down, the creature took a big breath of my scent, growled deeply, and lunged at me.

My whole body froze again in shock, despite being overwhelmed by an urge to flee.

A long moment passed, and since nothing touched me, I slowly opened my eyes. I saw the hands trying to grab me, but they couldn't reach me. Then I discovered that the creature was being held captive in midair.

It opened its mouth and a long tongue came out, the sight more disgusting than anything I had seen before.

It opened its mouth wider and wider, while its fingers desperately tried to reach me.

I realised that something was holding it back. I spotted another set of fingers on its chest, between the rib bones, holding the creature back with a firm grip.

I relaxed a little, but when I tried to move I found I still couldn't, so my feeling of ease was short-lived.

I was curious to find out who my helper was. The new creature's eyes were closing and opening, studying me intently. They glowed with anger. I could see them more clearly since the creature in front was no longer obscuring them with its flailing limbs.

I watched as the other creature strained to save me. Its sharp tusk-like teeth were visible. It fought hard, breathing out so harshly that it accidently spat. That's how I noticed how much saliva it was producing in its struggle to hold on.

Just then the first creature took a step forward, and the stairs made such a loud screeching sound that I understood how heavy it was.

What woke me from my state of mind was the sight of the creature's hind paws moving down the stairs, getting closer.

I started to realise that the empty eye sockets of the first being in front of me contained eyes after all; the creature behind had made me comprehend this. I deduced that the creature in the back was actually holding the creature in front; that it was in fact its phallus.

It had miscalculated; it was shy of reaching me by a few centimetres. This realisation in itself made me see through the darkness. Now I could fully recognise the creature.

I started to grieve over everything. The feeling of betrayal made me tremble even more. Maybe because I wanted to run away too.

If I had to confess, I would say I had not recognised it earlier because the creature's condition had changed so much. The brown, furry skin was gone, only the flesh remained. The hair was gone too, and the skin had claw marks all over it.

I can't imagine what had happened, but it was the first time in my life I had felt so powerless.

I argued internally about the end result, since it felt like I was eventually going to point a finger at myself.

The inevitable happened: the traitor grabbed me, and it would not let me go, but bit me on my neck. I must have bled, because I felt the creature's warm tongue against my neck. I tried to scream the pain out of my body.

As it started to drag me up the stairs, I saw how the fire from my broken oil lamp had engulfed the floor.

I was turned upside down as we entered the darkness. All I could feel was the pain of being bitten over and over again.

I first lost consciousness when it broke my back and split me open.

Was it my fault? I sang that spell and planted the seed to awaken the creature, but then it returned to me.

ICELAND

THE SHAPE OF STONES

by Hildur Knútsdóttir

June 16th

~~Dear diary,~~

No. That was a bad joke. And a terrible way to start what is supposed to be an appendix to a serious, scientific project. What a way to ruin a beautiful, pristine notebook! I really should try thinking about the words before writing them down. Anyway. What I meant to write is that I am doing a research project, and these are supposed to be my personal notes about it.

First, a little background: When I was small I used to read about the Aztecs and their horrific human sacrifices. And later I learned about how some countries hide the dark and bloodier parts of their past by writing it out of their history books or not teaching it in schools. I thought them equally barbaric.

Imagine my surprise when I learned that the settlers of Iceland were actually pretty big on human sacrifice too, and no, I don't remember ever hearing about it in school. But there are plenty of tales about it in the old Sagas.

In *Eyrbyggja* it says: "Í þeim hring stendur Þórs steinn er þeir menn voru brotnir um er til blóta voru hafðir og sér enn blóðslitinn á steininum." That would translate to something like: "In that circle stands the stone of Thor where they broke the men that were sacrificed and the color of blood can still be seen on the stone." (There is probably an official translation, by someone whose English is a lot better than mine, but I don't have it at hand so mine will have to do.) So the settlers of Iceland slaughtered men and broke their backs on stones.

And that is my research project. I am going to spend my summer trying to find those stones.

We have a pretty good idea of where the stone mentioned in *Eyrbyggja* is, so that is where I will start. It is supposed to be in Þingvellir, an old gathering place for chieftains, where they met to settle matters. This Þingvellir is in the Snæfellsnes peninsula and is not to be confused with the other, more famous Þingvellir. (Sorry, it's complicated.) The Þingvellir that interests me is located in Þórsnes, or Thor's peninsula. But the problem is, there are a lot of stones there. So here I am, in a guesthouse in Stykkishólmur, the nearest village, and tomorrow I will head out to examine them all. I don't really know what I am looking for—will the moss on one stone be thicker than on the others? Will the earth around it be more fertile, enriched by all the blood that was spilled? Or will the color of blood still be on that stone?—but I believe I will know it when I see it.

June 17th

ICELAND WAS SETTLED by Norwegians. They brought slaves that were probably taken from what is now Ireland,

Scotland, and England. Genetic research shows this, and so does my red hair.

Anyway, I wasn't going to write about my ancestors, the raping Norwegians, but their neighbors the Swedes. There is an account I read about them and what they were doing in the first century that has stayed with me because I think they were really onto something. In Uppsala, in around 380, the weather had been pretty bad for a few seasons, which led to failing crops and bad times all around. There was a tradition of human sacrifice to the Æsir, the old Norse gods, there too. They mostly sacrificed animals and slaves, but things had gotten so bad that they apparently decided that some more drastic measures had to be taken. So they sacrificed their king, Dómaldi, and let his blood soak the ground.

I am not saying that we should start killing our politicians. I don't know what I am saying, exactly. I am in a really foul mood. I spent all day mapping stones. It was a long day and the results of it are that there are exactly fourteen stones that are big enough to be the one I am looking for, and thirty-seven that are too small.

June 21st

I HAVE DEVISED a methodology to examine the stones. But it is quite tedious, and well documented in my scientific notes, so I will not bore these pages with the details, other than to say that it involves a lot of scraping off moss and gently lifting it from the rock, just to put it down again, hoping it will keep growing, and so far it has not been fruitful. The farmer who owns the land is nice. She came up on her tractor and brought me coffee and kleinur, and after chatting for a bit we discovered that she went to school with my cousin Ástrós. It is always like this here; you always find a connection. You can't escape being known. I often wonder what it must be like to live in a big city and be able to disappear into a faceless crowd. Here, the danger of running into someone you have slept with, or worse—their parents—is ever looming. It must be nice to live somewhere where you can have a meltdown in a public place without word of it reaching both your ex and your boss, and probably along with it the reason why you were having a meltdown in the first place.

The owner of this guesthouse I am staying at, for example, is my uncle's wife's cousin. If I were to have a tantrum here and break some furniture, word of it would surely reach my parents.

June 22nd

THE STONES STAND in a field close to the sea. It overlooks the Breiðafjörður bay, and the view is beautiful. They say that the islands here cannot be counted, and as I understand it, that is mostly because people cannot agree on what counts as an island. Like the small skerries that are sometimes visible and sometimes underwater, depending on the tides. There are so many birds here. And today I saw seals, their black heads bobbing in the water.

We are lucky that the stones have not been dragged away and the field plowed. The farmer who brought me coffee said that the people who lived there knew not to touch the stones. They were probably familiar with the history of their land and the Sagas. We have long taken great pride in them because those manuscripts are the only thing we have left to be proud of. The traditional

Icelandic house was a turf house, made from rock and dirt. Most of them have just rained away. We have no old cathedrals, no roads, no bridges, no marble statues. Those words scribbled on vellum are the only thing we have from our past.

Today, as I was about to go home, I found something. I don't know what it is, maybe it is nothing, but I will investigate further tomorrow. I am excited. Hopefully, I will sleep.

June 24th

I THINK I'VE found it! The stone, I mean, THE stone. It stands in the middle of the field, and I guess you could, with some help from your imagination, say that the other stones form a kind of circle around it. It is not a neat or perfect circle, maybe more of an oval and a lopsided one at that, but still, the shape is there. And there is no way of knowing if it is like that naturally or if the stones were put there by people. Anyway, the stone that stands in the middle is the one that I thought most likely to be the one I was looking for. But I did not start with that one, because I wanted to be methodical about it, as per the method that I devised but did not explain here. Shit, I am rambling. So much for thinking about the words before writing them down.

This stone in the middle is the perfect height to bend a person over. By that I mean that it comes up roughly to the small of my back if I am standing facing away from the stone. And if someone were to push me over it, and maybe then pull down my hands from the other side, I can imagine my back breaking quite easily. The stone is… thin? I do not think that is the right word for it, but I mean that it is not round, but rather shaped like a leaf, and on top there is an edge that is quite sharp. Writing this, I have now realized that I have a very limited vocabulary in English to describe the shape of stones. Perhaps that is not something my English teachers imagined I would ever have a need for.

Anyway, if somebody were to push me over that stone, then pull on my hands, or maybe push my shoulders down, my back would undoubtedly break, and my neck would be exposed. It would only take a stroke of a sharp blade to let out my blood so it would flow freely. And that is how you please a god.

I spent my day very carefully removing the moss and lichen that grows on the stone. What I am hoping to find are some markings. It took me all day to remove the lichen just from the top, and I am pretty sure that the stone there has been chipped away, making the edge even sharper. It might be weathering, of course, but then again it might not be.

June 26th

It has been two days, I know. But I have been really busy. My work is time-consuming. The moss comes off pretty easily, but it is harder to remove the lichen without scraping the stone. When I drove home yesterday evening I stopped at the farm and asked the farmer if she would be okay with me pitching a tent in the field by the stones. She looked at me a bit funny, but then she said yes, so I did, which means I can now work through the evening and into the night. The summer nights are so bright here in the west. The sun doesn't really set; it just dips down beneath the horizon for a moment and then it rises again. We sleep a lot less in the summertime. There have been studies on this, and to be honest I barely feel the need to sleep at all.

The soundscape here is out of this world. The birds screech and sing and trill and tweet in a cacophony that has its own kind of harmony, and underneath is the constant rhythm of the waves breaking on the beach. The farmer told me that there is an eagles' nest close by, but she also told me not to tell anyone about it. The eagles are endangered and their nesting places are meant to be kept a secret, so maybe I shouldn't even write this down in my notes.

June 27th

I HAD A weird dream tonight. I dreamt I was lying in my tent and that I heard deep voices outside. The pitch and the rhythm of their language was familiar, but I could not make sense of their words. In my dream I decided to go out and greet them. And I must have risen, because I woke up halfway out of my sleeping bag with my hand on the tent zipper. It took me a long time to go back to sleep again.

June 28th

THERE WAS AN eruption in the Reykjanes Peninsula in the night. That is the next peninsula to the south from the one that I am on. If I were on the other side of this one I could probably see it. It's not a very big one, as far as eruptions go, and no one is in danger. I was listening to a geologist from the Met Office on the news earlier. He said that this volcanic system in Reykjanes has been dormant since the nine hundreds, but is now active again, and will presumably stay so for some years, possibly even decades. He talked about the volcano as if it were a living thing, a beast that had been woken from its slumber and we would now feel its wrath. It struck me that the last time this volcanic system was active was around the same time that they sacrificed people on the stone right outside my tent. And now I can't stop wondering whether something might lie dormant in this ground too, and what would happen if it should wake.

We have tales of beasts, the landvættir. I don't know the best translation for that, but it is a beautiful word that means a being that protects the land. Supposedly Úlfljótslög, the oldest Icelandic law, thought to date back to 930, stated that ships with mastheads that had gaping maws had to take them down before land was sighted, so they wouldn't rouse the landvættir. And ships don't have mastheads anymore to wake them.

If they are still here, they have been sleeping for a long time.

I am making progress on the stone. Just now after dinner, I found a peculiar indentation just above what could be described as the center of it. It looks like a ring has been hollowed out. And up from it there seems to be a trace of a line, a groove, up to the sharp edge of the stone. It might just be how the stone is shaped naturally, but then again, it might not.

June 29th

I THINK I know why that line is there. Maybe I should not write this down, but it actually came to me in a dream. I know dreams are not a way to divine the future. I don't believe in any of that. But that is not to say that they are meaningless. Dreams are just another interpretation of our reality, from a different part of the mind. I don't know if 'subconscious' is actually an accurate term, but what I am trying to say is that perhaps my brain had already made this connection, but I just didn't realize it. Because obviously the blood is supposed to flow down the groove and into the ring.

I will not describe the dream that made that clear to me here. It is not fit for an appendix accompanying a scientific paper. But let's just say that I think I now have a better understanding of what it might have felt like to lose your life on that stone.

June 30th

I FOUND CARVINGS! Definitely, DEFINITELY carvings! Made by human hands. They are weathered and eroded, but they are fuþark runes and they spell Þór. And this is Þórsnes! It all makes sense.

The runes were quite hidden, down at the base of the stone, and nearly covered with grass and soil. I had to be very careful removing it. And under the runes I found a serpent carved into the rock. It is long and its tail disappears down into the ground. I had to take a break after I found it—I was quite overcome with emotion—and I also had to decide if I should call my supervisor or not. Because this is a big find, a huge one. ~~But my supervisor is… Well, I just know that if I called her now she would swoop in and she would take all the glory. And I don't want her to get the credit for all my hard work.~~

In the end I decided to excavate the base of the stone myself. And then I will call my supervisor. There is no need to get her all excited before I know exactly what it is that I have found.

I had another dream last night. It was the same one as the night before, but the roles were reversed. I guess I could say that now I also have a better understanding of what it might have felt like to sacrifice someone on that stone. ~~It felt surprisingly exhilarating. When I woke up my heart was hammering in my chest and I felt a kind of joy coursing through my veins. But maybe joy is not the right word for it. It was a feeling of a job well done, and the certainty that I would soon be rewarded for it.~~

~~Writing this all down I realize that is probably a very wrong and twisted feeling to have in that context.~~

I did not like that dream.

July 1st

A WEIRD THING happened. As I was excavating the base of the stone, I was surprised to find that it is actually a lot bigger than I thought. It seems to be rooted deep in the earth, almost as if it is growing from the bedrock underneath. I thought it was shaped like a leaf, but I seem to have been mistaken. It is more like a tooth, or a fang. I have dug away quite a lot of soil from the base, but the carving of the snake just keeps on going down, down, down.

The earth around the stone is very red. I know it is probably not from all the blood that has been spilled here, that was so long ago. Most likely this field was once a bog. They used to mine bog iron here. Supposedly it was backbreaking work.

But the weird thing happened this afternoon. I was on my knees, digging at the base of stone, and then the earth started shaking. It came in big heaves.

I know that it was an earthquake, and probably connected to the eruption. The land here is constantly moving and changing. But it didn't *feel* like an earthquake. I have experienced many in my lifetime, but none like this one. This didn't feel like tectonic plates grinding together, or like magma pushing its way to the surface somewhere far away. This felt localized. It was like the earth directly underneath me was shifting, as if a great, sleeping beast was suddenly stirring. And for a moment it even felt like the stones around me were its teeth and I was standing in the middle of a giant maw that would now close and devour me whole.

But then the earthquake passed.

A little while later the farmer came on her tractor to see if I was all right. She had felt the earthquake too. She became very angry when she saw what I was doing. She said that her people had known better than to touch the stones and that I should too. She said that I had no right to desecrate the stones. But I told her that this was a great find for science. This is our history, our only legacy, and we deserve to know its secret. She just stared at me for a long moment, then she shook her head, stomped back to her tractor, and drove off without a word.

I had another dream. It was the same dream, but now I was the stone, and I was so thirsty.

I have still not found the tail of the serpent. It lies much deeper than I thought possible. Tomorrow, when I wake, I will keep digging.

July 2nd

THERE WAS ANOTHER earthquake in the night. When it woke me I was already outside of the tent, standing in the hollow that I had dug out at the base of the stone. It felt as if it was coming from directly beneath my feet. When it was over I saw that the earth had shifted. I can see the tail of the serpent now. But that is not the end. For underneath it is another carving. I am not sure of what exactly, but I have my suspicions, and I will write them down once I have them confirmed.

I am going out now to dig. I don't know what long-hidden secret I will uncover but I am convinced that it will change my life forever. Something great awaits me at the base of that stone, underneath that dark, rich, red soil.

Tonight, I will write it all down on these pages.

YOU SEE ME, DON'T YOU?

by Nanna Árnadóttir

Flash.

I DON'T know when I became aware of the darkness or my presence within it. Perhaps just before the light flickered, bringing with it searing pain and a suffocating heat, too thick to breathe.

Flash.

That first time, the light's boiling blaze evaporated instantly like steam rising from a pot. Too fast for me to gain my bearings. Not that I especially wanted to understand what was happening. Like anyone stunned by a sudden, sharp pain, all I wanted was for it to go away. The darkness that then swallowed me felt like an embrace, its tenderness as surprising as the blistering light had been.

Flash. Flash.

For a while that's how it was. First blackness. Then a white flash filled with stifling agony. Flash. Pause. Flash. Pause.

Heartbeats of torment.

After a while, the light lingered long enough for my eyes to adjust. I had wondered—when I rested gratefully in the dark—what had actually taken place around me, but I admit I then existed in an in-between state of sorts. Since the light and the accompanying horror was so unpredictable, I spent all of my time worrying about when it might come upon me again. *Now?* I thought. *No now. N-n-n-now. NOW!* Was it easier? Knowing it *was* coming? Is the fear of suffering worse than pain itself? Perhaps not, but it is more tedious.

The first time I was able to see beyond the harrowing flashes, I spotted my house. So I was home. I hadn't even thought about the house, or my family, or my life before that moment, something that would puzzle me when the darkness returned and I was once again free from fear, pain, and the fear of pain.

In that first instant though, my mind, numbed by the scorching heat that accompanied the light, merely catalogued what it saw: my little concrete house—with the green tin sheet roof I'd proudly painted myself one summer years ago—was being devoured by a rushing river of luminous lava.

I had always assumed that lava moved slowly but now a flood of it crashed against the back of the house. A spray of tiny molten rocks popped against the roof, like a great wave flinging itself against cliffs. Just like the waves at Svalþúfa. I'd seen them as a young girl, when my parents and I stopped for a break during our trip down south to visit my father's family outside Reykjavík. Looking down at the raging sea as it beat the shore of Svalþúfa, I had imagined myself plunging into it. The fear of falling had felt like a fishhook in my rear, yanking me back from the edge. I had the same feeling when I saw the rush of fire bury my house but I could not pull away. I could not breathe enough to scream, could not move my feet.

The green tin buckled as the lava reached the top of the roof. First, the thick windows I'd spent two years saving up for blazed from within—as the wave gobbled up my lifetime's worth of carefully collected objects—and then they exploded, the glittering glass raining down onto the ground. The rising tide of glowing liquid fire had surrounded the house like an advancing wave might cradle a large rock on the black beach.

Mercifully, the dark came back, obscuring it all from my view, and bringing with it the soothing cold, the emptiness. Maybe you think I immediately started to question where I was, what was happening to me, why I was wherever I was? All people—myself included—think they'll be logical when something unexpected happens, but that is not my experience at all.

Instead, I drifted into the dark, my mind in a fog. The absence of the searing heat was such a relief I felt almost incoherent. Confused, I could not form a complete thought. Instead, I felt a truth gnawing at me, a certainty that begged to be acknowledged, but I could not think clearly enough to handle it. Of course, what I had seen in the light had felt familiar, because it was my house melting, my roof crumpling, my windows cracking, but the details, the context, was missing.

FLASH.

THE LIGHT arrived quickly the next time, and this time it lingered. That was when I learned that I was in the same place. I understood that I had probably stood rooted here every time the light had flashed: in front of my house, with the lava spilling across the landscape around my home.

Over the disorienting noise of my pain and the oppressive heat, I heard the hiss of the lava as it fried the wet grass, the roar as it melted through the concrete walls as easily as fire burning through plastic, the metallic groan of my roof as it gave away to the heat, the crackle of sparks searing new freckles onto my face. Screams, I heard the faintest screams, though I was not sure where from. Certainly not mine; it was so hot by the house I could not even breathe.

I saw the darkness reaching for me from above, and my eyes followed it, desperate for its stillness. Knowing that the pain would soon end—that just as the light always came, the darkness would eventually return—made my situation bearable. This time I *did* wonder what was happening to me, but I did not have time to think further before the relentless burning revisited.

FLASH.

I REALISED that the light was a wall in front of me, illuminating the horrific diorama I found myself imprisoned in. It was as if a guillotine had sliced through the world itself and all that had been on the other side of the blade had fallen into a bright void. The lava disappeared into it like a molten orange wave topped with black foam.

I looked down to find myself knee-deep in its tide. The pain overwhelmed me. Not inside my legs—I didn't feel them at all—and I knew that somehow, they did not exist anymore. Every nerve, muscle, or bone had been liquified and swept away. It seemed clear that I was trapped in the seconds prior to when my legs gave way completely and I collapsed into the sea of fire that Krafla regurgitated from her earthly entrails.

No, it was the rest of me that was straining and burning. Above the lava flow, my nightdress had burst into flames, which licked my thighs, and the cuffs of my sleeves. Perhaps it was a good thing I could not breathe; I do not think I could have endured the smell.

When the darkness finally enveloped me, it brought with it the kiss of sleep. At least, as close to sleep as I have come here. Perhaps a better way to describe it is an absence of thought and feeling, reminiscent of the emptiness I felt at my mother's deathbed, where we waited for days for her to die. I would look out the window, my gaze unfocused, and the hours would pass as easily as the minutes. Time itself lost its shape and weight, and my siblings and I were both terrified of the moment she would take her last breath, and at the same time certain that her laboured breathing would go on forever, torturing us. Of course, it could not continue; my mother died, and the light returned.

Flash.

This time, I was determined to find the borders of this nightmare, though not for a way to escape. I knew that was not for me: I could not move, I could not breathe, and time seemed frozen in the seconds just before I would collapse into the lava and die. I was stuck in a single instant of pain, unable to fully understand how I had got there.

I studied everything I could see, hoping for a clue. There was my house again—the walls that had kept my children safe from the winter storms and the black fog of biting gnats that hovered over Lake Mývatn in the summer—succumbing to lava. Further away, I could see the lava slipping across the grassy lawn, smothering the house next door. Inside, Kalli Gamli and his wife Heiðrún would be in bed. Kalli Gamli, who shovelled and salted the path outside my door when it snowed. Heiðrún, who watered my plants when I travelled south to visit my children in Reykjavík. Could I hear their dog, Drifa, barking? Begging them to wake up and run, or was I imagining it?

I HAD NOT lived such a bad life. I did not delude myself into thinking I was a particularly good person, but I had never done anything I could think of that deserved hell. Because that's what this was, I decided. It's not like I had ever murdered anyone, nothing as interesting as that. Wished someone was dead, certainly, but what woman hasn't?

When my ex-husband drank himself to the point of stupor, shouting and threatening, and frightening the children, I absolutely wondered if it would not be easier if he just died. That way I would never have to worry again, when I came home from work or the shops, whether he'd said or done something to them that I could not forgive myself for, because somehow it would be my fault if he did something bad. It always was. In the end, it was easier to just leave him. He made a big fuss and made things difficult for a while, but then he sobered up and met someone who made him much happier, and now they'd been together three times longer than we ever were. As if he'd saved up all the kindness and love he had and just didn't want to waste it on me. The worst part was that he became the father I always knew he could be when we broke up. A shameful part of me wanted him dead all the more because he had the audacity to live the version of life we were meant to share but did so with her instead. Was that why I was here?

As darkness fell, I began to sift through the memories from my uneventful life, searching for serious sins that might explain my circumstances. What I found was simply recollections from my life: lying on a blanket of silvery moss, watching arctic terns swoop above my head and swearing to remember the view, running my fingers through my ex-husband's hair, his breath in my ear, the peal of my best friend's laughter, the taste of a soup I once made on a whim but never managed to recreate properly, the pride in my heart at my children's graduations, the cold plunge as I dove into the pool for my daily swim.

I could recall no crime worthy of this agony, no petty jealousy I might have nursed over time. Like anyone, I was guilty of the occasional ill-timed criticism, a cutting remark here or there, but was this to be the punishment for that?

FLASH.

THE MORE often the light arrived, the more I remembered from my final night. I had been at the hotel to train the accountant who'd take over from me when I retired. I had worked there for almost four decades, long enough to have known the original owner as a young man, watched him grow old, attended his funeral and comforted his children as they sold his life's work to a foreign hotel conglomerate. It was understandable; they had lives of their own.

I had finished work, stopped at Bónus to buy milk for my morning coffee and loaded up on some extra groceries for Kalli Gamli and Heiðrún to save them the walk in the drenching rain. I remember pulling the hood of my coat over my head to shelter from the downpour as I carried the bags over to their house. It didn't help, because I stood on their front steps for so long, insisting that I couldn't come in for a drop of coffee, that I was completely soaked by the time I got through my own front door. I showered, roasted potatoes and a limp broccoli floret in the air fryer, and ate it in front of the TV. My eldest had bought the air fryer at Costco in Garðarbær the last time I visited, insisting that it would change my life. It was fine. I had considered ice cream for dessert while watching the news but hadn't indulged in it. Oh, how that haunted me now!

I fell asleep on the sofa while scrolling on my phone. When I woke up, I didn't quite understand what had woken me up, but now I realise it must have been the tremors that preceded the eruption. Earthquakes happened on and off, so it was hardly unusual. I did not think about rushing outside or checking the news, I simply went to the bathroom because my bladder was calling me, brushed my teeth, took my vitamins, and put on my nightdress. By the time I heard the thick, syrupy sound of a hungry fire, it was already too late. I went to my bedroom window to investigate and found fingers of lava already reaching towards the houses of our street, a hand of it crawling towards Mývatn where it would explode into an immense cloud of ash. At the sight, I clung to the curtains and my knees almost gave way. I took a few shuddering breaths before I bolted for the front door, but as you know, it wouldn't matter. The flood was too close to my car, so I had to flee on foot. I did not look back as I darted out of the driveway. I did not dare jump over the tendrils of fire to alert Kalli Gamli and Heiðrún, realising I would not make it, and neither would they. The lava sloshed against my ankles before surging and swallowing my knees. I tried to scream but couldn't.

At this moment, I looked up in time to see a flash go off somewhere in front of me, in the near distance. Damned tourists! Only they would be crazy enough to stop in the middle of the road and take a picture of an oncoming lava flow as it tore through the streets to greet them.

I can't remember more than that—not my own death, although I am certain it followed shortly after—and it feels unfair in a way. I feel I am entitled to it. Instead, I am here, with you, and you, and you, and you.

IT TOOK ME a long time to look straight ahead instead of looking around. To school my gaze away from the burning ruins of my life and instead fix it on the wall of light in front of me. I frowned at it and there it was—the face of a man I'd never seen, floating past me, rising from the boundary where my street ended and the wall of light began, but soon disappearing again. It felt as if I were in an elevator, and on each floor, I passed a new gigantic face, a new room, then another and another.

Flash. Flash.

At times, someone like you, stops and stares at me.

Stares at that moment I relive over and over again, considering the pain on my face, the distorted features, my peeling skin, the flames climbing up my nightdress, the wave of fire spilling over my home, erasing all evidence of my life.

I suppose this is what I will be remembered by. I wonder when you look at me, what you discern, what I mean to you as you are confronted with the instant before my death, not having any context for my life.

I think most people don't even notice me. Honestly, their faces are a blur as they scroll past me to a more pleasant or banal photo of an influencer's breakfast or a snide cat passing judgement on a toddler failing to walk for the first time.

But you did not move past me. You saw me, and you hesitated. A part of me wishes you had not, so that I could disappear and the pain could vanish, so that the peace of obscurity could embrace me and let me die, really. But I know that won't happen, that even after you have moved on, I'll have to relive this moment.

Have my children seen this picture? I have not seen their faces flash before mine, and I have not decided whether I am grateful for it or not, but you see me.

You see me, don't you?

LITTLE BOY

by Steinar Bragi

Translated by Quentin Bates

1

WE GOT OUT of the car in a suburb. The streets were long and straight, six of them stretching out from a central point where a glowing glass dome flew a white flag from its roof. A similar building stood at the end of each street, with the pattern repeated as far as the eye could see.

David explained that these were each district's community centres, where I would get to know my neighbours. "Or get to know them afresh," he added amiably.

These were all two-storey houses lining the streets, built of wood and painted white, not all precisely the same but with understated variations, differences in the design of the windows and doors, and the pitch of the roofs. The plots around them were green with grass and a few plants, but what most attracted my attention was that behind the houses appeared to be a park of some kind, a long strip of greenery with trees and birds that stretched out to the horizon.

"This is where you live," the man said, nodding his head towards the house nearest to us. I saw a large garage, and a woman and a child standing in the doorway of the house, and I recognised neither of them. "That's your wife and child, and I gather you hadn't wanted to remember them?"

I said nothing.

"They have been informed of what you are undergoing and will show understanding. Don't hide anything from them, that'll just complicate things for you. Be honest and be open. If you don't know what to do, whether that relates to your domestic situation or social circumstances, then ask people around you. We are so grateful for what you have done."

I didn't know what to say. I just raised one eyebrow, which David seemed to find amusing, although I found this unbelievably irritating.

We went up to the house. The woman clapped her hands in delight and said that she had missed me, then threw her arms around me and kissed me, while the child clung to my leg and buried its face against my hip.

"There, there," I said when the woman began to weep. She said she had been so frightened for my sake, and before I knew it, she had picked up the child and put it in my arms. This was a boy of around nine years old, and I saw right away that his face resembled mine, with a sharp, imposing nose and crinkled black hair.

"Love you, Dad. I've missed you so much," he said. His eyes brimmed with tears.

"Wipe the tears from his eyes," the woman said, her voice quivering.

"There," I said, doing as she asked. The boy laughed, the sound affectingly sharp, reminiscent of a lamb's bleating.

"Come on, I want to show you what Bragi and I have been doing. We've been making careful preparations for your arrival!" She took hold of my hand and led me into the house. A banner with my name on it hung on the living room wall, welcoming me home, and the table was laid with all sorts of snacks and cakes, soft and alcoholic drinks.

"Mum has been baking," the boy said. I had immediately forgotten his name.

The woman led me upstairs, asking the boy to wait, as she meant to show Dad something exciting.

On the first floor were a bedroom with a double bed, and one child's bedroom with no toys and no books, just a bed and a desk. The walls were white with a faint sheen. The woman pulled me into the bedroom.

"Make love to me. My sweetest darling, love me. It's been so long."

She lay on her back and pulled off her underwear, which appeared from under the red dress and tangled around one of her high-heeled shoes. Then she parted her knees, reaching out with her hands, and again asked me to love her, gazing at me with such passion that I almost gave in. Instead I said that I wanted to be alone, that I needed to rest after the journey.

"Of course, my love. Whatever you want. I understand that you need more time to compose yourself." She pulled her knickers on and stood up. "The guests will arrive soon."

"What guests?"

"Our neighbours. You can rest here in bed. I'll let you know when they arrive. Is that all right?"

I nodded.

* * *

TRY AS I might, I couldn't bring myself to meet these people. I heard the increasing frequency of the doorbell's ring downstairs, and then a knock on the doorframe was enough, with a greeting called out over the chatter of conversation. The woman came up twice and said that the guests were asking after me, and wouldn't I come down? I asked to be allowed to rest a little longer. The third time, a tall, elderly man came up, extremely broad-shouldered and with piercing grey eyes. He said we had been friends, but I didn't recognise him. I asked them to all leave me be and huddled under the duvet.

The house gradually emptied and I listened as the noise faded and then couldn't face the woman returning to the room. I jumped to my feet, turned the key and locked the door from the inside. She could sleep with this boy who was supposed to be my son. A little later, the door was tried, I heard her speak my name a couple of times, and then she gave up.

2

AS SOON AS it was daylight I got up and tiptoed down the stairs, hoping the woman wouldn't wake. In the kitchen I boiled water and made myself coffee. When I heard movement upstairs, I slipped out for a stroll around the neighbourhood.

To begin with I followed the street, looking at the houses that were all the same, apart from details that made no difference. I came to a footpath between two houses and went along it to the botanical garden I had noticed the previous day. This park stretched out in a straight line between the back gardens of the houses, which also formed a straight line bordering it, even though it had appeared to me that the layout around the community centre was circular. A stream flowed through the middle of the park. Birds twittered in the trees that stood in thick copses in some places, and butterflies flitted between the flowers.

The path I was following meandered gently through the park, sometimes dividing to lie in the direction of little bridges spanning the stream. I decided I would keep to the grass, and if I were to walk far enough, it occurred to me that maybe I'd leave this district behind me. I had no plan of how to survive on my own, but maybe that wouldn't be any worse than living with strangers who pretended to know me.

A mountain rose on the horizon. I was so used to seeing nothing but variations on the same theme that I stopped dead. The mountain loomed over the rows of houses and dome-roofed community centres, and the verdant, stream-crossed, fertile flatness. Its sides were sheer and came together in a peak that should have been sharp but was flat, as if the mountain had been decapitated. Above its peak hung a mist, or a shimmer of great heat that was slightly mesmerising to watch.

I continued on my way, barely taking my eyes from the mountain. Unlike everything else about this district, it seemed familiar, and after a while I set myself a good pace, while my circumstances or where I was heading barely crossed my mind. It was good to maintain a course. I felt I could make out movement on the mountain's sides but couldn't be certain.

There was no sign of life in the houses on each side. I got the occasional feeling that I was being watched, but whenever I glanced at a window, nobody was to be seen.

After walking for a while, I lay down on the grass and

dozed, I've no idea for how long. Then I took a drink of water from the stream and continued until the daylight began to fade. I still hadn't come to any crossroads, although the path occasionally divided to lead off between the houses, as if it wanted to draw me back home.

It was by one of these snickets that I came to a house with a somewhat larger garden than the others. The house was grey with a blue-painted fence marking the extent of the garden.

"Good afternoon."

The greeting came from a woman behind the fence who appeared unexpectedly, and who must have been stooped over something on the ground.

"Hello," I said.

"This ball bounced away. I've a dog here."

She held up the ball and nodded to me. I could make out an imposing gas barbecue behind her. The aroma of the meat reached me. I swallowed and could barely contain the raw greed that welled up inside me. How long was it since I had last eaten?

"I'm grilling some chops," the woman said, and I followed her along the fence to a gate. "You look tired. Been walking long?"

"Since this morning."

"Do you live nearby?"

"No, unfortunately." I realised how strange I sounded but hadn't the energy to make up any kind of story and hadn't thought it through. There was a chill in the air and dusk was creeping up on us.

"You have somewhere to stay tonight?" the woman asked as she opened the gate, as if she already knew the answer. I shook my head and followed her into the garden.

The dog was one of those little ones that bark at anyone and anything, although this particular one kept quiet.

Beside the house was a veranda with a table and chairs, laid for one person. The woman went inside and fetched cutlery to add a place for me. To cap that, she handed me a bottle of beer and got one for herself.

The meal was fine, but practically after the first mouthful my appetite was gone, and by the time I had cleared my plate I was half drunk on the beer the woman brought from inside the house. She said she was a cook at the nearby community centre and that she liked experimental cuisine and exotic recipes.

"What are exotic recipes?" I asked.

"Szekely goulash with asparagus. Hummus from Belize. Grilled kangaroo with couscous. That sort of thing."

"We've been eating kangaroo?"

"Not now, no." She shook her head, as if this was something unthinkable.

When she had cleared the plates from the table we sat in silence and drank wine from tall glasses. As usual when there's an uncomfortable silence, my thoughts went to words I was sure I had misunderstood, such as 'stage fright'. I guessed that this referred to anxiety about some upcoming event, with a meaning that was primarily metaphorical, or was it?

There was nothing for it but to go to bed. I saw little of the interior of the house, but in broad terms it was the same as the one I had left. We moved to the bedroom and undressed, and the sex that followed was better than I expected. The woman straddled me and set a rhythm so rapid that I wondered if she was a machine that had been sent to envelop me in warmth and suck me dry. She came almost immediately but continued until I had orgasmed twice. Then we both fell into an exhausted sleep.

3

I STAYED FOR a few days with her, until it felt time to move on. Almost every one of our conversations led to sex, and if she wasn't talking about cookery, I had the feeling we were speaking at cross purposes, misunderstanding practically everything. If I turned the conversation to—I don't know—the context of her life, or the world, where she was from or where she was going to, it was as if it was dead before it started. Sometimes she got angry with me, not that I understood why, and then she'd be silent for a long time. All the same, the thought hung in the air that Selma, which was the woman's name, wanted to tell me that she loved me, but I couldn't allow myself to reciprocate. She wasn't like me. I wished it could have been otherwise but knew that such a relationship would never work.

Early in the morning, before Selma woke, I wrote a farewell message on a note that I left in the kitchen. Then I went out into the garden, clambered over the fence and continued the march towards the mountain. Over its higher slopes lay thick banks of cloud that shivered at intervals, as if something was stirring them. After some time, the sun rose and the birds began to sing, the stream chattered to me and I no longer felt as if a gorilla sat perched on my shoulders.

I had been on my way for some hours when I heard a squelch to one side and saw a woman sitting by the bank of the stream. She splashed her feet in the water and looked enquiringly into my eyes and then smiled.

"I haven't seen you before... How long have you been here?"

"A few days."

"I knew it!" She laughed. "Nobody here but us goes outside. An arty type, are you?"

My first instinct was to say no, but I still replied with a yes. She scrambled to her feet. Her hair was dark and reached half-way down her back, fringe cut straight, brown eyes. I had never seen her before.

"A new arrival here in paradise. And you don't remember who you were before you were planted in this place, no memories of the family that was so unbelievably glad to see you. You think there's something strange about all this, don't you?"

Now it was my turn to laugh, almost overcome with delight to hear someone who... I don't know... had a presence, said something with meaning, that hadn't been dreamed up by someone else and placed in the person's mouth for it to dribble from their lips.

"How long have you been here? Well, I don't know where to start. Where are we? Why are we here?"

"What were you told when you arrived here?" She shook the water from her feet and took out a little yellow cloth that she wetted in the stream and used to wipe her face.

"I was in an institution, as far as I recall. Then I was told that it would take some time for me to remember properly who I am, that I'd be able to rest once I was home, that I'd get more support to make a recovery. So I don't know..."

"And you don't feel like you're at home?"

"That's just it! I've never seen any of this before. The house, the streets, this woman..." I left out mentioning Selma.

"Do you have a child?"

"A son. He resembles me, but all the same, it seems..."

"It'll all come back to you. Don't worry about it."

The woman said her name was Laureen. Her face was left flushed by the cloth, which she folded and put away in a satchel that hung from her shoulder.

"I don't have a name,' I said, not knowing why I lied. "Well, I was told that I'd get better. I can't get comfortable with having no memory. It's like you recognise some things, even though you don't recall exactly. You feel a connection. I just think it's so unlikely that I could have forgotten my own wife and child... Am I dead?" The question leaped out of its own accord, although I knew it had been there in my head for a long time.

"Let's walk a little," Laureen said, and I followed her. She halted on one of the bridges that gently spanned the stream, leaned forward over the rail and pointed out the trout that barely moved as they kept station in the water. One lifted its head above the surface to swallow a fly, and I wondered if it was real as I saw the dark patch on its head, the innumerable delicate insects hovering in the air, the undulations of the tails, the sparkle from the water and stalks of grass waving on the banks. Somewhere behind the buzz of insects I could make out a low tone, light and airy, that I couldn't be sure wasn't just in my imagination. This was a motif that brought to mind the lobbies of hotels, scheduling announcements on TV—

"Look, there's a rabbit," Laureen said, pointing down the stream. A brown rabbit sat up, chewing something held between its front paws, absorbed completely in what it was doing as it lifted morsels quickly to its mouth. Unless it was listening to the music that carried from above? "Amazing, isn't it?"

Laureen said she was taking a walk, as I was, and that this was nothing unusual.

"What do you mean? Are there many of us here?"

"Like you and me? Not many, no. But we're here now and again."

"Until what?"

"I don't know. Until we go to one of the houses, I suppose. I haven't been here much longer than you."

She asked if I was heading anywhere in particular and I fudged answering the question. It seemed pretentious to talk about the mountain, although there was nothing special that I sought there, let alone that there might be something artistic there that could be complicated to explain. We all need aspirations, and yes, more than likely I was drawn by the mountain because there was just this one. I could see no other mountains anywhere.

We walked side by side and made good progress, although it didn't feel like the mountain was getting any closer. Dusk began to fall and Laureen said, "Well, let's see what happens now." She looked around more than she had up to now, into gardens and up to the windows of houses. A low mutter of crickets could be heard from the grass and bushes.

"Where are you going?" I asked, as her demeanour told me she was looking for something.

"We need a place to stay." She stopped by a three-storey house painted a neutral colour. To each side of it were storage sheds with small, square windows. A low chatter of conversation carried from inside the house, as if of people engaged in furious discussion. I followed Laureen into the garden and from there through a door into a living room full of chattering people. They all held glasses and finger food from a table at the end of the room. None of them paid us any particular attention.

"Just make yourself at home." Laureen picked up a bottle of sparkling wine, filled glasses for us and we started on the snacks. "Cheers," Laureen said, raising her glass. "For my abstinence that's now over." We clinked glasses and toasted each other, and she said she had been sober for ten years.

"Are you an alcoholic?" I asked.

"I just took a break."

"How has that worked out for you?"

"Ach. It was pretty effective, but boring. Sometimes you need to lift your mood, don't you?"

"Lift your mood?"

"Lose yourself. Be someone else, or I don't know, challenge yourself. Give yourself a push."

"Is it difficult to put into words? Are you really that drunk?" I asked, and after a moment we both burst into laughter. The bubbles in the wine made us careless and had us laughing constantly. The guests sent an occasional glance in our direction, but not in any hostile manner. They spoke the same language as we did, and there was nothing about their demeanour that seemed unfamiliar. I caught the occasional reference to something familiar in politics or the arts, but it was oddly flat and two-dimensional, like kissing your own image in a mirror, and it did nothing for me. I had no words to describe how I felt; it was all somehow timeless.

Laureen and I took our bottle and she led me up the stairs to the first floor where there was a room used as an office and a deserted lounge with magazines laid out on a glass table. There was a large bedroom on the second floor, with a balcony that provided a view over the whole settlement, the rows of streets that circled out from the domed roofs of the community centres, but in a straight line bordering the park. Several of the nearby houses were lit up, with the sounds of chatter and music carrying from them.

When the bottle was half-empty, we kissed and ended up in bed. The vibe was pleasant, and before I knew it, I was telling a story without knowing how it ended. To get out of it, I asked if the owners would mind us lying there.

"We're left in peace here. I don't know why."

"Someone must live in this house?"

"It's like we drop in to fill the gaps," Laureen began. "We're not here in the same way that they are. They step aside and leave us alone, in a way that's convenient for everyone, so there's no explosion. Or so I thought to begin with. But now I feel they don't want to have anything to do with us and the best way is to let us do as we wish, not that we get anything. So, no. I don't know."

"Not easy to put it into words?"

"We don't share a world with them. I don't want to, and I think the feeling's mutual."

"Agreed," I said, more heartfelt than I had expected, although I barely understood what we were talking about. I recalled how I had felt with Selma, and those few days that had felt like a month, leaving me drained. "They live their lives in a different way to us," I added.

"Us?"

"Like me and you and the others who are like us, and I thought there were more of us?"

"That's right."

I saw she was sleepy and drew the duvet up over her, and huddled close to her. She smelled of cinnamon. I sipped from the bottle until I no longer wanted to and fell asleep.

4

THE NEXT MORNING she was gone. I awoke alone in bed and by the time I was finally on my feet, with a pounding headache, Laureen was nowhere to be seen. She wasn't anywhere on the lower floors, or out in the garden. There was debris everywhere, left over from the previous evening's party, empty bottles and overflowing ashtrays, food leftovers, trash.

I had no reason to be here and didn't hesitate to be on my way. It was hotter than before and I lay on the bank of the stream to splash my face with cold water.

"Aaah," I sighed. "That's so good. Here's me... A man on a river bank, making the best he can of..."

A bird sang in a nearby tree. The leaves were still and there was a tranquillity to the place; the sun, the grass and the water. The music, that I had been sure I had been able to hear and which had been like muzak, had fallen silent. I lay there for a while, half-waiting for Laureen to show up, and then made off in the direction of the mountain.

There were houses on both sides.

Fences.

Gardens.

Hills.

Colours.

Now I could see the mountain was closer than before. There was no mistaking it, with that familiar flat top, a heat mirage hovering over it like a gap in the mountain. Was it full of machines? Love, intimacy and sex?

The day passed as had the others: I walked. Except that in the evening I curled up under a hedge, having pinched a blanket that had been hung out to dry in one of the gardens.

One day I came across a shabby character who seemed to be searching in the grass for something. Not far from him, on the other side of the fence, stood a woman with an awkward look on her face.

"It's all right," the woman said. The laughter of children could be heard from the house.

I offered a greeting and asked if I could help.

"I lost my purse in the garden, or rather, my child claims to have thrown it over the fence. This gentleman is helping me," the woman said.

"Don't mention it," the man said, without looking up, and continued to search. He gave off a strong earthy aroma, his hair was grey and unkempt, his clothes had not been washed for a long time. *This could be me in a few weeks*. Without something to aim for, the process could be even quicker than that.

"What sort of purse?" I asked, looking around in the grass.

"It's a little red one, a purse for coins."

"Aha."

"There's no need to make a big thing of it. May I invite you into my garden?"

I accepted the invitation, as it had been a long time since I had eaten, and the tramp mumbled something to the woman that I took as agreement. We sat at a table in the garden and let ourselves bask in the sunshine, while I felt a warm draught carry from inside the house.

The woman came out again with a full tray of bread rolls and cold meat, juice in a large pitcher. She had changed into a red knee-length dress that clung around her waist, and yellow rubber boots, too low to allow her to wade in water or be around the stream. I guessed she wore these for gardening, as the garden was well kept, with flowers in neatly tended beds.

When we had eaten, two silent children came out of the house and played in the garden with sticks and a ball. Elma—that was the woman's name—and I tried to engage the shabby man in conversation, and while he seemed willing enough to speak, we couldn't understand much, until he stood up, brushed himself down and said his farewells. I was relieved. We watched him leave, patting one of the children on the head, before making off in the opposite direction to where I was headed. I felt a sudden surge of despair, thinking of all the days it would take to return to where my journey had begun.

"He was weird," Elma said, slipping lower in the chair. I gazed at her small breasts and her legs that were splayed apart, her bare knees and sun-tanned limbs. One day I would be old and indifferent, or the remnants of libido would lurk in my body like an echo. If I became senile, I'd maybe stare relentlessly at some waitress without having the sense to be ashamed or to hide my desire, which had in fact long since been extinguished: even our most fundamental urges manifest themselves in the form of habit, keeping going even though that spring has long run dry, as we resemble a shell around something that has disappeared.

"I'll put the children to bed," Elma said as dusk fell. Afterwards she switched on the lights in the garden, a mixture of red, yellow and green, and we drank the same brand of beer as I had seen before in the houses. The thought of another round of sex hung in the air, and although I couldn't really be bothered, I knelt before her in the chair, pulled down her pants and set about fingering her. I worked my thumb angled upward and could hear that Elma liked this, spreading her legs further. I let the back of my hand rub her clitoris at the same movement. After a few minutes a fluid spurted from her as I felt a warmth spread over the back of my hand, softly like a mist, and when I withdrew my hand, it was coated with slime. Some of this had dripped into the yellow boots.

There was plenty of furniture in the living room and a large computer screen stood on a table. The children's rooms were upstairs, while Elma slept in a small room adjacent to the living room, on a sofa bed. We lay on the sofa and she switched on a speaker from which a woman's voice whispered, and she ran a comb through my hair. Elma tried to explain to me how this whispering woman would banish anxiety. Afterwards she said she worked on developing character movements in computer games and dreamed of releasing her own game that was to be called *Hiroshima*, a perfect reincarnation of the city of Hiroshima in three dimensions on the day the Little Boy atomic bomb was dropped. The game was designed to collect items, and to save as many people as possible from death,

I finally fell asleep.

5

WHEN I WAS a child, I followed the shore of a lake. I don't recall the circumstances, but I suppose I had been with my parents at a summer cottage. There on the grey sand I came across an older woman, which means that she could have been twenty or thirty, or forty, for that matter.

She had reversed a small jeep down to the waterline and behind it was a trailer. On this was a long tube that the woman was busily directing up into the air or to one side, depending on the readings from a screen that sat on the roof of the jeep. I asked what she was doing.

I'm at work, little one, she said.

What sort of work?

I search for lost people.

She showed me the tube and let me climb onto the trailer to look down the tube.

In a moment you'll be happy not to have your head just there, she said with a note of humour in her voice.

Why's that?

She opened the back of the car, where there was a box full of big, heavy balls.

These are cannonballs, she said. *You know what we do with balls like these?*

Put them in a cannon.

Quite right.

Then she opened the breech at the base of the barrel, lifted one of the balls over to it and dropped it inside. This landed with a heavy clunk, as if it were the whole lives of grown-ups packed together, to be carried out over the lake, imparting it with a sadness and a form that contained nothing. Of course, it wasn't until much later that I was able to put this into words.

After a few more turns and checking the screen, the woman asked me to step away from the car and cover my ears. I did as she asked, pretending to put hands over my ears. There was a resounding report from the cannon, ruffling both hair and the surface of the water beside us, and a sour-smelling smoke filled the air.

Look, the woman whooped, pointing out over the

water, and her voice sounded distant. I saw a plume of water reaching skywards far out in the lake. The woman adjusted the cannon, added another round and fired again. Report, splash. Report, splash. In between shots, the woman picked up a pair of binoculars and peered through it out over the water.

Are you finding lost people? I asked.

Hope so.

She fired a few more times until she found what she was searching for. I could see that by her expression. She squinted through the binoculars, and then let them drop, peered at the lake and nodded.

There he is, she said finally. She handed me the binoculars and helped me point them in the right direction until I saw what she had seen. It looked like a floating log in the water.

That's a man who went out into the water and died, the woman said. *All his friends have been searching, and now we've found him. Now we can bury him.*

I CONTINUED MY trek and sensed that it was about to come to an end. Or rather, I saw that the mountain was much closer, so that soon I would reach its foothills and begin to climb. At the peak I would presumably be able to look inside the mountain and could then decide what the best next step would be. Drawing closer, I made out a sound from the mountain, a rhythmic pulsing, like a dry *dunk, dunk, dunk* noise, as if someone were dry-retching, but so fast that nothing could be seen to emerge. On an unusually still day I made out streaking jets above the mountain, vertical, straight lines out into space, not that there was anything to be certain of.

The houses on each side were the same as before. The grass was just the same, as were the birds, the trees, the stream, the fish, and the little bridges between one bank and the other. The water was cool and sweet, the sun hot. On my long journey I had met people, made love and acquired a tan. I didn't know what else I could have desired. My stamina was better than ever and I no longer wallowed in thoughts that spun in circles with no answer to be had, and what could be called emotions—a primitive and possibly clearer version of thought—made increasingly infrequent appearances the less I sought the company of other people.

Closer still to the mountain I began to notice a sound other than the *dunk*, softer and more regular. At dusk I sat under a tree and allowed this sound to flow with my bloodstream, a circuit through my body, to and from, and suspected from where it came. I curled up to sleep beneath a bush, huddled in the blanket, and at dawn I folded it to set off on the last leg of my journey.

I came to a shore. A beach, narrow and sandy, took over where the houses came to an end, stretching further than I had expected towards the mountain, which stood on an island off the coast. From the peak of the mountain shot a series of these things that were wanted gone, disappearing at the speed of light—or so I described it to myself—up into the blue sky and out into the darkness.

I sat on a rock on the beach and rubbed my face.

"So do I swim?" I said, to try out the notion on myself. But the distance was too great. I hauled myself to my feet and walked along the beach, with the idea of seeing around the edge of the mountain in case there might be some protruding point that I could approach by continuing on my way. After all the time with houses to left and right, it was confusing to have them now on one side. To my left was a regular row of houses, seen now side-on instead of from behind, while in the other direction lay the shimmering sea with its smells of salt and seaweed.

Dusk was falling and ahead of me, on the shore, I saw the outline of a man. He stood, awaiting me, hunched and looking sick, so that I felt I could practically make out his trembling movements. Closer to him, I could see his face, leathery and wrinkled, and there was a glint in quiet eyes beneath a protuberant, placid forehead. He leaned against a shovel and looked to be exhausted from some toil. I followed his gaze to the house nearest to us. Sand from the beach had been blown by the wind onto the grass in the garden and the wall that faced us was weatherbeaten. No fence encircled the plot and there was a hole in the middle of it.

"What are you looking at, old man?" I asked and didn't wait for a reply. I went over to the garden and inspected the hole. It was the length of a man, and deep enough to bury one. A mound of earth stood beside the hole, which I assumed the man had dug up to create this grave. Maybe he was in a hurry to die.

I sensed a movement behind me. Something collided with my head and I raised my hands, but it was too late. I felt the blood flow from them, and from the whole of my body. I sank to my knees, blinking. The hole was right before me. For a moment I saw every detail of it as if a flare had been lit in the sky above, sandfleas skittered about the walls with a rustle, a worm slithered into a hole in the wall, and shimmering water filled the bottom. I could hear the old man gasp close by my ear, realising that he was holding me under my arms and trying to roll me into the grave. I tried my hardest to resist, but it was too much for me.

I fell and the world turned on its head. A blow landed on my back and everything turned white for a moment, until the darkness closed in from the sides, leaving a little gap of a window. The old man's head appeared, peering in through this opening, and then vanished. Earth came tumbling down to me, in bursts, as if the old man had remembered how to use the shovel. I thought of my life—and while it had seemed to be a long one and somehow compelling while it lasted, there wasn't much that I exactly missed. And along with the fatigue that came as part of keeping everything going, keeping active both inside and out, it was a relief to no longer need to—after that long walk to lie and feel the earth settle around me, and to become nothing.

I'm so sorry.

THE FAROE ISLANDS

THE RAT

by Sólrún Michelsen
Translated by Matthew Landrum

HE USUALLY LEAVES it in the garden. Covers it with mulch. When the last remains of summer are long-gone and autumn fades toward winter, he covers his heart the same way he covers the most fragile flowers, covers it well, so the frost won't finish it off completely.

When spring returns yet again, he exhumes it from time to time and listens to the weak heartbeat together with the small stirrings of different seedlings and root vegetables.

When summer comes, he ties his heart to a string and hangs it around his neck. Then walks in and out of doors. The heartbeat weakens every time he enters the house, but this time of year he is outside so often that it doesn't matter.

It's different in winter. Then he has to be inside so much that his heart can't stand it. That is why he buries it.

Even though he pines for his heart, there's lots to keep him occupied during the winter. Such things that don't require a heart. Such as multiplying and adding sums.

All winter long he counts. Page up and page down with numbers that are only numbers. They are exactly the same, once you have counted to nine. Just repetitions.

And he fixes up the house in the winter. Paints and hammers and sets mousetraps in the pantry. No heart's required for this.

He also picks at candlewax. He likes candles so much. He keeps them burning all winter all around the house, but they leave lots of stains, both when he blows them out and when he moves them. So that's work in and of itself.

More than once he's thought about getting himself a candle snuffer, but he holds off. He needs the work. Wintertime passes, and he can think about the spring and summer as he's picking.

His wife ran out on him two years ago. Then his heart grew sick and was only comfortable outside where he tried to nurse it.

When the first shock of her leaving had subsided, he'd expected that his heart would start thriving again, but it didn't. He tried several times. He didn't really want to believe that it was so bad but was shocked to admit that his wife had given his heart a wound that wouldn't heal.

When the longing gets too strong and spring is a long time coming, he goes out and puts his hand on the place where his heart lies.

That sometimes helps a bit.

Then he goes in again and pours himself a big glass of schnapps. It warms the black hole where the roots of his heart were once planted.

He often stands by the window and looks out over the wet, frost-covered garden, as if he wants to will spring to arrive and the flowers with it.

This has made his neighbour feel uncomfortable, and he's put up curtains in the window that faces the street.

He doesn't bear a grudge. He just knows that he has to watch.

Winter drags itself out, not like summer which just flies by.

Once he tried to shorten the time by building a stone wall outside, while snow was still lying in drifts, but this gave him visions of the garden, more beautiful than ever, and that started him longing for his heart again, so he had to let wall-making be and head inside again.

He sighs every time he sees the stones strewn about in a heap. But when spring comes… When spring comes, he will start construction again and then he'll plant flowers so they'll grow along the wall, and the stones will soak up heat from the sun so the flowers will be even more beautiful than before. He can hardly wait.

One cold winter day, he goes to the pantry to fetch a dried leg of lamb and he sees that there's a bit missing. Someone has nibbled off a big piece. He starts back and looks down on the floor.

There he spots the culprit.

A big rat sits curled up in the corner of the pantry. One of her front legs is stuck in a mousetrap. He looks at her for a moment and wonders what he should do. She stares back. She sits stock still.

He backs out of the pantry and closes the door. Then he fetches some thick gloves and an old birdcage he has in the attic.

The rat tries to escape with the mousetrap on her front leg. She runs right toward him and is just about to escape between his legs when he captures her.

She struggles to escape but he manages to hold her

while he releases her from the trap. Then he sets her into the cage where she settles to lick her wounded front leg. She is extremely thin. Maybe she'd been stuck in the trap for days.

He gets something for her to eat. She's famished and gorges herself on what he sticks between the bars.

While she eats, she peers out suspiciously.

The longer he watches her, the more lost in thought he gets. He feeds her and talks to her, but she only looks at him with that insidious look that makes him think about his wife.

He begins to call her by his wife's name, Alma. Yes, Alma. That'll be her name. He sighs. He never did manage to tame that wife of his. God knows he tried. And in the end, when he locked her up, she had run away. And not just run away. She had also wounded his precious heart.

But now he feels the thrill again. The thrill that came from the quiet battle between them over all the small everyday things. Vicious as she was, she often said that he liked making everything into a battle, and that she couldn't let him win every time. And for every loss he suffered, his resistance against her grew stronger.

He feels alive again. He has to admit that he has missed this game more than he realized.

While he stares at the rat, it occurs to him that he has been given another chance to get this right. Yes, if he uses the correct method, he might be able to liven up his heart again, so that he can keep it inside all year round.

Now he has Alma where he's always wanted her. This time she won't succeed in escaping. And when he has her properly trained, she won't even think about running away.

He gives her loads to eat, and she fattens up and grows calmer.

Or lazier might be the better word, he thinks. He talks gently to her, and she looks at him and puts her nose up into the air so that her front teeth are showing. He starts to feel a certain affection for her.

First, he moves her from the pantry into the kitchen, where he spends the most time, but after a while, he also takes her up with him to the bedroom when he's going to bed.

It's so nice to hear someone rustle in the dark and to have someone to say goodnight to.

It doesn't matter that she doesn't answer. She never has.

Time passes and one day he decides that the time has come to try the next step. Alma shows good behaviour. She sniffs at him when he comes close and seems mostly friendly. Yes, certain signs even indicate that she understands what he says to her. He smiles and praises himself for his great patience. He has managed to build up a good sense of trust between them, yes, better than ever before, so now he should be able to touch Alma.

She is so sleek and beautiful. He looks at her affectionately. Her fur reflects the light. This is something completely different than that poor dishevelled thing he saved from the trap.

He doesn't hesitate any longer but carefully sticks a finger into the cage to stroke the rat's back, but she suddenly turns around and bites him on the finger, drawing blood.

He curses and kicks the cage so it bounces along floor.

He wraps the finger in a handkerchief and goes out into the cold garden to try to calm down.

He's agitated and very hurt. But what else could he expect from Alma? She's always been a beast. She's never been anything else. This is the second time she's done this to him, but this time he's given it his all and really done his best, and all for nothing. He feels tears in the corners of his eyes.

That he should ever have met her…

He stands awhile and looks at the place where he's covered his heart with sod, missing it dearly.

Then an idea strikes him.

If he buries Alma the same way he buried his heart, maybe he'll be happy with her when he digs her up next spring.

He feels warm inside. Maybe everything isn't lost anyway. This could teach her once and for all. Now he can get two birds with one stone.

He is so excited that he doesn't notice the cold, even though he's in his shirtsleeves.

He fetches a shovel from the cellar and digs a pit right by the place where his heart lies.

Then he fetches Alma, who, thick and fat, runs inside the overturned cage, carries her out and puts the cage into the newly dug hole.

He looks at her, and she looks back with her black eyes.

Then he fills the hole with dirt and covers it with mulch. He tamps it down with his hands. He stands there for a while and wipes his dirty hands on his trousers and, smiling, goes back inside to hang up the shovel.

WHEN THE ANGELS CAME

by Rakel Helmsdal

1 May 2036

I AM PALMA Jákupsdóttir, 41 years old. I am recording this in an attempt to understand the unfathomable that has happened to my world since the first pandemic, 16 years ago. It has exploded into pure madness these few days since the Flag Day Revolt, 25th of April, where the president is said to have been killed.

When the Angels came 10 years ago, I thought they were wonderful; we both did, my husband Grias and I. The drones were going to watch over everything, especially the children—Lona and Jón were 12 and 10, and it was impossible to get them home before bedtime. I worried. It was all crazy downtown, everyone said.

When it was announced that we all had to have a barcode tattoo, for the Angels to work, I was taken aback.

"Seriously, Grias," I said. "Do we all have to have a tattoo—like *her*?" I whined, but I couldn't help it. It felt so gross. And it would never disappear, but of course, that was the point: the Angels should be able to scan and read us forever and for all time, until the tattoo rotted away along with the rest of us in the coffin. I felt like throwing up.

"Calm down, woman," Grias snapped. "Tattoos don't hurt. Otherwise, all those weak losers wouldn't have gotten them." He smiled but I saw how the left corner of his mouth twitched, as it always does when he thinks I'm being difficult. "And everyone is going to have one. This is going to be decent—*comme il faut*." When he starts using the only French words he knows, he is about to lose his patience.

"Sure, sure, my dear." The smile stretched my dry lips. "It's gonna be really smart." I quickly cleared the table but was unable to get the image out of my head: all those distinguished ladies sitting at the hairdresser's, proudly showing off their new barcode tattoos.

Of course, it was a piece of cake when the time came. I just took an extra pill. For fun I asked an artificial intelligence tool to make an illustrated children's book about it: *Lina, the Angels, and the Barcode Tattoo*, one of those repulsively over-educational ones, to help small, cute kids being poked. I printed it out so the children and I could have a laugh—we have the same sense of humour.

But then, a while later, a package arrived with '12 author copies' written on the box. I can't describe the shock I had when I saw its contents: copies of my book and a thank-you letter from Tindur Lambhús, the president himself. I ran to the bathroom and vomited until there wasn't anything left but bile. Grias had sent my ridiculous joke to the government and they had printed it.

I felt so humiliated that I didn't leave the house for long, though my silly friends called and praised me, and Grias proclaimed: "Look at that! That is quite something! Palma Johannesen—a true supporter of the government!" He has taken everything, even my sense of humour and my name, but at that time I no longer dared to speak up.

After we got Angels and barcodes it was no problem getting the children home at night. The drones located people as long as it was daylight; hence the curfew was implemented. Anyone who was not at home before dinner time was registered and lost points. Grias did not accept that the children lost points. After all, it wouldn't have looked good for him since the workplaces had started to announce how many points each household had.

For a long time, I thought all was fine… or maybe I have forgotten… there are gaps in my memory… The pills Grias forces me to take for my nerves, they make me forget, and I've taken them for so many years. But I stopped on Flag Day.

Now, I am slowly waking up. Last week I found some old photos. As I flipped through them, I suddenly remembered things from my childhood, such as the joy of playing hide-and-seek in the twilight summer evenings in Sandvík. No one called us home before midnight.

Lona and Jón have never played outside after the late summer sunset.

I can never confide my thoughts to anyone; the government will hear of it, and I will lose many points. They'll punish our family, take away our rations, and maybe even move us to the blocks. Grias would kill me—I mean, he literally would.

My children are young adults now, Lona is 23, Jón

21. They are nice young people, really, and down to earth, working every day, home before the curfew, no nonsense—exemplary, if you ask the government. But happy? No. Both have had partners, but Grias didn't accept them as potential in-laws. He found something to report on them—there is always something. Anna, Jón's girlfriend, lost so many points that they couldn't be seen together. And no one has seen Lona's boyfriend for a long time: Sundar Orrason, Nita and Orri's boy, a handsome young man, intelligent and gentle. I think Lona knows that her father is to blame. She looks at him so strangely, not just angry—I believe she hates him. I don't remember why Grias dislikes our neighbours so much—it often doesn't take much.

I haven't seen Nita for a long time. She used to walk past our window with her beautiful smile.

"There goes *that one* again with her loser tattoos, so annoying!" Grias used to say. "Smiling and grinning stupidly! So damn happy all the time. As if writing books makes anyone happy. You certainly weren't, woman! But maybe that's why the government gave the book series to someone who can actually write." He would usually laugh mockingly and throw the rest of the contents of his coffee cup at me.

My ridiculous book has developed into a long series of educational Lina books: *Lina and the Curfew*; *Lina and the Point System*; *Lina, Remember, Daddy Decides!* and so on. The latest in the series is *Mommy, When Will I Get My 4th Little Brother*? The books are distributed to all households with small children. The guy that creates them with artificial intelligence has become stinking rich. I didn't get a penny, but Grias suddenly bought himself everything.

It used to make me happy to see Nita smiling in the street. Orri and she were always holding hands and looking lovingly at each other. Grias was about to choke just seeing them.

"Who the hell goes around being ridiculously in love after so many years? They got married before us! And she must absolutely be kind to the birds too. Feeding them in the garden, just so they can splatter their droppings on our windows. What a cow!"

No one has seen Orri in more than three years. Grias made sure he lost all his points, and one day he was suddenly gone. Nita hasn't been out much since, and after Sundar went missing too, I haven't even spotted her in her garden. I rather expect her to be driven to the blocks any moment. One person can't have a house for themselves; it makes no difference that her great-grandfather built it. Everyone must have an affordable roof over their head, says the government. One should also be worthy of a house—in other words, have served the community. We have. Grias has reported on someone almost every month for several years and forced me to have Pandemic Knitting Club, Pro Life Knitting Club, Safety Knitting Club; to organise cake raffle after cake raffle for the benefit of the Angel Army—in short: I have been a model wife.

"Good for her!" Grias says spitefully. "Sitting there alone, with the husband fled and the son thrown into the nick!"

But there aren't any prisons any more, says the government. The Angels ensure that no crimes are committed. If someone misbehaves, they'll get a Guardian Angel hanging over them all day and night. The government sees and hears every scrap, but there is little to hear anyway. No one wants to be seen with criminals; it means losing points.

Grias sometimes says that Orri and Sundar have killed themselves out of shame. It may well be—there are so many who have done just that, but I think it's not out of shame, but out of grief for this crazed country.

For two years, we have been told that the terrible pandemic Dream Death is responsible for the many fatal accidents. More than a thousand are infected and hospitalised, or locked up at home, putting their families in a completely unreasonable situation. The patients do not fall out of their dreams when they wake up. Instead, they walk around dreaming continuously, doing completely insane things without realising it. Like that woman who smashed a man's head with a jar of red cabbage in the supermarket because she dreamed that he was an axe murderer.

Last week it was announced in the news that it has all been a big conspiracy against the government: the Dream Death doesn't exist. No one is sick—they are all members of the terrorist group Mótrák. They pretend to be insane, so they can walk around killing without being punished.

I have never heard a bigger load of poppycock. Many more have ended their own lives than those who have killed anyone.

5 May 2036

This morning we heard in the news that Glasir, the high

school, has been shut down. The 2000 pupils have been instructed to join the voluntary workforce while they still receive support. Then they have to look for work—or, for the girls, get pregnant.

It feels unnatural that a government doesn't want an educated population. It seems Lona and Jón were lucky to get their diplomas. Grias says that all this schooling is exaggerated! Girls who go to university don't get a husband, he told Lona. Lona wanted to study chemistry, but *Daddy decides*... Jón would have liked to be trained as a carpenter, but he still has no apprenticeship. Both have worked at the fish factory and had odd jobs since they left school.

Then the afternoon news came; it was broadcast live:

First, we saw a group of the black-clad police officers, who were first seen when they violently suppressed the Flag Day Revolt. Now the reporter called them 'The Sons of the Fatherland'. The sight sent shivers down my spine, and I still can't believe what happened next: *the police stormed the Psychiatric Hospital,* herding sick people out like sheep! Many patients were dragged out, some by their hair. The sick shouted and cried, and some threw themselves down on the asphalt, holding their heads, screaming. The police officers kept pushing them forwards and were hitting those who didn't move quickly enough with their batons.

Fortunately, people came running to protect the patients and move them out of harm's way. Everyone looked totally shocked, but no one dared to raise their voices. It's been only nine days since Flag Day.

All evening, ambulances, police cars and fire engines have howled through the streets, and people have been ordered to stay indoors.

It feels like a horror movie, what we watched on the news today. No one can pretend so perfectly to be insane, not even desperate rebels. They were ill and raving crazy. The town is full of pure madness.

In the replay of the news just before midnight, they had cut out the distressed patients from the footage and only left the recordings of the ones that acted aggressively. Another retouching of reality. This country has gone nuts. I think that those who were thrown out of the psychiatric ward today are indeed mentally unbalanced, but there *are* some who are even more deranged than them.

I HAVEN'T BEEN out of the house since Flag Day. Grias forbade me to leave the house that day, even though all able-bodied persons have a legal duty to listen to the president's speech. Grias didn't tell me why, but he must have known something. "Don't you dare go out that door until everything is back in order," he said.

I feel so helpless. I only know of what is taking place from the news, and I know by now that the news can't be trusted. I haven't dared to think this before now. The pills Grias has forced me to take, prevented me. I have no one to talk to. Jón works all day as a bin-man and comes home too tired to do anything but sleep. Why are there so few people doing all the work when they say that the population has grown so much larger? Lona is locking herself in her room as soon as she comes home. I can see the hateful stares she sends Grias when she slips inside. She will soon have no points left, having neither husband nor children.

Grias and I never talk. I speak and at best he ignores

it. He speaks and I obey like a proper wife. That's how it's supposed to be, says the government. Grias wasn't like this when we first met. This all started after the government closed the country.

7 May 2036

JUST WHEN I think it can't get any worse, something even more gruesome happens:

A neighbour knocked on the door while Grias was at work today. I waved her around the house so the Angels wouldn't register her but I couldn't let her in. More than a year ago, I discovered an Eye right above the front door. But she didn't mind, she was just here to rejoice in bringing me the bad news.

Lona has reported Sundar and he is now charged with rape. She was of course lying. Lona wouldn't hide important things from me. And why would Sundar harm her? They are head over heels in love. Can something—or someone—have made her turn him in?

When she came home, I went to her bedroom door and knocked gently. She didn't open it.

"It's Mum, Lona love, please open the door," I pleaded.

No response, just sobs.

"My dear, you know that you can tell me everything," I assured her, "just like you always can."

"No, not this time." I hardly heard the words; her voice was so muffled by tears.

"You can, my sweetheart," I tried. "I'll..."

I was yanked away from the door.

"Don't you interfere!" Grias shouted. "Now she has finally done the right thing, you are not going to ruin it! Go bake a cake or something, woman!"

I am lost for words. Something is very wrong! It's such an alarming feeling. For a moment, I had the strongest urge to take a handful of pills, just to make me stop shaking, but I persevered.

Why have I let myself become so numbed all these years? I think I have known all along what Grias' pills do to me, but everything just became so unbearable when the new government came to power—to witness how all our rights were withdrawn little by little, while we powerlessly watched it happen. The pills took the weight off and gave me indifference. Life was just easier if I didn't care. But I should have cared! I should have stood up to Grias when he started to change. I loved him once, but I did nothing when he went off track and lost himself—or did he? Do I really know him? Maybe he has always been like this: fixing what he thinks needs fixing, there are no feelings involved. And I have been lazy—it can't be said more nicely—mentally and physically lazy. And therefore, accessory to what he has done.

9 May 2036

TODAY WE WERE in court.

I so revelled in the feeling of being outdoors for the first time in two weeks, that I almost forgot why I had been released from my detention. The bright light hit my eyes, and it felt wonderful: the wind on my face, the sun on my skin. But to be among people… I felt exposed, like everyone was staring at me, all these people who were just going about as usual—walking, cycling, going to work, shopping…

"They are staring, Grias," I whispered.

"Don't be such a bloody moron; they don't give a

shit about you," he hissed. "You're nothing to look at anyway."

As usual I let it pass. I had dressed up in a nice black dress, styled my hair, and put on makeup. The people in the street looked at me but it was probably because of the way Grias held my arm, locked so tightly to himself I couldn't walk properly upright. He is a head shorter than me and today I was wearing high heels—my little drop of revenge. This is what I have come to: stupid spitefulness that makes no difference.

The trial was a farce. The authorities were directors and actors, and my family and the neighbours' son extras.

It was tragic to see Sundar; he was unrecognisable. His clothes were torn and dirty and he was thin, pale and haggard, as if he hadn't had sunlight, food, or sleep. He, who used to be so handsome and fair-hearted.

When he and Lona caught sight of one another, something perplexing happened. They headed straight towards each other like sleepwalkers. When they were a metre apart, they froze and stood staring at each other, like statues. I couldn't see Sundar's face, but the sorrow in Lona's was heartbreaking. Grias quickly shoved Lona into the courtroom but I heard what she whispered:

"I'm so, so sorry, Sundar, I couldn't do anything."

It was at that moment I began to understand. Oh my God, I have been so stupid.

What went on inside that courtroom was incredibly ugly. Lona was asked all sorts of nasty questions, and her answers ate at me as though I was eating broken glass. How could she say such things? Her voice was flat, mechanic, as if one of the Angels were speaking. Others also came to testify, and most of the accusations against Sundar had nothing to do with rape—and all were totally unbelievable: he has been violent to others too, has stolen and cheated, and is furthermore accused of being a traitor and part of Mótrák, the terrorist group behind the Flag Day Revolt.

Sundar looked like a beaten dog.

"I plead not guilty to any of these charges," was the only sentence he managed to say throughout the trial. There were no witnesses in his favour. He didn't have a chance. Lona knew it too. She wasn't home when we arrived back at our house.

"Nicely sorted!" Grias said, pleased, as he scooped the fifth spoonful of sauce onto his plate. He set the spoon aside and took a piece of paper from his pocket and laid it on the table in front of me.

Lona's score card: full points in total, plus a bonus. Yesterday it was nearly empty.

I clenched my mouth shut.

She didn't come home until long after the curfew. Fortunately, Grias snored in front of the TV. I rushed out in the hallway and tried to hug her, but she pushed me aside, took the stairs up to her room three steps at a time, and turned the key in the lock on the inside.

I now fathom the depth of Grias' betrayal, but there is still much I don't comprehend, especially the judge's verdict: "A chance to defend himself in the Arena."

What is the 'Arena', and what did the judge mean by 'defend himself'? Grias wasn't surprised, but I can't ask. You can never know who is the next one to *defend* themselves in the *Arena*.

EVERY DAY I take my five pills and grind them to powder. I pour the powder into an envelope and put it at the back of the bottom kitchen drawer. He mustn't know that I am not sedated any more. My head feels clearer, so most of the drug must be out of my system. It has been hard; my body has been screaming for the poison, but I have restrained myself. I owe it to my children—and to this country, that I used to love so much.

I've been asleep long enough.

Why did I let him control me like this? I see now what I didn't want to see when we became a pair: everything has always been about him and him alone.

And then this, which I've been wondering about all these years: how does Grias benefit from the snitching? We are not rich. We don't have a car; the house is small and in poor condition; there's nothing special about living in this part of town. Everyone knows this is the next neighbourhood to be demolished to build apartment blocks. He works no less than anyone else: eight hours a day doing tedious registrations, and then all those hours watching surveillance footage at home. I have often considered that maybe he's just pretending to work in the office—in fact, I have no idea where he goes when he leaves home in the morning. Maybe he has another family somewhere? But who would want him?

I am going crazy just staying here and not being able to do anything! But if I leave the house or do anything, the Eye at the front door will inform him—them—immediately. And there might be other Eyes I haven't spotted yet. The only difference between me and a prisoner is that I haven't been given a fair trial—as if fair trials still exist…

13 May 2036

For a long time, I have thought about ending it all—or

disappearing out into the night never to return. But I have nowhere to go. My friends have long since been taken from me. Some simply disappeared, and then it didn't take long before the rest realised that the only common denominator in the first cases was that Grias didn't like my friends.

It's three in the morning. Grias has taken his own medicine—literally. He lies comatose on the couch. I don't know when he will wake up again—or if he ever will. I couldn't care less.

THE TV NEWS this evening was so atrocious that it wasn't really a decision I made, but a pure reflex: I have to get away with the children, I don't know where, just away... We cannot remain in this hell on Earth.

"What great entertainment!" Grias laughed so hard that his belly bumped against the edge of the table, causing the glasses to jingle. "Those guys are good. Killing two birds with one stone. The miserable traitors are killing each other off and we get free entertainment. Cheers to the government!"

Lona and Jón were speechless with shock, and pale as corpses. I pinched my thigh to keep from screaming, and the decision made itself:

"Say, shouldn't we open a bottle to celebrate this?" I got to my feet. Jón stared at me as if I was an alien. Lona stirred, a spark kindling in her eyes.

"You're absolutely right! What a good little wifey I've got myself!" Grias clapped his chubby hands, excited. "Make it a good one, woman!"

I almost ran to the kitchen, opened a bottle of liquor, poured the powder from the envelope into it and shook it vigorously.

"Put this in too." I froze in shock, but it was just Lona. Two steps behind her stood Jón. He nodded as I took the syringe Lona handed me, and I emptied it into the bottle. Three pairs of eyes met in mutual understanding—a silent pact was made.

Lona's voice was but a whisper:

"Glasir is not the place they call the 'Arena'. Glasir is just the beginning. It's going to get much worse…"

I carried only one liquor glass back with the bottle. It's been years since he announced that 'a mother doesn't drink in front of her children'. I filled the glass full to the brim. He gulped it all down without tasting it first, then shovelled an enormous amount of sauce and mutton in behind it. Another glass quickly followed. Soon the snores from the living room mixed with the sounds of the shots and cries from the re-transmitted news.

We didn't wait for his snores to fade.

We just left.

WHAT WE WATCHED on the news this evening is too cruel, too appalling, too inhumane to describe, but then again, only humans can behave like this... I have to tell, even if the words are hard to say.

I didn't immediately recognise where the footage was taken, but Jón gasped and whispered "Glasir."

There were gunshots and screams of terror, people running, some desperately trying to flee, others chasing them. There were injured and dead, and everywhere weapons: rifles, knives, sharp hooks, shuttles, shotguns. Our living room was filled with horrible sounds and images: shouts—screams—shots—screams—running—falling—crying—screams—glass shattering... The images were blurry, likely from surveillance cameras inside the high school. One time there was a view of the outside: the building was surrounded by a heavily armed police force. Inside the building there were no uniforms, only prisoners forced to kill each other. And we just knew: no one is going to get out of there alive.

The almost hysterical voice of the reporter still rings in my ears:

"As you know, the government decided earlier this week to send the pupils at Glasir home, because the building was to be used as a prison for the Mótrák terrorists who attacked a peaceful crowd on Flag Day and killed our beloved president, Tindur Lambhús. Fortunately, our skilled Sons of the Fatherland had all the terrorists arrested in no time.

"The intention was, of course, that Glasir would only be a temporary prison, until the trials against the terrorists could be held, but as we can see from the footage from Glasir today, this will probably be useless. They are not humans, but animals! They planned to destroy our beloved country, but now they are killing each other instead!"

THE FOOTAGE FEATURED children! There were people of all ages, old and young, men and women, all in utter distress and chaos. The images were out of focus, but we could clearly see that these were not people who had been arrested only a few days ago. Many looked starved and miserable in the same way that Sundar had. Some could barely walk. These must be the many who, like Orri, have 'gone missing' in recent years.

I couldn't bear to watch, but I couldn't close my eyes.

* * *

I CAN'T BELIEVE this is happening here in my peaceful little country.

They have turned us into monsters—by fear!

Why did we vote for them?

… there was blood everywhere…

The text is transcribed from recordings found in a scrapyard. It has not been possible to verify what is described in them, since there are no archives left from this tragic time period.

NORWAY

ALL THE FRIENDLY PEOPLE

by Tor Åge Bringsværd
Translated by Olivia Lasky

Once I'd yawned three times, I felt like I owed the other people in the compartment an explanation. "I didn't get much sleep last night," I said. "There weren't any free berths onboard, so I had to make do with three wool blankets and a deckchair."

"Oh, you poor dear, why don't you sleep here for a bit?" said the old woman smoking a Roth-Händle. "Wouldn't that be alright?" She looked around.

The bald man and the young couple nodded in agreement.

"I can never sleep on trains," I said.

"Nonsense!" the old woman protested. "Just shut your eyes, don't you mind us one bit."

The bald man set his newspaper down and peeled a banana.

"Feel free to put your feet up here," the old woman said. She and the young couple scooted apart a bit to make room.

"No, thank you," I said. "I should be fine." Then I yawned again.

"If we all move over to one side..." the old woman continued, stubbing out her cigarette.

The bald man stood up and sat down next to her.

"Look, now you can stretch out properly."

All four of them smiled at me kindly. "Don't be shy. Make yourself comfortable. How far are you going?"

"Munich," I said.

"That's over three hours away. Don't worry, we'll wake you up. With plenty of time to spare. Go ahead and get some sleep."

"I don't think—"

"Look, now the whole seat's free! Make yourself comfortable."

"This is really very nice of you," I said.

"Try to sleep now. We moved for your sake."

The bald man took hold of my legs and set them on the seat. I tried to get away, but he held them firmly in a freckled vice.

"Thank you," I said. "Thank you all so much."

"Relax," the old woman cooed. "Just shut your eyes and relax."

"Try to sleep now," the bald man grunted, his face red.

"It's really not *that* big of a deal..." I mumbled.

The young couple shook their heads with a sigh and kissed each other.

"Oh, stop. It's better this way, isn't it?" The old woman lit a new cigarette. "Now you can get properly comfortable."

The bald man wouldn't release his grip on my feet. Beads of sweat were forming on his forehead. "Shut your eyes and sleep," he said hoarsely. "Go to sleep, dammit!"

I tried to get up, but the old woman put a hand on my chest. "You just stay put," she said with a smile. "It doesn't bother us one bit. There's absolutely no shame in being tired."

The young couple stopped kissing each other. The boy shoved the old woman aside.

"Allow me," he said politely, and pressed both hands against my chest. It was getting harder to breathe, and I could no longer speak. I kept opening my mouth but couldn't get a word out.

"Please, stop trying to talk all the time," the old woman said. "You shouldn't feel obligated to make conversation with us." Then she placed a kind, wrinkled hand over my mouth.

"I can't hold him much longer, dammit," the bald man said. "My arms have nothing left!"

"Wouldn't it be better if we sat on top of him?" the young girl asked. Those were the first words I'd heard her say.

"Fantastic idea!" the bald man said.

And then they sat on top of me. The bald man sat on my feet. The young couple took up the space from my thighs to my chest, and the old woman spread out her skirt and sat on my face.

"Now, now, dear, do try to lie still, won't you?" she said. "Just relax."

And somewhere far in the distance, I could hear her lighting another cigarette.

WRECKED

by Aleksander Brun
Translated by Olivia Lasky

"Ma-ma?"

THE WHISPER was soft, but it was enough to wake him. Despite the voice being so quiet and careful, the sound seemed to fill the entire room. It was on the verge of overwhelming. He rolled over carefully. A headache pounded against his forehead. Nausea crept up his throat. Fresh sweat covered his skin like a layer of oil. He opened his eyes, struggling to find focus in the darkness. It was like the room was spinning around him. After a few seconds, he spotted the white IKEA crib his wife had chosen, the one he'd reluctantly put together. He saw a shape between the bars of the crib: a small bundle of a person. He couldn't see the face, though, and deduced that the little girl was lying on her stomach. His gaze wandered further along the crib until it met two dark eyes, shiny as marbles, staring straight into his own.

"Ma-ma?" she repeated, her voice toneless. She lifted her hand and pointed a tiny finger in his direction.

"Mama isn't here," he snapped, feeling an inferno

building up somewhere deep inside. What had begun as a deep grief had, over days, been fed and cultivated into a malignant rage—like a wound that never scabbed over and healed but instead festered with infection and pus. He saw the little girl's hand sink slowly towards the mattress, as though she had both received and understood the message. But just before her hand met the sheet, it flew back up and hung in the air, still pointing in the same direction.

"Ma-ma?"

Furious, he slammed his hand against the bed, so violently that even though the padding from the mattress dampened the blow, the bedspring still let out a considerable creak. He rolled onto his back and pulled a pillow over his face. *Just go to sleep, you little monster*, he thought, barely managing to resist the temptation to scream the words into the damp pillow. Its stale stench of sweat and alcohol filled his nostrils, and the revulsion it stirred made him want to vomit. He took a few deep breaths of the enclosed air. *I didn't mean to call you a monster*, he thought. His shoulders relaxed as he realised that he was being sincere; he really hadn't meant it.

Along with his breathing, every sound around him seemed to be trapped in a vacuum. He could hear his organs gurgling, pumping fluids, blood, and air through his body. But he could also hear something else: a faint rustling, almost identical to the sound of someone shifting beneath a blanket. It came from just to his left—from the other side of the bed. It stopped quickly, but a trace of unease had still managed to creep beneath his skin. He knew it was just his imagination. Or wishful thinking. He would have put together a hundred cribs in a row if it could have made that wish come true. Because no one had slept beside him for days. Not since his wife had gone to visit her parents.

He'd decided to stay at home that evening. There were homework assignments to grade, but he ended up playing video games instead. The darkness of winter made it hard to tell how late it actually was when he finally looked up from his computer. It was already dusk when his wife had left around four. Now, when he looked out the window, he saw the thin layer of ice on the asphalt glittering beneath the streetlights. The sight left him with a sick feeling in his stomach, almost like a warning, a bad omen. He glanced at his phone. It was nearly eleven.

Shouldn't she be back by now? He'd repeatedly told her to text him before she left for home so he'd know when she'd be arriving. She always forgot, but then again, she always came back home in one piece with a laugh and an excuse about how she'd simply been distracted or that she'd forgotten to text in the chaos of saying goodbye.

Starting to get nervous, he began scrolling on his phone. He went through his usual routine of social media and online news outlets. But when he got to the local news site, he froze. The words blazed up at him from the screen: *BREAKING: CAR IN COLLISION WITH LORRY*. He tried to steady himself at first, to think rationally. She was most likely just stuck in traffic. Nevertheless, he called her.

"The subscriber you have called has switched off their mobile or is in an area with no coverage," responded the cheerful, pre-recorded female voice of the mobile operator. His hand was now shaking so hard the phone trembled. The screen was slick with sweat. He tried calling again and again, but the same message kept playing each time. Then he called her parents, who told him she'd left over an hour ago. They lived only a half-hour's drive away.

It didn't take long for his fears to be confirmed. When an unknown number appeared on his phone screen, he somehow already knew what was waiting for him on the other end. The car in the article belonged to his wife. She was the one who had been in a head-on collision with the lorry. Her car had been completely destroyed. She'd been pinned in the wreckage. He had seen the vehicle afterwards himself. No one who had been inside it could have possibly survived.

THE DAMP PILLOW felt suffocating. Gasping, he tossed it aside and smacked his lips. All these thoughts made him thirsty. His tongue felt too big for his mouth, like it was disproportionate to the rest of his body. He tried moistening the back of his throat with saliva, but it only made it worse. The bitter, rancid taste of half-digested beer swirled around in his parched mouth. He rolled over again. The memories of the car made him restless. It was precisely those images he was trying to suppress with all the drinking. It started with one thought, but then, much like an avalanche, everything came tumbling down.

But avalanches stop eventually, he told himself.

The past few days had been a whirlwind; he hadn't been able to process everything. There wasn't any time to either grieve or digest what had happened. Instead, he'd had to get in touch with family and friends and accept condolences and go to bereavement counselling and contact the funeral home and plan the ceremony and identify his wife and…

Once again, he heard movement coming from the sheets behind him. It lasted longer this time, as if someone was turning restlessly, unable to find a comfortable position. And this time, he could feel the faint vibrations of another body shifting.

Hell, my imagination is running wild tonight.

He tried to shake it off, but it wasn't all that easy. Doubt had taken root, burrowing into his awareness. Feeling at a loss, he hurled his pillow towards the foot of the bed. He found himself facing his daughter once again. She was lying motionless in the darkness, her body stiff, her eyes fixed in one place. She was still staring in the same direction—towards him, but not at him. He stiffened as a low, guttural moan spread throughout the room. It resembled the sound someone makes when they get the wind knocked out of them, only this seemed even *deeper*, if that was even possible. Sweat beaded from his every pore. Behind him, the movements in the bed continued, followed by a gasp—a desperate, choking gasp, as though the air itself had been cut off, or a windpipe was being crushed. Fear rushed through his veins.

Suddenly, he felt a weight against his body. Something was pressing against his back, clumsy and trembling. It seemed like it was using every ounce of power it had in its body to get close to him. He felt skin against skin—his warm and sweaty, the other's cold and sticky.

This isn't happening, he thought, squeezing his eyes shut. *This isn't possible!*

He felt the frail, broken limbs of the uninvited guest embracing him. All he wanted was to flee, but he couldn't move a muscle, reminiscent of the time he'd been under anaesthetic during surgery, fully awake but unable to act. Now the terror paralysed him, as if the *thing* had such a strong hold on him that he couldn't escape. He heard—and felt—the creature's rasping, inhuman breath at his ear. It was starting to feel claustrophobic, like there was no longer any room for him in the bed. He kept his eyes shut as though his life depended on it. He convinced himself that if he couldn't see it, it couldn't be real—that was the only hope he had to cling to. In a wild panic, he tried to summon an image of his wife as she had been when she was alive: her warm smile, her cute, slightly pointed nose dusted with lively freckles. But the vision shifted quickly, twisting into the last image he had of her. The smashed nose. The bloody lips. The teeth missing from her gaping mouth.

"No..." he wheezed through gritted teeth. His sobs echoed against his ribcage like a hammer against a concrete wall. Tears forced their way through his clenched eyelids. Then, something sharp pressed into his side. A cry of pain tore from his throat. It felt like someone was trying to cut him with blunt scissors or grab him with sharp claws. Rough, jagged shapes dug into his back, piercing his skin. They felt like broken branches—or jutting ribs. The creature was trying to crush him like rubbish in a compactor. Or no, it was as though it were trying to force itself *inside* him, to merge the two of them into one being. Was it seeking comfort—or was it dragging him with it to the grave? Blood started to stream from his new wounds and pool around him. He had to do something!

His eyes snapped open. Focusing was now even more difficult than before. His daughter was no longer lying down in the crib. She was standing upright, her face pressed against the bars, her little hands gripping them.

Oh my God... was all he managed to think. A chill ran through his body. It was like every bodily function was shutting down. Now, he was nothing but a passive onlooker. He saw his daughter's eyes—coal-black and glassy, like a porcelain doll's. Her short, chubby legs trembled as they fought to hold her up against gravity, but it seemed like they were about to buckle at any moment. The few muscles left intact strained to keep her twisted frame upright. Her mouth sagged slackly, like her jaw had been knocked loose. The rest of her head was deformed, caved in with unnatural hollows, like dents in a crumpled car.

"Ma-maaaa?" she croaked, her voice slurred and hoarse as if being dragged out with her final breath.

He gasped for air, his consciousness rapidly fading. Cold and despair were all that remained—as if his soul were leaving his body—when he realised what he had managed to forget in his haze of sleep and drink: his little girl had been in the car that night, too.

SMOKE AND SHADOWS

by Jon Ewo
Translated by Olivia Lasky

THERE WAS ONLY one solitary cross at the back of the old cemetery. It was at the bottom of the slope, half a metre tall and made of iron. It might have been painted at some point, but the paint was long gone. Now, the cross was rusting, and the grass around it was stained reddish-brown.

The reason nobody else was buried here wasn't because it was so steep or shadowy. It wasn't because it was too far away from the old stone church. It was because Martens was buried here.

Martens was hanged 154 years ago. He was a murderer who'd stabbed seven people to death.

Some people kill in self-defence.

Some kill by accident.

Martens murdered seven men because he enjoyed killing.

He liked watching other people suffer. It made him smile because he felt like it gave him power. And he liked sinking his teeth into his victims. He particularly liked the taste of their blood.

Martens was an evil person. Some might have even said he was barely a human, but rather a monster. Either way, no one wanted to bury their relatives beside him. He was condemned to lie there at the edge of the cemetery—alone.

If Martens had still been alive, that would've been perfectly fine with him. He despised other people.

Even in death, he enjoyed the solitude.

Because even though his body had been hanged 154 years ago, there was something inside him that wouldn't die.

Three black-clad judges had sentenced him to death, but the evil and bloodlust inside Martens was a flame that refused to become grey smoke and charred wood. When he'd murdered those seven men, the malice had been like a bonfire inside him. That didn't change when they captured him and put him in a cell. He sat there in the semi-darkness, chewing inedible food and drinking stale water. He got a rush of joy each time he thought about how he'd gotten the blacksmith, about how he'd surprised the shopkeeper, about what he'd done to the ship captain.

During his long trial, the bonfire of monstrosity was occasionally reduced to embers, but the mere memory of stabbing the knife could make the embers glow again. When they took him to the gallows in the middle of the town square, his hatred for all other people continued to burn inside him just as intensely. Just as it did in his last seconds, when the hangman strung him up on the gallows.

Maybe that was why the evil continued to live on in his heart after the doctor had seen his body and declared Martens dead? Even after they'd placed him in the very cheapest casket? Even after six trusted men had carried him to the deepest grave that had ever been dug in the district? Even after they'd spat on his casket at the bottom of the grave?

It took several years for the corpse to rot. As small animals ate him and worms wriggled their way through his skull, the maliciousness flowed into the soil around the grave, looking for ways out. The groundwater took it further down the slope. Minuscule fragments of evil accompanied insects, water, and voles towards the buildings on the other side of the hedge—a primary school with over 400 pupils. What remained of Martens collided with the basement wall two metres under the gym and found the microscopic fissures in the stones.

The evil and the desire for blood lived a life of its own. It looked for sustenance and found it—a little animal fat, some mould, the rotting remains of a mushroom, a few rodent bones. There were plenty of possibilities in the basement, which was large enough for there to be forgotten corners that had hardly been visited since it was built.

But the evil still didn't really have a body. It was just smoke and shadows. Something whirling around a small, glowing core. Something that was growing slowly and that now managed to make a faint sound that sounded like "Mmarrteens".

Many years passed, and the smoke and shadows took on a miniature form resembling a combination of a doll and a rat. It often sat near a narrow window close to the ceiling, listening to the children playing out in the schoolyard, watching the human bodies darting back and forth in the sunlight, thinking about others' deaths—and others' blood.

One day, it spotted a fly on the other side of the windowsill. The insect was enjoying the summer sun and rubbed its front legs together before it made its way up the window. The fly's antennae probed the air while it shifted restlessly, like it could sense something was creeping closer.

The smoke and shadows spotted a long pine needle on the windowsill, glided over to it slowly, and took hold of it. The fly continued its way up the window, but then it came right back down.

The fly's antennae probed at the pine needle uncertainly. It took a step towards it, turned away, then turned halfway back.

And it was at that very moment that the pine needle was lifted and driven straight into the fly's right compound eye. The animal flapped its wings wildly before it tipped over as the pine needle was driven further into its body.

The fly's legs flailed and its wings quivered for a few seconds as its life came to an end.

The smoke and shadows attacked the insect's corpse, boring its way through the hard exoskeleton. It chewed into the fly's soft body, which was still twitching with death throes.

The hazy being that had once been Martens became something more tangible as it ate the fly's innards, leaving only the exoskeleton. It grew larger.

It continued to grow and eat more flies as the years passed. It now had a regular hangout on the windowsill with a view of all the children playing outside. But it was still too small. It needed even more sustenance to be strong enough.

The smoke and shadows had long had its eye on the enormous spider spinning its web in the corner—a hairy beast that lived off the flies down here in the basement. But the flies had become fewer and farther between. The indistinct form that had once been Martens had been taking the spider's food. That meant war.

If the spider had been driven by a clearer sense of purpose, it most likely would have won. It was strong, fast, and much bigger than the smoke and shadows entity. But the basement was so enormous that it was easy for its foe to get away.

The spider had waited to ambush it several times. It had spun delicate, sticky threads that could alert it to where its rival was—but hadn't yet lucked out with that strategy.

That is, until one night, when the spider surprised it at the base of a dusty old storage shelf. The smoke and shadows was at the back of a corner—with no escape. The spider blocked the way out, and its foe was trapped.

The spider crept closer, placing one leg slowly in front of the other until it was ready to attack. Its fangs snapped slowly.

Then, the smoke and shadows entity spotted something twinkling close to the wall. It was almost completely covered in dust. It glided over and picked up half of an old needle that had been broken in two.

The spider realised it had to attack straight away.

It scrambled quickly towards its rival, opening its mouth wide and lowering its upper body by bending its hairy legs.

The smoke and shadows creature turned abruptly. It slowly raised the needle, but it was so heavy—heavier than anything it had lifted since it ended up here in the basement and got bigger.

The shadowy being that had once been Martens knew

this would never work. Its pathetic life was about to end right here, once and for all. It managed to make the needle stand up on its end just as the spider launched itself over it and impaled itself on it.

The point slid through the black body and tore through the underside. Something wet ran down and covered the smoke and shadows, bathing it in the spider's fluids.

It gave it new strength, new power. The smoke and shadows creature bit through tough skin and into the body and feasted on the dead spider for several days.

It was intoxicating, and a mind with a clearer thought took shape inside it, a still-weak thought that only whispered: "I… was… Martens. The murderer… Drinker of blood… Martens."

THE YEARS PASSED, and what had once been an obscure form was now a solid life form around the size of a mouse. The school was redone, and the basement was used for storing old desks, schoolbooks, and supplies. Small animals snuck in when doors and windows were opened—right onto Martens' platter.

No longer the human he once had been, but a savage creature of indescribable terror, Martens ate mice, attacking them with sharp nails and raging teeth. He hurled himself at the rodents' sides, ripping out fat chunks of flesh, and reattacking before his opponent had a chance to defend itself, biting until the blood gushed so freely that both of them were slick and sticky with glorious red.

Martens grew and eventually ate the basement empty of other animals. Mad with hunger, he tried to pass the time by counting the children in the schoolyard, all the while longing to sink his teeth into one of them.

Until a fox strayed inside one day. It had been an ice-cold winter, and the animal had gone without food for a long time. It ventured down towards the town during the quiet days after Christmas, and the empty schoolyard stirred its curiosity. The fox sneaked onto the school grounds and sniffed around. It eventually discovered that the hatch covering the opening down to the back of the basement beneath the gym had a wide opening after more than a metre of snow had gathered on top of it, weighing down the doors.

The fox was a more formidable opponent than the rodents and insects. It had believed it was fully in control when it came upon the rat-sized creature in the darkness of the basement—until the small attacker sank his razor-sharp teeth into the fox's belly. And no matter how much the fox flailed with its paws, it wasn't able to save itself.

ONE DAY, JUST before the summer holiday, Martens heard the hatch to the back entrance being opened. The janitor must have forgotten to lock it. Eager footsteps echoed on the stairs, and the creature—which had once been a cold-blooded murderer—hid in the shadows. A girl of around nine giggled happily and crouched down, peeking through the crack between the hatch and the ground above. She was playing hide-and-seek.

Suddenly, she darted down the stairs and into the darker part of the basement.

She didn't notice the creature creeping behind her—a creature the size of a full-grown dog.

Just then, the hatch made another sound, and two boys' voices rang out. The girl vanished into the darkness, and one of the boys shouted: "Greta? We know you're down here!"

But the girl neither moved nor made a sound.

"Ugh, it's creepy down here," said the other boy.

"Are you a sissy or something?" said the first, coming all the way down the stairs. Martens could see the outline of a boy in the dim light. It was the first human he had seen up close in… many, many years. And a craving rose in the small creature, one that felt impossible to resist. He felt the urge to sprint the ten metres over to the boy and tear into his throat, to taste his flesh and blood.

All his senses sharpened at once: he heard the boys' hearts pounding, smelled the sharp stench of anxiety sweat, felt the warmth of sunshine on their clothes, sensed the girl's fear of the darkness around her.

"She's not down here," said the first boy. "Let's look somewhere else."

And with that, they hurried up the stairs with relief and slammed the hatch shut behind them.

Martens, however, remained still for a few seconds. Then he turned and walked deeper into the dark. He could smell the girl. There was no need to see her. He could sense her sweat and nerves, and the faint giggle hovering on her lips. She could hear someone was coming.

"Olav?" she whispered into the darkness.

The creature didn't answer, but he started to creep forward with even greater care.

"Olav…" the girl whispered, sounding more nervous now. "I think I can hear you…"

Martens was now only a metre away. He reached towards her at the very moment she took a step forward.

They met in a murderous embrace, and Martens went

straight for her throat. He feasted on human flesh for the first time in so very long.

It took two days to devour the girl entirely. Martens burned with a feverish thirst for her blood. He dragged her body far back into the basement's darkest corner and consumed her—bones and all.

MANY YEARS PASSED before the creature finally grew to the height of a man. Martens' skin was white as snow, unable to bear direct sunlight. His hands were thin and bony. His lips, blood-red against a snowy white face, looked like a brutal scar with his teeth and black-red gums exposed. He wandered restlessly through the basement, muttering his name: "Martens… Martens…"

The creature vaguely remembered that he had once lived, but it was so long ago that the memories felt like faint pencil sketches. What made him feel almost human was the memory of the seven murders he had committed while Martens was alive. The quick, violent thrusts of the knife. All the blood he had drunk. He remembered these things more clearly than anything in the many years he had spent down here in the basement.

In the meantime, the school was remodelled once again. The pupils were moved to nearby schools, and the life and bustle of the schoolyard that Martens had loved watching was gone. The workers kept indoors in the cold, and everything seemed dead and deserted. That was when he thought he might die a second time. No animals to feed on. No blood to drink. And at his size, the creature now needed a certain amount every day just to be able to stay upright.

Martens didn't actually know what had happened to

his food source. Maybe he thought that the school was being shut down, especially when the workers tore down one of the wings.

He walked hunched over, wanting to howl every hour, every minute. The hunger for fresh blood made him desperate. He was on the verge of attacking the workers themselves, but whenever they came down to the basement, there were always two or three of them at once. He didn't stand a chance against that many people.

Could he find another building? Another basement with more food?

He ate flies and a spider, which was about as filling as dust and dry leaves. One day, he found a lunchbox one of the carpenters had left behind and wolfed it down. But he vomited only seconds later. Martens' body could only handle fresh food.

The creature felt himself growing thinner, saw the bones of his skull standing out more clearly with each day when he caught his reflection in the windowpane.

On the last Tuesday of January, Martens was crouching down to ease the hunger gnawing at his gut. He whimpered like a small animal each time the cramps seized him.

That was why he didn't hear the steps on the basement stairs.

That was why he stayed put, crouched in his own private hell.

Then, a voice sounded behind him: "Hello there. What are you doing down here?"

The creature straightened up as quickly as he could. He knew the light was behind him, making him no more than a dark silhouette against the window. Grunting something, he took a couple of steps closer.

The man was maybe around fifty. The creature was reminded of the shopkeeper he had once stabbed several times in the stomach, the one who had coughed up pink froth as he gasped out his final words.

Martens took another step forward.

"Are you here for the fire inspection?" the man asked. "Then you're terribly early."

Martens grunted something incomprehensible. He stepped sideways and pointed into the darkest corner, trying to lure the man away from the stairs and towards himself.

"Is something wrong?" the man asked. But now he was looking at Martens more than the place where his finger pointed. "Are you… all right?"

Martens turned away from him, pointed again, and barked, "LOOK!" The man took a few steps closer and looked.

Martens sprang forward. His muscles were coiled springs, charged with a brutal strength. He struck the man hard in the stomach, causing him to double over and fall to his knees, gasping for breath.

Then Martens pounced, aiming his teeth at the soft flesh of the man's neck. He took an enormous bite and buried his tongue in the blood. This was the best prey the creature had tasted in as long as he could remember. This was real food.

The man was dead within minutes.

Martens walked carefully up the basement stairs and shut the door. Then he laid the man on an old blanket and dragged him deep into the part of the basement that had once been the coal bunker. He went back to the stairs and noticed the blood on the floor. The creature lay down and licked the stones clean so nothing would go to waste, then scattered dust over what remained. He glanced out the window. A man in overalls was crossing the schoolyard, and only seconds later, he was at the top of the basement stairs.

"Evan!" the man shouted. "Where are you?"

Martens slipped back to the coal bin where the worker's body was bleeding out onto the blanket. He waited in silence, feeling his strength returning.

"Are you down here, Evan? We don't have time for this. The kids are coming back tomorrow. Everything has to be ready."

Martens lapped at the still-warm blood, gathering strength—more strength than ever before. He listened as the man descended the stairs. He lapped and gathered strength.

"EVAN!" the man bellowed.

Martens could track the man's steps as he wandered aimlessly, calling out twice more. Then he heard the man mutter: "God knows where he's gone. But he'd better have everything ready by tomorrow!"

The workman went back out into the January cold.

Martens took a smaller bite now. He cradled the body in its arms, knowing it had hours of pleasure ahead.

Tomorrow was Wednesday, and the school would be opening again.

That meant hustle and bustle in the schoolyard once more.

Martens was saved. The creature's food supply would soon be filled again. He lowered his mouth and tore a long strip of flesh from Evan's arm. A delicious sense of calm washed over him.

SWEDEN

THE STORM

by Boel Bermann

Translated by Heather Jonasson

THE SOUND OF the alarm cuts through the storm. The signal resonates for seven seconds at a time with fourteen seconds of silence in between. At first, no one takes any notice. They're all used to hearing it during test runs and the sound is dampened by the snowfall. It takes several minutes before people realise it's serious. Only when the sky turns pitch black and the clouds rush forward do they start to react. I didn't believe it would happen so soon, or maybe I thought it would never happen at all.

When the alarm goes off again, I know that it's happening in all urban areas with more than a thousand inhabitants. Sound transmitters scream out their warning from the rooftops across Sweden. All landlines ring and play a pre-recorded safety message. My phone vibrates; a part of the national system that sends texts with warnings. I don't read it. I already know what it says: an appeal to people to go indoors as soon as possible. Instructions to close all doors and windows and turn off all ventilation. Listen to the radio, watch

TV or follow the news on the internet for real-time information about the crisis. A call to stay calm, that the situation is under control. A blatant lie that they hope people will believe.

Intense beams of light illuminate the winter darkness in the middle of the snowstorm. Lightning streaks through the sky like an air raid and the thunder is deafening. I should get to safety, but it's impossible to stop watching. All the people I see on the streets are moving quickly now. They run, a surge of people falling over one another. I see some of them jump into their cars and drive away, but the roads will soon fill up, and the traffic will prevent people from moving any further. One group of people runs towards the nearest building. I can see them struggling to squeeze through the doorways. In the harsh wind, visibility is obscured by falling snow and coarse hail. I can't take it all in. It doesn't feel like anything I'm seeing is real.

I remember the day I broke apart inside, the catalyst that led to this. I know exactly what triggered the storm, but I have no idea how it will all end.

IT'S TIME FOR coffee with my colleagues and I'm late. I'm stuck in a meeting with the Norrland office. I fill my cup with the dregs of burnt coffee from the machine and sit down with the others. They're discussing an article in today's newspaper. I can tell they're upset.

"Three days without electricity and the whole of society collapses..."

"Stop, I don't even want to think about it."

A colleague sees the questioning look on my face and hands me a paper with the article folded in front. The coffee cools in the cup while I read the text from beginning to end. I hear the others continue to talk in the background, frustration in their voices.

"It's like everything we do is completely meaningless..."

"In a way, it's good when a storm, like the one last week, knocks out the electricity. Those who were affected are going to be more prepared for the next catastrophe."

But all my colleagues look downcast. There are a few scattered words as people leave the room, but most are quiet and composed as they disappear back into the open office landscape. Back at my desk, I realise I'm still holding the paper in my hand. I read the headline and introduction again.

Half of Swedes Not Ready for a Power Outage

A winter storm has knocked out electricity for thousands of households in southern Sweden. The forces of nature show how vulnerable modern society is. Most of us are so used to electricity, telecommunications networks, running water, sewage and other vital functions that we rarely think about what would happen if the supply were interrupted. A new survey shows that half of Swedish households have made no preparations in the event of a long power outage.

I've only been working at the Swedish Civil Contingencies Agency for a few months. I switched jobs because I couldn't handle all the pitying looks and mumbled words that meant nothing.

One of the first things I learned in my new job is that all Swedes should be ready to fend for themselves for at least three days. Everyone should be prepared with water, food and heat in case of a power outage. That's the rule of thumb, the minimum amount of preparation. But I think about my own home and realise that I myself am still not prepared. I have a few water jugs in the basement, some blankets and extra duvets. And of course I have some dry goods in the pantry. But I haven't even read the checklists. If I, the person working on these questions, am not prepared, how can I expect others to be?

Impulsively, I pull up the checklists from the website and read them carefully. Under the heading Communication, I read: *have a battery-powered radio, extra batteries for a mobile phone and keep a landline*. I feel a pressure in my chest and it's difficult to breathe.

I continue to work on routine tasks for the rest of the day, answering mail and struggling to finish the report that has a deadline today, but it hurts inside. I don't want to and can't think about what's happened. Instead, I focus on how bad things are in Sweden, in concern for all the people out there. I think about how fragile our society is. After just a few days, we could experience a total societal collapse. I think about the number of people that will die when there's a real disaster, because they don't take it seriously.

I see it all before me. It's so clear that it feels like it's already happened. The dark, the cold, the panic, the hunger. In a crisis, our resources won't be enough for everyone affected. I know that the authorities' efforts will be prioritised and go to the most vulnerable. Everyone else will need to survive on their own. To get by for at least three days. But what happens if a disaster continues for weeks, months, years before everyday life returns to normal? These three days are all the state requires of its citizens. And we can't even manage that, despite living in such a vulnerable society… For the first time, I realise that my work can make a difference and save lives.

* * *

My partner Sara calls, but I don't answer. She's called several times already. I ignore her every time.

I sit at my desk, surrounded by reports and evaluations. Large stacks of paper surround my computer screen. My desk lamp is the only light in the room. The rest of the office is dark, the ventilation is turned off, and I'm the only one left. This is how it's been for the past few weeks. I have been maniacally committed to my work. And it's all because something happened to me when I read that news article and saw the lists. Before, everything was overshadowed with grief. Now, I see too much. I see things clearly. That an upcoming disaster could threaten lives. The article has triggered an obsession. I must save people by making sure they're prepared when the disaster comes. It's not a question of if, but when.

I start working harder, coming to work earlier and going home later. My overtime is escalating. I don't miss any days, and I don't take any time off. In the evenings and nights, I work in secret and from home on my laptop. When I started at the agency, it was just a new job. A way to escape people's pity. But now I realise it's a chance to save lives.

My new colleagues are worried about me. I'm called in to see the boss. She suggests that maybe I should take some time off, asking if everything is OK. I try to sound relaxed to signal that there's no problem, I'm just very committed to my work. But it's more than that. I can't think of anything else.

I wake up on a plane and have trouble at first getting my bearings. I look around, dazed, and next to my seat is a smiling flight attendant. But her smile looks strained and stiff.

"We're about to fly into some turbulence, so I'm afraid I need to ask you to fasten your seatbelt and put your seat back to an upright position."

She notes that I understand the instructions and quickly moves to the next row of seats. I make the movements routinely, struggling to remember the dream that's slipping away. It was something about thunder, strong forces in motion.

I sink into the soft embrace of the chair, take off my shoes and press my socks against the floor of the plane, feeling the vibrations of the motors throughout my body. Work has been hard on me lately. I've been travelling around Sweden constantly for the past month, staying in cheap hotel rooms, airports, train stations with overpriced dry sandwiches, or stuck in bland meeting rooms at various authorities. I am exhausted, but the conviction that I must do everything in my power to prepare Sweden for a disaster permeates my waking thoughts. I know it's not normal, that I should do something about it. But work is the only thing I have left.

I'm thinking about contacting a therapist when I get home. Sara has asked me to do so several times. I'm dangerously close to my breaking point. She's right that I need to talk to someone, that I could explode at any second. Right now, I want to take off my seatbelt, tear off the jacket and shirt that are suffocating me. I just want to stand in the middle of the aisle of the plane and experience the turbulence—let it take me and break me into pieces.

The headache is returning. It's been with me this whole trip, a throbbing pain focused near the front of my head. At any moment I'm going to burst.

Ever since Sara left me, I've agreed to be the one to go on domestic trips to talk to authorities. At first, it was just a relief to get away from the empty house. All my colleagues have children. That's why I offered to take the trips, so they could be with their families. Travelling to godforsaken places for over a day and being forced to listen to lame excuses about why the local office didn't lift a finger in order to get a disaster preparedness plan in place. Would I mind going to Örnsköldsvik, Perstorp, Rättvik? I've always said yes, I just wanted to get away. Away from my empty suburban villa filled with memories.

Lately I've been dreaming a lot. Maybe it's because I change places, beds, rooms and cities constantly. I dream of hail and lightning, thunder and raging snowstorms. I dream of things that shake the world. As I wish she had shaken me. Sara. She should have screamed at me, accused me, and hit me with clenched fists. It was my fault. It's all my fault. Instead, she fought to keep the relationship together and make us move forward despite the grief. I couldn't take that from her. I hated her because she never blamed me. Then, I buried myself in work, shut her out and just stood by silently as she disappeared from my life. Because I knew that what we had was gone. Because of me.

I went to work the day after she left me. I should have taken time off, spent time with her and tried to get us back together. But people's lives depend on me doing my job. I couldn't do it. Instead, I took on so many tasks that I wouldn't have time to think.

But travelling has given me too much time alone, too much time to think. Like the moment she left me. I think about it over and over again. I can't let go of that moment. I wonder if it would have changed anything if I'd released the entire storm of emotions that was just below the surface. She said I shut her out. That I refused to understand she was grieving too and that she couldn't stand it. Then she left. I try to imagine a scene where she walks out the door and I actually do something. My headache gets worse just by focusing on that memory, but I struggle to hold the thought, to imagine I'd do something differently. The way I would grab her wrist, open my mouth and say how I feel. My entire inner storm is exposed. The pain in my head is rushing, piercing through my head like lightning.

The plane shakes violently. The water glass spills over me, the liquid running down my legs and forming a puddle at my feet. Lights flicker; handbags are thrown around. People scream. Yet I'm barely aware of how we're all being tossed back and forth in our seats.

There's another flash outside the window, a bright light stinging my eyes. A loud bang comes from the wing right outside where I'm sitting, something hitting metal. A massive white light blinds me, and a sharp pain bursts through my body.

In front of my face an oxygen mask falls down. I shut out everything in the cabin and think back to that day. I think about my daughter Maja for the first time since it happened.

MAJA IS OUTSIDE *playing in the sunshine. I should be out there with her, but I really have to work. Sara isn't here; it's my turn to stay home. Maja has been sick all week, but now she's more or less well. We decided to let her stay home an extra day, just to be on the safe side. I was supposed to take the day off, but a deadline is approaching. Maja kept bothering me. I told her to go out and play in the garden.*

I look at her from time to time through the window. What could happen?

Then the power goes out, and the laptop automatically switches to battery. I only notice the power outage when I can't send emails, and I start swearing when the laptop suddenly turns off.

Frustrated, I go and check the main supply panel, but everything seems to be in order. When I pick up my phone to see if it says anything about a power outage, I notice I've forgotten to charge it. I feel stressed, but think it's probably just temporary. The power will be back soon. I look out the window into the neighbourhood. It's empty on the street, which is normal for a weekday afternoon.

I sit down at the kitchen table again, from where I can see Maja playing on the lawn. I've told her to stay at the back of the house where I can see her. Then I pick up my bag and pull out the printed quarterly report. Time passes. I look up from time to time. Maja seems to be able to entertain herself. I see her jumping on the trampoline, kicking a ball or digging in the flowerbed. I'll head out there with her soon, I just have to finish reading…

I read numbers and analyses until the light quickly becomes too poor. I look up from my papers. Through the window I see that the sky has suddenly been covered with grey, rushing clouds and that it's starting to rain. I run up from the kitchen table, stick my head out the kitchen door and call for Maja. I'm not worried, I'm mostly concerned about her getting wet and cold. As long as she doesn't get sick again, I really can't take more time off from work. She doesn't answer. I sigh, thinking that she needs to stop being so troublesome. I don't have time for this. Head of Department's Quarterly report. Responsibility. Rummaging up my raincoat quickly, I go out.

"Maja, you have to come inside. If you want to be outside, you have to put on your raincoat and rubber boots."

Hearing how irritated my voice sounds, I feel a twinge of guilty conscience. I try to soften my voice.

"Honey, please, it's time to play indoors. I can get you a cup of chocolate and some snacks."

I don't see her anywhere, and I feel a worry growing inside me. The rain is heavier now, obscuring my vision. Where is she? I keep calling, moving quickly across the damp lawn. Anxiety creeps into my voice. Why isn't she answering?

Then I catch a glimpse of something in the corner of my eye, and I feel coldness spread through my body. Yellow sneakers and a turquoise jacket. Maja is lying on the ground. I run to her, throw myself down on my knees and shake her. She doesn't react. Her skin has a pink tone and there's a whitish-green spot on her cheek. She's breathing, but her breath sounds weak and wheezy. When I lift her eyelids, I see that her eyes are red. I carefully pick my daughter up in my arms and feel her warm, delicate body that's still and lifeless. I realise that I can't call for an ambulance, I only have my mobile phone that's dead. I thought it was unnecessary to have a landline; we got rid of it just a few months ago. I don't remember what to do, I can't think straight.

I don't understand what happened, I just know it's serious. My daughter could die if I don't do something.

In my desperation, the only thing I can think of is to carry her to the car, belt her up and drive to the A&E. I drive as fast as I dare. Sweat is pouring down, despite the coolness of the air conditioning. I look straight ahead and focus on the road, fighting to not let panic take over. I turn on the radio and hear something about a spill. I try to process the words.

"The first alarm came in at nine oh four a.m. Several units from emergency services are on the scene, working with chemical diving and cleanup. Residents near the facility are being asked to go indoors, close all doors and windows and turn off the ventilation. All schools and preschools are keeping the pupils indoors. The preschool closest to the accident site has been evacuated."

I cast a panicked glance at the seat next to me where Maja is strapped in. She doesn't move; her eyes are closed. I turn off the car's ventilation and try not to think about the possibility that she might die. I reach the hospital and rush in, screaming, "Please help me! Someone!"

The staff comes running and takes my daughter from my arms. Quickly and efficiently, they put Maja on a stretcher and examine her. Someone asks where we live and what happened. I stammer out our address, say she was playing outside. The nurse straightens up and shouts something to the others. I can't make out exactly what she's saying. I hear words like release, risk area, emergency treatment. My gaze is fixed on my daughter's face, on the green-white stain on her skin, as the stretcher rolls away across the room.

Someone asks if I've rinsed her off. I shake my head and see a shadow of fear cross the nurse's face. She rushes after the stretcher, shouting something to the others.

I feel an arm on mine and hear a voice asking if I was outside too. The stretcher with Maja disappears from sight and I look up.

"Just a short while, I was mostly indoors working."

I think I see a reproachful look, or so I imagine, that he's thinking about what kind of father would let his daughter play alone in the garden.

It was a private garden, a warm late summer day, what

could happen? But I didn't have time to play with my child. Bad parent.

I am passively led into another room for examination. I mumble that someone needs to call Sara. My wife must be here. They take off my clothes, put me in a shower and rinse my body. Then they make me breathe in oxygen over and over again. I'm powerless, I just do what they want me to do. It's hard to breathe. There's a pressure in my chest.

They put a hospital gown on me and wrap me in a blanket. I sit on a hospital bed while they ask me things, but all the words are so faint, as if they're being said from afar. Didn't you see the warning on the internet? Didn't you hear about the alarm on the radio? Didn't anyone call and tell you to stay indoors? Power outage. Dead mobile phone. No home phone. I knew nothing.

Sara comes rushing through the door with wide eyes and a pale face. She throws herself into my arms and holds me tight for a long time. She mumbles that she went home as soon as she heard the news and that she had tried to call but I didn't answer the phone. When she lets go, I see a doctor standing in front of us. He looks serious. I can't breathe from the worry, the hard pressure in my chest. I feel fear running through my body. The doctor looks at us and opens his mouth. I don't want to hear what he's going to say.

I SHOULD BE dead; I don't want to live. All around me I can see the outlines of people thrown around, trapped and lifeless. Hell is in this airplane cabin. The plane has crashed. I pull myself up from the floor and stand up laboriously. The cabin is tilting. Slowly, I begin to search for a way out of the inferno. The air is filled with smoke, flames light up the airplane cabin at the far end. I feel an indescribable pain in my chest, strong and persistent, radiating into my arms, back and neck.

I climb through the wreckage, trying to make out people and see if I can help in the chaos. But I can barely stand upright because of dizziness. The world consists of shadows of arms, bags, legs, airplane seats and dead stares in the darkness around me. The air is filled with sirens and screams. I shouldn't be alive. I remember the turbulence and how I sat frozen in pain. How people were thrown around. How the pilot spoke to us, trying to sound calm and collected, but how panic cut through her voice. That we were flying straight through a thunderstorm, that the plane had been struck by lightning. She explained that the metal was a protective casing that guided the lightning out. The lightning couldn't hurt anyone in the plane, but the electronics had been knocked out. She urged everyone to belt up and prepare for an emergency landing.

I cough from the angry, feverish smoke that obscures everything and makes my eyes water. I fall to the floor, struggling to breathe. Then I feel the darkness descending. To survive a plane crash and die of smoke inhalation. I should never have stopped smoking. I might as well have enjoyed the cancer sticks; it's not that kind of smoke that's going to kill me now. Yet I feel calm. Now I'll get some rest. I'm thinking of Maja. I'll be there soon, Maja. Soon you won't be alone anymore.

The ECG monitor starts pulsing again. I open my eyes and see the doctor's pupils dilate in surprise above the mask. Back from the dead. I saw the shadows spread, felt myself being drawn there.

My chest hurts and I cough. I look straight at the doctor, but I can only see her eyes above the mandatory mask. Her big grey eyes, with iron in her gaze. She says nothing but somehow, I can tell that she was the one who refused to let me die. I feel confused and disoriented, with the taste of blood in my mouth. Somehow, I am fully aware that I was dead. That the doctor made me come back.

I see the nurse checking my values and hear the doctor say something. I think she is saying that they were dangerously close to losing me. The nurse attaches a nozzle to my lips and lets the gas flow with a hissing sound. My eyelids start to flutter, and I try to form words. I try to say that I feel different, as if my body is pulsing with power. But the moment passes before I can make a sound. I slip back into unconsciousness.

THERE'S BEEN THUNDER in the air, saturated and suffocating, ever since I woke up. I've been discharged from the hospital. They wanted me to stay longer and examine me more thoroughly. I died and was revived, yet they couldn't find anything physically wrong with me except for the superficial burns and bruises.

I refused to stay. Now I'm standing outside my house, and I want to turn around. I'd rather be anywhere than where I call home. The fatigue permeates my marrow and bones; I can barely stand upright. I fumble for the key in my jacket pocket and try to focus. Sara didn't know I was on the plane. No one but my colleagues knew. They've been calling like crazy. I've said everything's fine a thousand times, and even though it's a lie, there's nothing else to say. I feel the frustration and confusion erupting again. I hear the thunder grow louder above my head.

The damn lock on the front door that I can't open is the last straw that makes everything overflow. I start to cry uncontrollably. I collapse, sobbing, leaning against the door with a taped-together cabin bag next to me. Above me, the snow-mixed rain pours down on the world, cold and persistent. I feel my clothes getting heavy and cold, my tears mixing with the rain. I feel lost in time and space.

Finally, I gather myself enough to get up and unlock the door. The house is quiet. It's just me here. It takes me a few minutes to collect enough strength to stop crying. Through the window, I see the rain falling from the dark sky. I take a deep breath. I don't have the strength to handle this; I'll figure it out later. Not now. I feel it inside me. Something is wrong. I don't want to stay in the house, so I turn and walk out.

I snort, acting like a child, and wipe the snot off my sleeve. Walking towards the commuter train station, I decide to check into a hotel for the night. I need to get my bearings, find myself again. Right now, I'm nobody at all.

I WAKE UP sick in a vomit-soaked bed in an anonymous hotel room. I drank everything in the minibar yesterday and passed out. Over and over, I kept thinking that it would have been better if I hadn't survived the plane crash. I should be dead. But now I'm alive. Staggering out of bed, I lose my balance and fall hard onto the wooden floor. I use the bedside table to pull myself up, having to remove the dried vomit from my T-shirt, cheeks and hair. My head is pounding with pain.

When I step into the bathroom I stop and look at myself in the mirror. There are dark shadows under my eyes, burns on my face and large bruises all over my body. I almost died of cardiac arrest, which is why I had chest pain. No one can explain what happened to me. Airplanes are designed to conduct electricity away. No other passenger has the same type of injuries. Only I have symptoms of lightning being passed through me, even though it's impossible. They can't explain how the electrical current from the lightning could enter the airplane or my body. How the electricity could pass unhindered through the heart and penetrate the nerves, muscles and blood vessels.

After I've collected myself, showered and changed clothes, I muster the courage to call Sara. I stand looking out over the quiet landscape with my mobile phone pressed to my ear. When she answers, I don't say anything about the plane crash. I just want to talk to her, try to explain that the reason I've become so absorbed in my work is so I can save people's lives. But Sara doesn't listen to me. I tell her I love her, that she must try to understand. But all she cares about is me and us. She doesn't see the bigger picture. My anger almost cracks under my skin.

I start screaming into the phone, even though I know I shouldn't. She has to listen to me. Disaster is near and we must prepare for the worst. Thunder begins to roll outside the window. Suddenly, lightning strikes right outside. I withdraw, completely taken aback. The call ends. And suddenly the sky clears, the clouds part and the starry sky spreads out. I look out at the quiet darkness and suddenly I feel completely calm inside.

An urgent meeting at the end of the day. I'm sitting in the conference room with all my colleagues. None of us know what it's about, but these types of meetings are unusual. It's rarely a good thing when everyone has to gather at short notice. The room is chilly, the hairs on my arms are standing up. We sit silently side by side. Everyone looks wide-eyed and worried, crowded around the large conference table. There's a tense atmosphere in the room, as if we know something bad is about to happen.

Our boss comes in. She looks sad but tries to hide it. Instead of starting a PowerPoint presentation like she usually does, she stands in front of us all. She tries to look relaxed in her grey suit and neat white shirt, but her jaw is tense, and she clears her throat several times. She seems to be having trouble finding the words. But eventually they come.

I try to listen to what she says, but it's as if a red fog has taken over my entire consciousness after the introductory presentation. She says that the authority will have reduced resources next year. That the new directives state that the main focus of our work will be shifted to Vision Zero for everyday accidents. That disaster preparedness will be downgraded.

My whole body is tense. In the end, I can't stop myself. My hand is shaking with suppressed anger; I squeeze it as tightly as I can against my knee.

"Is there anything we can do to prevent this?"

She looks at me and swallows hard before answering.

"It's not my decision. We simply have to do the best we can under the circumstances."

"This is insanity. We have to protest!"

I say it angrily, slamming my palm on the table to emphasise the words. Outside, lightning flashes and a loud clap of thunder is heard. My boss flinches at the sharp sound in the silence.

"I've done all I can. I hope you understand."

I can't bear to say anything more. A few brief questions follow, but few answers are given. More information will come soon. She thanks us for coming. I take a deep breath to regain my composure. A sudden gust of wind blows open one of the windows, papers fly around in chaos and coffee cups tip over. A colleague and I rush to the window to close it. My colleague mutters to me, almost in a whisper, as we press it shut: "You're absolutely right, but those damn politicians don't get it. I don't know what it will take for them to understand how important our work is."

After people have collected the papers and wiped up all the spilled coffee, they leave the conference room. I remain by the window until I'm alone in the room, looking out over the grey car park for a long time, staring into nothingness.

I GET OUT of the car at the car park and walk the short distance home. My body is buzzing with anger after the meeting and I'm deep in thought as I walk, my eyes fixed on the ground. I've started smoking again since the accident. I take out a cigarette and struggle to light it in the snowstorm. My fingers are shaking. Once I've succeeded, I look up while taking a deep drag. At first, I don't understand what I'm seeing.

The air is roaring. Snow falls from the sky as the wind lifts it from the ground around me. Everything is circulating around me. It's unpleasant and unlike anything I've ever experienced. The snow is spinning around me as if I'm the centre of a vortex. I stand still, holding my breath. The snowfall stops and the snow hangs in the air, as if frozen in time. I throw away my cigarette, walk to the house, but stop on the porch steps. I feel snowflakes against my face. Turning around, I can still see the empty outlines of my body hanging like a dark tunnel in the snowstorm.

I can no longer control myself. I slam my clenched hand on the banister with all my strength. As if on an unspoken order, lightning strikes the parked cars in the street in front of me, and the snow swirls to life. I punch mindlessly, over and over again. The evening darkness is lit up by violent flashes of lightning in time with my blows. I turn around, unlock the door and flee into the house. The wet snow steams from my body. I tear off my shoes and walk into the living room. Each step leaves scorched, smoking footprints on the parquet.

A GENTLE SNOWFALL fills the air, settling like a white film over the world before me. My palms are covered in cold sweat. I feel like I want to smoke a cigarette, even though I've just smoked one. I know that I'm just trying to postpone the inevitable. I'm going to do this. It feels like everything I've done in my entire life has led up to this very moment. It doesn't take much to affect the entire population of Sweden. One big storm, one that knocks out electricity and paralyses society. Like a warning signal. Now I'm trying to summon the courage to create it. Either I try this now or I never think about the idea again. The air vibrates with pent-up energy. I haven't released all my anger yet.

I've done everything I could at work, but it's not enough. Now I'm prepared to do something that goes against all my principles. I'm going to create a disaster.

I've been thinking about whether I'm really doing the

right thing. There's a calm over all of Sweden, the calm before the storm. But something is already on its way, something that will destroy everything faster than anyone can imagine. It will tear down what has been built and destroy lives. I don't know when the catastrophe will come or in what form it will hit us all. But the calm is apparent and without any real danger, people will never prepare for a disaster. So now I've decided. I must create a temporary storm that hits the whole country for a few days, so that they're prepared when the real danger comes.

What I'm about to do now will have enormous consequences. Or maybe I've gone crazy to think I can control the weather. I don't know anymore.

I stand on the roof and watch the grey sky, the snowflakes and the silence. I look out over the city. Then I raise one hand straight above my head. I close my eyes and think about how I want to help people, that I'm doing this for their sake. I've never felt like this. Unstoppable.

I let all the frustration about people being unprepared pour out of me. I vibrate with anger, electricity crackling between my fingers. When I open my eyes, the dark clouds have gathered above me. Pitch black, they move in a vortex just above my head, as if waiting for my orders.

I clench my fist tightly, watching the clouds tighten even more. Then I pull my hand down in front of me, fingers spread out, with all the strength I have. The clouds move violently, bumping into each other, being thrown out in all directions. The wind picks up. It starts to hail. I clench my hand so hard that my knuckles turn white. Lightning flashes. Razor-sharp lights cut through the air, hitting me on all sides, surrounding me. A tree below the house starts to burn. Thunder fills the air. On some level I realise that I'm the one doing this. On another level it all feels surreal. The sound of the alarm cuts through the storm. The signal is heard for seven seconds at a time, with fourteen seconds of silence in between.

I STAND OUTSIDE in the winter darkness on the porch steps and look out over the street. The sun has just set. Everything should be still and quiet; the dark blue shadows should cover the world.

But the sky is moving, the clouds are impenetrably black, and everything is lit up by white flashes of lightning, over and over again. The lights along the road are out, and there are no more shining Christmas stars hanging in the windows. In the first few days I could still glimpse flickering warm lights from candlesticks in neighbouring houses in the brief moments between storms. Thick smoke billowed against the sky from the houses that had wood-burning stoves and ovens. But I see fewer and fewer lights. The temperature is constantly dropping, the coldest winter that's ever hit Sweden.

The silence that arises between the waves of thunder is deafening. The street is dark and deserted. No cars are moving on the road. I breathe in and out, trying to keep panic from taking hold of me. I wonder how many of the houses I glimpse are cold or starting to approach the limit of when the wood supply runs out. Which ones are on their last candles, and which will not be able to eat anything hot for the rest of the winter. With the sub-zero temperatures, people have at least been able to empty their fridges and freezers and put the food out in the garden or basement, hiding it away. Inside the city, everything is probably harder. I wonder how many people will die from cold, hunger, disease or in senseless accidents this winter. I don't think it will be long before people start attacking each other, trying to take what they can to survive.

Every grocery store was cleared out and emptied after just a few days, as were the pharmacies. No new deliveries arrived, money could not be withdrawn, the electricity was out. Almost no one has a landline and mobile phones died quickly. There were queues and congestion as far as the eye could see, panicked people looking for whatever they could get their hands on: blankets, sanitiser, cigarettes, alcohol, cans, chocolate bars, anything. But there were few who thought logically, who managed to cover everything they needed in the crowd and chaos.

The few who have battery-powered radios listen to the news, but there is no break in the storm in sight. I've seen people running out to their cars to listen to the radio. Not that listening helps much, the people on the radio don't seem to know what to do either.

I had no idea how much the storm would affect everything. How it would escalate. How it would spread further out of the country. It has no end in sight. I gave the storm perfect conditions and now I have no strength left. I'm just a normal person now. The weather warning is constantly set on Amber. I don't understand how the storm could get so strong. But I put all my anger and sadness into it. When I was done, I was drained. One charge. One storm. The perfect storm raging is my creation.

ECHO

by Madeleine Bäck

The mountain stretched out before us, steep and clad with mighty trees. Strong, straight pines and shy white birches, crowned with deep, lush midsummer green. The last beads of summer rain still clung to the grass and ferns, making the forest glisten in the hazy afternoon sun. It was stunning, but so damp and chilly it made me shiver. My socks and trousers were already soaked. Every step squished. Evelina slid up beside me and put her arm around my shoulders.

"Just like when we were kids, right? I'm dying of heat and you, you skinny bitch, are becoming an icicle. Want to borrow a jumper?"

I nodded.

"That would be great. Thanks."

"No worries. I always overpack. You are honestly doing me a favour, taking some weight off."

Evelina dropped her backpack, popped the lid and pulled out a bright pink fleece. "So stylish!" she exclaimed.

Evelina knew I hated pink, always had. Ninety per cent of my wardrobe is pitch black. The other ten per cent is some shade of grey, probably because the clothes used to be black, and I am too lazy to throw them out. But then again, pink was better than freezing.

"You're a doll," I said, and pulled the jumper on.

"Oooh. I like this colour on you!" Saga was suddenly behind me, panting like she'd run the last stretch. "Jesus. Is this a marathon or what? Can't you guys move at a normal-people pace?"

She crouched beside us and took a deep breath.

"Steady there, Silver," Evelina smirked. "We wouldn't want you to have a heart attack."

Saga raised her hand and extended her middle finger.

"But seriously, Liz," she said. "Was it always this far and steep? So unnecessary, if you ask me."

"Sorry, darling. I don't believe the Kungsberget mountain has moved since last time," I said. "Nor has it gotten any smaller."

I could understand her question. These woods were not *home* to her and Evelina, the way they were to me. I had been hiking the forest of northern Gästrikland for as long as I could remember. Grandma brought me here as soon as I could walk. We picked berries and mushrooms under the tall, mighty trees, while she filled my head with stories. She told me about the leaf ladies who lived in the crowns of the big birches, how they howled to warn of disasters. About the lantern man, luring wanderers deep into the darkness with his bewitching light. About the woodland fairies dancing their enchanting—but deadly—dance in the morning mist. There were hundreds of others too, creatures both kind and cruel, hiding in the midst of us.

It was Grandma who first spoke of The Rock of Whispers, high up on Kungsberget. When the time was right, she brought me there to ask my first questions.

Now I had come to ask the mountain about Tove.

She was with us that one and only time I had brought my friends here, right after our high school graduation three years ago. Back then, we'd all been at some level of drunk, and—understandably—my friends had been more focused on snapping funny selfies than noticing how far we went, or where.

Two weeks later, Tove had gone missing.

"It's weird being back here without her."

Saga said what we were all thinking. Around us, the air seemed to shift. None of us said anything. We just stood there for a moment, catching our breath, our gazes drifting across the trees. Then Evelina laughed, just a notch too bright to feel natural. Even so, a small part of me dared to relax.

"God, that summer was chaos," Evelina said, still smiling. "Remember when we thought it'd be smart to grill hot dogs inside the tent."

Saga snickered, but the grin didn't quite reach her eyes.

A dark, hollow feeling tugged at my guts. Coming here was probably going to be harder than I had expected. Yes, I wanted to ask the mountain about Tove, to see if it spoke more than vague whispers of the future, but I also hoped this trip would heal us as friends. Nothing had been the same between us since that horrible summer. Tove had vanished overnight. The police, the military, even the whole community, had searched the woods and the nearby villages for weeks. No one ever found anything. Not a trace.

After that, we all started drifting apart. No more

lakeside parties, sneaking into clubs, or camping trips with barbecues and too much beer. I wanted to change all that. The forest just seemed too dark, too evil.

"We'll be there in half an hour," I said.

"Half an hour at our pace or Saga's?" Evelina asked, half-smiling.

Saga rolled her eyes, stood up and slapped something in the air. "Okay girls. As much as I'd love to stay here and hear Little Miss Cheerleader crack jokes, I say we get moving. Or maybe you'd prefer to wait for the mosquitos to drain us like juice boxes?"

IT FELT GOOD to be moving again. The heavy feeling of Tove's absence drifted off as we settled into an easy pace. The morning chill gave way to a mild summer breeze. I could shed Evelina's hideous jumper and feel like my usual pale, dark-clad self.

Bright green ferns and blueberry bushes brushed our legs as we climbed up the mountain trail. Somewhere south, a cuckoo called. I inhaled deeply and let nature fill me. This was my holy ground. My lush embrace of serenity, stillness and magic. I briefly closed my eyes and felt myself healing. Coming here had been the right decision. Everything would be okay. It had to be.

"Hold on. I need a minute!" Evelina stopped, set down her backpack and picked up her water bottle. She took a long sip and sighed with relief. "That's better."

She handed the water to Saga, who took a deep chug, then held it out to me.

"It's okay," I said. "I've got my own."

Saga shrugged and returned the bottle to Evelina.

"So," Evelina said, brushing a strand of hair from her

face. "How is university treating you both? It's so sad we ended up so far apart. I mean… Umeå, Saga. Why?"

"Well, first of all they've got a great law school," Saga said. "But more importantly, the rate of pearl earrings, blond bombshell blowouts and Louis Vuitton bags is far lower than at other universities."

"But still," Evelina pouted, "you should transfer to Lund. Be closer to me. Share an apartment. I miss you!"

She formed a heart with her hands.

"As much as I'd love to pay half of your rent," Saga said, "I have a hunch there wouldn't be much studying in our mutual house. I mean, you work in a bar. You are up all night throwing after-parties."

"I am not!"

Saga gave her a good hard stare. "Social media sure says you are!"

Evelina put her tongue out.

"Social media also says you're a bitch."

I laughed, realising how much I'd missed their bickering. Still, I knew what Saga meant. We both loved Evelina, but being too close to her always put your heart at risk.

Evelina was a master flirter, and she wielded that gift like a loaded weapon. We were all collateral damage. Or, in Evelina's words, "saved from evil". Boys, she believed, were there for the play and the dance, not for the ever after. All through high school she did her best to rescue all of us, using her own body as means of salvation.

"Over there!" Evelina stopped and pointed at a gigantic moss-clad rock on the left side of the trail. "I remember this place. Liz, this is where you threw up!"

Saga gave me a gentle pat on the shoulder.

"I'm sorry, Liz, but *goddamn*, you were drunk. All

thanks to the moonshine booze from that disgusting dude in Hofors."

"Harta, yeah," I said, recalling the feeling of being completely helpless, holding on to a tree for support. "He was a real ray of mafia sunshine. I'm glad you both remember the important things from our hike."

Evelina frowned.

"He was one scary son of a bitch. Whoever took him out did Gästrikland a big favour."

"A bloody favour too," Saga said.

We fell into silence. Harta's killing was the closest we'd ever come to a gang-related murder. Someone had gotten tired of his shit and took him out in the goriest way possible. The police still hadn't figured out who.

Just as they hadn't figured out what happened to Tove.

I tried to shake the thoughts from my head. *Soon I will know*, I told myself. *The mountain will help me. It has to.*

"Girls, we're almost there," I said. "Look!"

Here, near the top of the Kungsberget mountain, the forest opened up like a gate. The trees parted on both sides, the white birch and willow branches intertwined, forming an almost perfect arch. Beyond it, the mountain top levelled out into a breathtaking viewpoint, complete with a fireplace and sturdy logs arranged for seating.

Even Saga, who was usually more cheek than charm, let out a low whistle.

"Wow," she breathed, like the word had snuck out on its own. "I had forgotten all of… *this*!"

"I know," I said. "If I ever marry, this is the place. The Gate to Heaven."

Evelina threw off her backpack, stretched like a cat, and let out a whimper of pleasure.

"Jeez! Let's pick somewhere close to civilisation next time," she said and shook her hair back. "So, I volunteer to serve shots and snacks if you two pitch the tent."

"It's not even five o'clock," I said. "Are you ready for hard liquor already?"

Evelina raised an eyebrow.

"Working at a bar doesn't make me an alcoholic. Despite Saga's beliefs, I hardly drink. Being with you, though, calls for a celebration and that calls for afternoon shots."

Saga bent over to hide her quiet smile. She knew, as I did, that Evelina never stayed away from what she enjoyed. Boys and booze, especially.

I let it pass. "It's the best of celebrations," I said.

IT TOOK US under fifteen minutes to pitch the tent, all thanks to Saga's solid outdoor skills.

"Seven years of being a Scout," she said, sheepishly.

Meanwhile, Evelina did what she'd promised, and more. She got the fire going, and soon the scents of summer—warm grass and fresh pine—blended with the sweet, smoky aromas of a barbecue.

"Come and sit down," she shouted. "And hurry up. I'm starving!"

We all were. My stomach felt like a dark hole and I honestly couldn't get to the fire, the food and the drinks fast enough. The sun was blazing now, and before sitting down to eat, I peeled off my still-soggy trousers and socks, draping them over the log furthest from us and the fire.

"I'm sorry. I hope you don't mind me eating in my knickers."

"Not unless you plan to sit on my face," Evelina snorted. "I can't have sweets before savoury."

Saga rolled her eyes. "Can you dykes just hand me a hot dog?"

"But of course, ma'am," Evelina said in an overly polite and servile voice. "Big and thick, just like you straight girls want 'em."

But she didn't just make hot dogs. As we wolfed them down, she grilled, then scooped delicacies from the grill: corn on the cob, halved sweet potatoes—all soft, mushy and steaming, and skewers stacked with glistening bits of red pepper and chunks of halloumi.

"How on earth did you manage to carry all of this?" I asked, surprised.

Evelina shrugged.

"Nah. This is nothing. Saga was the muscle hero, hauling all the alcohol."

She reached behind her and handed me a lukewarm can of beer, and a liquor bottle of golden-brown schnapps to go with it. She poured me a shot in a plastic glass.

"Sorry. I forgot the ice."

I raised my shot glass.

"Cheers and Helan Går," I said and downed it all in one go.

The herbal scented vodka made my mouth dry out completely.

"Woah," I said, wiping my mouth. "And thank you for fixing all this. I really appreciate it."

Evelina kept smiling, but something in her expression faltered. Her eyes flicked between me and Saga, restless and glinting, as we ate. Like she knew what was coming but couldn't say it.

When she began fidgeting with her nails, I knew I

wasn't imagining it. In school she'd bitten them to raw stumps. Now she scratched at phantom dirt at the back of her long, bright pink stiletto nails.

Something was off. I was about to ask what, when she dropped the bomb.

"Guess what, girls. I invited Jonathan and Rasmus over."

I froze.

Rasmus?

My Rasmus?

EVELINA HAD PULLED her rescue stunt on me several times during high school, most of the time I could take it. But what she did with Rasmus really hurt.

He was in my parallel class and from day one we kept eyeing each other in the hallways. Two shy kids, blushing, barely daring a hello. Then, during the summer between first and second year, we both ended up at the same holiday music camp. I sang. He played guitar. We kissed on the second day. By the end of the two weeks, we were a couple.

When school started, we held hands between classes, kissed in hidden corners. People kept saying we were the perfect fit. Sweeter than candy.

Everyone except Evelina.

She just scoffed.

"Seriously, Liz? *Him*? You can't be that naive. A guy like that won't stick around. He'll get bored, or scared, maybe both. Why give him that kind of power over you?"

It wasn't advice. It was a warning.

Around mid-term that autumn, she made sure it came true.

She'd thrown a big Halloween house party, magical forest theme. Dressed as an elven queen, Evelina bossed us into showing up as creatures from Norse mythology. She served us strong, sweet mead she swore was home-brewed. Somewhere in that sticky alcohol haze, Rasmus and I fought over something trivial, blown up by drink and heat.

He stormed out.

Evelina followed to "calm him down".

And that, she did.

I found them in the playground behind her house. She was straddling him on the dripping wet metal of the roundabout, his face buried deep between her naked breasts, her head thrown back in ecstasy. Her crown of black twigs and moss swayed wildly with her movements. I remember thinking it must be alive, glistening and growing, drawing the darkness of the autumn night closer.

As I stood there, too shocked to move, Evelina opened her eyes and stared straight at me.

She didn't stop.

She didn't flinch.

She just smiled and kept moving on top of Rasmus.

I DIDN'T SPEAK to Evelina for days. Actually, I didn't speak to anyone. My heart felt shattered in a way I couldn't explain, not just broken but hollowed out.

It was Tove who made me forgive her. She had a gift for finding kindness in the darkest places, in the darkest people. Around someone like that, anger never lasts.

By Christmas the silence was over.

Evelina and I never spoke to, or about Rasmus again.

So what was he doing here now?

I stared at Evelina, hoping for eye contact, but she clearly avoided me. Instead, she clapped her hands together and jumped up and down.

"Surprise!" she squeaked, like we were at a birthday party and not halfway through a minefield. "Isn't it fun, getting back together with the old gang?"

Saga cleared her throat.

"Ehm, so, when exactly did you invite these guests?"

Evelina squinted at her phone.

"Oh, just yesterday," she said, all breezy nonchalance. "I thought… It's been ages since we were all together. So, I asked and they happened to be free."

I opened my beer can and took a long sip.

"You know Rasmus and I haven't talked in years," I said. "Not since…"

I just couldn't say it out loud. The scars on my heart were too thin, too easy to tear open. I held my breath and swallowed the pain.

"Exactly," Evelina cut in. "That's why it's fine. It's ancient history now."

She was still smiling, still performing.

"I mean, we were only kids back then. We're different now, right?"

I didn't answer. My stomach clenched like a closed fist.

"Okay," I said, pushing to my feet too fast. "I'm sorry but I desperately need to pee. Don't eat all the corn."

I didn't wait for a response. I grabbed a half-empty napkin roll, ducked behind the tent and made my way through the undergrowth to the back side of the ridge. Twenty metres on, I crouched behind an uprooted tree and pulled my knees towards my chest. My heart was pounding like a hammer in my ears.

This had been a mistake. I'd let myself believe in the comfort of old friendship, that healing the rift between us might give me the strength to ask the mountain the only question that mattered: *where is she?*

I had tried and failed every year since Tove vanished. This time, I'd hoped we might ask together, that a stronger request would bring a stronger answer. Now, all I wanted was to go home.

Fucking Evelina.

"Hiiiiiiii!"

And there it was. Her high-pitched voice said we were no longer alone.

I wasn't ready to face anyone, least of all him. But I was out of time. Soon they'd start calling for me, maybe even come looking. I didn't want any more drama than I was already choking down, so I stood, brushed pine needles from my thighs and followed the voices back to the camp.

Jonathan saw me first. As I stepped into the clearing, he beamed like a golden retriever, like everything was fine and all I had to do was throw the damn ball already. He lifted his hand in a lazy wave, a can of Norrlands Guld clutched in his fingers.

"Liz! Shit, it's been forever."

"Hey," I said. It came out dry.

Next to him, Rasmus was squatting to unzip a backpack. He stood up slowly when he saw me.

"Hi," he said.

That was it. Just that one syllable, low and quiet, like he wasn't sure he had permission to speak.

Evelina was buzzing. That's the only word for it. She flitted between them like a spark trying to catch, nudging logs in the fire, brushing hair from her face, laughing too loudly at something Jonathan had said.

"See? I told you this would be fun," she beamed. "The whole gang, back together."

Nobody corrected her. Nobody said what we were all thinking: there was no gang. Not anymore. What was left of us wasn't whole. Tove was dead. Or missing. Or just… gone.

Saga gave the newcomers a cool once-over, then turned and tossed the bottle of schnapps to me. I caught it, barely.

"I think you need this more than I do," she said, raising an eyebrow.

Evelina kept going.

"Come on! Water under the bridge, right?"

She gave me a long, demanding stare. The message was clear: no protests wanted. Then she leaned into Jonathan and ran her index finger across his chin.

"Still growing that beard, huh?"

Jonathan blushed visibly and tugged at his scraggly chin fuzz.

"It's a work in progress."

Then the silence settled in. Just long enough to feel awkward.

"Didn't think you'd actually come all the way out here," I said finally, looking at Rasmus.

He met my eyes. Held them.

"I didn't either," he said. "But Evelina said it was important."

Evelina was already reaching into a plastic bag, pulling out marshmallows and skewers.

"Yep," she said breezily. "We need to toast things. New starts. Old friends. Closure."

Closure. The word hit me like a heavy stone on my chest. Behind us the wind rose, and the trees answered with a low, uneasy rustle.

"Where's your tent?" Saga asked, snapping the moment in half.

"Didn't bring one," Jonathan said. "We'll figure it out."

Evelina clapped her hands. "They'll share ours. It'll be cosy!"

I opened my mouth to protest, but Rasmus was looking away, his ears red.

The fire popped, sending sparks into the growing dusk. Saga shook her head, lips clenched together and grasped the bottle of golden-brown schnapps. "I don't know about you guys, but I suddenly feel the need to get properly wasted. Cheers!"

She raised her can towards the summer sky, kicked off her boots, and dropped down on one of the logs close to the fire.

"Liz, would you grab my Bluetooth speaker from the bag?"

It felt nice to have a task. I expanded it, dug it out, and spent way too long scrolling my phone for the right playlist, if such a thing even existed. In the end, I gave up and hit play on something cheesy and premade called *Summer Chill*. I winced as the first soft beat pulsed through the clearing.

"Who even designs these?" I muttered, settling beside Saga.

She put her arm around my shoulders.

"You okay?" she whispered.

"In all honesty?"

"No thanks," Saga said with a half-smile. "Let's leave it there. We'll get through this night, Liz, I promise." She snatched the bottle of schnapps from my hand and took another sip. "For what it's worth, I'm really glad you're here. I've missed you!"

"I've missed you too."

From across the fire, Evelina let out a sharp whistle.

"Hey, you! I was thinking, since we haven't seen each other in a while—let's play a game!"

She clapped her hands again, more insistent this time.

"Come on! It will help you loosen up."

Jonathan groaned.

"Please don't say it's *Spin the Bottle*. I refuse to be fake-kissed this early in the evening. My heart can't take it!" He dramatically put his left hand on his chest. "Also," he continued, "I didn't bring a bottle."

"Nooooo. You are very safe from a made-up romance," Evelina chuckled. "I was thinking about something more nostalgic."

She glanced at me, then at Saga.

"How about... *Truth or Dare*?"

Saga rolled her eyes, but she was already smiling. "What are we, twelve?"

"Yes," Evelina said sweetly. "Twelve, with beer and baggage."

Jonathan raised his can. "Subtitle of the summer."

There was laughter, the easy kind that covers up nerves. Rasmus didn't join in. He was still staring into the fire like he'd lost something there.

Evelina rummaged around in her snack bag and pulled out a gummy worm, holding it like a cigar.

"Rules are simple. No skipping. No cop-outs. If you don't answer, you drink. If you don't do the dare, you drink twice."

Saga scooted down on the ground and rested against the log, her grimace sharp.

"Sounds like someone's got an agenda."

"Of course I do," Evelina said. "It's called *fun*. Try it."

Evelina tilted her head at me.

"Liz? You in?"

Her voice was soft, but her eyes carried more: challenge, pressure, and an odd glint that felt older, darker, as if it expected something from me.

I nodded, carefully.

"Fine. But I'm not eating anything weird. Not again."

"Fair," Evelina said. "Though I'd argue that the dried reindeer penis from last time," she grinned, "was a delicacy."

Jonathan choked on his drink and started to cough, banging his fist against his chest.

Evelina hushed at him.

"Okay, okay," she continued. "Truth or dare. You chicken out, you chug. First to flinch sets the next challenge."

I settled beside Saga, my skin still humming with all I'd left unsaid, already drawn into orbit. I clung to Saga's advice: get through the night, ask the right questions.

The fire crackled. Shadows stretched, yet the sky refused to darken fully, midsummer's half-light holding the evening in its strange pause.

Saga took a deep breath and asked the first question.

"Okay, Jonathan, here goes… Truth or dare?"

He scratched his beard fuzz theatrically.

"I prefer to start out with honesty."

"Truth it is. Have you ever lied to get out of a date?"

Jonathan snickered.

"Good one! I have, actually. I once told a girl I had a rare allergy to dinner."

We laughed. He held up both hands.

"She wanted sushi. I hate sushi."

Jonathan turned to Evelina.

"Truth or dare?"

"Truth," Evelina said, popping a gummy worm in her mouth.

He considered for a moment. "What's one thing you regret from high school?"

A shadow flickered across her face, almost too faint to notice. "There was a boy," she said, her voice lilting like a nursery rhyme. "He followed me for weeks. Left notes in my locker. Wrote poems."

She fixed her eyes on the fire.

"One day, I told him to meet me in the woods after dark. I don't even know why. Just wanted to see if he would."

A beat passed.

"He did."

Another gummy worm slipped between her lips. Then her gaze lifted, eyes gleaming.

"I never saw him again!"

The group went quiet for a moment, then Evelina giggled, soft and airily.

"Or maybe I just regret that time I tried to dye my hair with lemon juice. Ended up piss yellow."

Laughter again, just faintly offbeat.

"But then you went bright red," I pointed out. "Fiery and fierce—like a fox, or that woman in *X-Men*!"

"Sure," Evelina said. "But without that super hero body."

"Not so sure about that," Jonathan added, eyeing her over his beer.

Evelina gave him the finger and leaned toward Rasmus. "Your go. Truth or dare?"

He shrugged. "Truth."

Evelina paused. "Why did you stop hanging out with us after graduation?"

Rasmus looked at her, then at me.

"We all left, didn't we?" he said. "Went our separate ways. It was just time to move on."

No one spoke for a moment. Then Saga snapped open a beer. She pointed at me.

"Okay, Liz. Truth or dare?"

"I know I'm boring, but truth," I said.

"What's something you think about way more than you should?"

The fire hissed. My eyes rested on the flames as I tried to gather my thoughts. They had been the same for the past three years. The same scenes looping endlessly, keeping me awake at night, keeping me from focusing on anything.

"I think about the night Tove disappeared," I said at last. "All the time."

A hush fell over the clearing. Saga shifted her weight. Evelina's eyes wandered away. Even Rasmus, who had barely spoken, seemed to flinch. Jonathan cleared his throat.

"Sorry," I muttered. "Didn't mean to kill the vibe."

"No, it's…" Saga started, but didn't finish.

"It's just hard," I said. "Last time, she was sitting right there." I pointed at Jonathan. "She had us meditate to the sky and to the mountain. She brought sage to burn, crystals, runes carved in wood. All kinds of shit. She had this whole routine prepared and she made us feel important, you know?" I sighed. "Like we could move heaven and earth. Like we had, well… power."

I felt the weight of their eyes on me. Everyone except Evelina. In the corner of my eye, I saw her staring off into the trees like she'd just remembered something she didn't want to.

"She thought it was serious. Tove, I mean. She always took the magical stuff to heart. You..." I paused, then faced Evelina. "I know you hated it. I remember how annoyed you were that night. Said it was all a bit too much. Maybe you were right. Then again, I think Tove believed in it. Whatever *it* was."

Evelina didn't move. She just sat there, still staring into the forest.

Saga reached out and pulled me into a hug.

"It was a great night," she whispered, stroking my hair. "But what do you say we try to move on and create some new magic, right here?"

I nodded. It felt good to be held.

"I'm sorry," Rasmus mouthed.

Jonathan leaned forward, resting his elbows on his knees.

"Okay, let's try again," he said calmly, his attention steadily on me. "Go a bit easier? Truth or dare?"

I hesitated. I'd assumed my story had killed the game but felt relieved he still believed in play. Some version of it.

"Still truth," I said with a shrug.

A flicker of something passed over his face. "You're the one who talks to the mountain, right?"

"Jesus Christ," Evelina muttered. "Easier, you said."

"I'm just asking," he said, waving an imaginary peace flag. "I've heard it talks back if you ask the right thing."

I didn't respond. The others didn't move.

Jonathan cocked his head, studying me.

"So why haven't you asked about Tove?" he said.

The fire popped. Someone's beer hissed open. No one drank.

"I mean," he continued, voice low, "if anyone could get an answer, wouldn't it be you?"

The air suddenly felt thinner. My skin buzzed, like it knew something I didn't.

I swallowed.

"Of course I have asked," I murmured, my voice barely held.

Silence followed, dense and expectant. I felt the others' scrutiny.

Then, quietly, from the other side of the fire: "Do you want to take a walk?"

Rasmus.

I lifted my head. He wasn't smiling, just watching me with that familiar, careful charm. It caught me off guard. I hesitated. That's when Evelina's eyes fixed on me, sharp and sudden. She wasn't smiling anymore. Something behind her eyes had become dark and still. She didn't move. Her body held the calmness of a hunter, waiting to strike.

A chill eased its way into my chest, slow and thick.

Whatever Rasmus was offering, I'd take it. I needed a break.

"Okay," I said, and stood. I pulled my hoodie off the log and nodded towards the trees. "Let's go."

We left without a word. Behind us the fire kept burning, but it didn't feel warm.

WE MOVED IN silence for a while, falling into an easy rhythm. Rasmus kept his hands buried in his jacket pockets, his shoulders hunched. The tension from earlier had begun to ease. I'd left without even putting my shoes on, and the freedom of it thrilled me. Each step sank into wet moss and pine needles; the earth felt cool and forgiving beneath my feet.

I'd always loved being barefoot in the forest. Grandma insisted on it when she told her stories, saying you had to let the ground touch your skin, or the tales wouldn't land right. *To feel them*, she said, *you have to open yourself up, lean into what is real and what isn't. Flesh to soil. That's how the veil disappears and how you truly see what the shadow world holds.*

I inhaled deeply. The air was cooler here, richer and scented with pine, earth, herbs and the memory of rain. Every breath I took softened me.

"Jonathan can be a dick sometimes," Rasmus said at last. "That wasn't fair."

I shrugged. "Doesn't matter."

"It does," he said. "Especially to you."

We went another few paces. A low thrum filled my ears, either my blood, or the wind threading its way through the trees.

Rasmus cleared his throat.

"Listen. I didn't come here to mess with you. I didn't even want to come, honestly. But Evelina really stressed the importance of us all reuniting, and I thought—"

"What?" I stopped. "That it'd be fun? A chance to lick our mutual wounds?"

His face tightened. "No. I thought maybe I could... I don't know. Say I'm sorry."

That stung. It shouldn't have, but it did.

"Sorry for what, exactly?" I asked.

"For how I handled everything. For not apologising, avoiding you..."

He broke off, his head dipped. "I should've told everyone what really happened."

"You slept with her," I said. "That's what happened. I saw you."

He didn't argue. He stared for a long time past my shoulder, as if there was something in the trees. When he spoke, his voice was quiet but wounded and raw.

"It wasn't like that," he said. "I don't remember anything from that night, Liz. Nothing. My memory is so blank, it's like I wasn't even there."

A silence opened up between us. Something weightless and slippery slid along my spine.

"I only know what people told me happened," he added, barely audible. "It's creepy."

"It's fine, Rasmus. I don't need an apology. Not now."

We stood there for a while, the hush between us folding into the sounds of the forest. Leaves rustled in the wind. A few birds chirped, stubborn against the approaching night.

Then something shifted.

It began as a prickle at the back of my neck. A faint pull under my skin, like static crawling, up my legs at first, then along my arms. The air felt strained. Charged. As if the mountain and everything on it was coming alive, breathing around me. In me. Wanting me closer.

"I need to go," I mumbled, almost to myself.

"Where?"

"To ask."

He looked confused but didn't follow me. The trees parted as I moved towards the ridge and the tingling under my skin intensified. Each step buzzed. I didn't need a torch. The path to The Rock of Whispers was all laid out for me, calling me through the very marrow of my bones.

I quickened my pace. Behind me, Rasmus shouted something, but his words scattered in the wind. I was already beyond them, my body humming with expectation.

As I kept going, the forest simply stopped. One moment, dense birch, pine and soft undergrowth pressing close around me, the next, open air. The sight stunned me, just as it had every time I'd been here.

The top of the mountain ended in a sheer drop, a vertical plunge so deep the valley below appeared unreal, like watercolour washed thin across paper. A dark sea of pine rolled out beneath me, stitched together by a river that gleamed like a silver blade. It all looked endless. Ancient. Like a place the world had forgotten.

To the west, smaller mountains and hills layered into each other in hazy greys and blues, as if the world over there was dissolving, disappearing. To the east, the dark cliff side jutted out, steep, narrow and unnaturally clean. It stretched a hundred metres or more before it hooked sharply inward at a right angle. It closed the view and formed the eerie sound barrier that could make even the softest whisper sound like a desperate cry, amplifying it beyond what should be possible.

As I stood on top of The Rock of Whispers, I could feel its tingling energy growing stronger, travelling across my skin. It wasn't just calling me anymore. It was reaching for me.

There was a rusted fence right at the edge, and as I approached it, the wind pressed harder, shoving against my whole body.

"Are you sure this is safe?"

I could suddenly hear Rasmus again. His words whispered against the mountain walls, through the wind.

Safe, safe, safe…

I curled my fingers around the cold, metal bar. The wind pulled at my t-shirt, making it flap against my back. The drop before us was dizzying. I had to close my eyes for a moment to regain my balance and give him an answer.

"The mountain clearly thinks so." My voice came out weaker and more unsteady than I wanted. "I've been here many times, and I'm still here."

Still here. Still here, echoed the mountain.

"Why did you run?" Rasmus said. "It was like you wanted to get away from me. Or like you were afraid of something."

Afraid. Afraid.

Then the echo shifted, becoming more than a simple repetition.

Ask me, it said. The words were barely audible, just a faint whisper through the wind. *Ask me. Ask me.*

Rasmus drew a sharp, trembling breath.

"Goddamn," he said, his voice unsteady. "Did you hear that?"

I nodded. My tongue clung to the roof of my mouth. The Rock of Whispers had always been cryptic, sometimes incomprehensible, but never before had it told me to ask.

"Where is she?" The words slipped out of me. "Tell me where Tove is."

Something stirred in the wind, as if the mountain exhaled. Then, in an instant, the air stilled and everything went silent. Everything but the echo. It came at us loud and clear.

She is here.

She is here. She is here. She is here.

Rasmus gasped and took a step back.

"Oh my God," he breathed.

Right then the wind hit us again.

"Hey, what are you guys doing?"

Evelina stepped out from the trees behind us. She flashed us her big, toothy grin. But above it her eyes were wide, black and unnaturally large in the faltering evening twilight. Like darkness had somehow taken root in them.

"Oh, nothing really," I answered, forcing my voice into breezy carelessness.

Evelina peeked over my shoulder, like she was searching for something in the void behind the fence. Expecting something to rise. Her smile faltered. She lifted her chin and inhaled deeply through her nose.

"The air is so fresh up here," she said. "Like it could just wipe everything clean, you know?"

Her dark eyes met mine, sharp and unreadable.

"So, did the echo say something interesting? Like it did that last time when it told Tove she'd be rich and famous?"

My heart skipped a beat. We had been here on that hike, three years ago. We had all been so deep into our rituals, our makeshift magic. Tove had shouted at the mountain like she could shake answers from stone. We had all laughed, but she was dead serious. Furious, even.

The echo gave almost nothing back. Only a faint, weak whisper of no meaning at all. Certainly nothing about fame and fortune.

But Evelina spoke with such rock-hard certainty. I knew better than to challenge her. Just like I knew I couldn't tell her why I was really here. What I'd sensed in the mountain.

"We're just playing," I said, trying a smile of my own. "You know this echo is a total diva? Half the time you can't make out a word."

"Yeah," Rasmus said and swallowed. "We're just messing around."

I could feel the tension in him, the effort to stay calm. His hands hung rigid at his sides, fists clenched tight against his body. He too was fighting to keep it all together.

Evelina's black eyes moved between us: me, then Rasmus, then back again.

"Is that so?" she said, sounding overly cheerful. "I never believed the stories about this place anyway. Kungsberget is just a mountain, albeit a good one. Why else would people ski here in the winter?"

She came closer. Patted the pockets of her mini shorts like she was searching for something. Then she let out a disappointed squeak.

"Goddamn. I thought I put a joint here somewhere. It must have been in my other shorts." She sighed and pouted her lower lip. "We could have used some nice weed now, don't you think? Something to take the edge off. We all miss her. So very much."

She sounded like she was reading from a script. And weed? Evelina knew how much I hated drugs, and as far as I remember, she did too. Now she acted like this was some American teen movie and that smoking marijuana was the most natural thing in the world.

Nothing about this situation was natural.

"Maybe you should try asking something then," I said. "Ask about Tove. Maybe the echo will respond better to you."

I tried to sound casual, letting the words slip into the moment like they belonged.

Evelina's eyes locked on mine. Was I imagining it, or had they grown even darker? I could barely make out the blue of her irises. An eerie, cold sensation pierced through me, as though the shadow in her eyes had coiled itself around my throat.

Ice-cold fear crept down my spine, spreading like a swarm of stinging insects along my nerves, raising the hair on my arms.

"And why is that?" she whispered, her eyes still fixed on mine, probing.

A sharp stab of pain exploded between my eyes. My vision blurred. I lost my balance.

Rasmus grabbed my arm before I could fall.

"What happened?"

I couldn't answer. The pain was too strong, like something inside my skull had cracked open. Her darkness was somehow in me now. It spread through my insides, thick as ink, infectious as rot, seeping downward and deadening everything it touched.

A wave of nausea rose in my chest. My stomach churned.

Suddenly, a rustle in the woods behind us. A branch snapped. Evelina flinched, whipping towards the sound. The pain vanished instantly.

"Anyone out here?"

It was Jonathan's voice.

"Say hi if you're there!"

Saga was with him. In front of me Evelina swung back to face me once more. Her eyes were normal now. Blue and sparkling. She put that wide, bright smile back on.

"Why don't you go get them, Liz?" she beamed. "They must be lost. We don't want anyone else to disappear, do we?"

Rasmus took one step forward.

"I don't think she is doing too well," he said.

Evelina laid her well-manicured, slim hand on his shoulder.

"But she is. I think Liz will be perfectly alright now,"

she said in her smoothest, most velvety voice. "And you wouldn't want to leave me all alone out here, right?"

Rasmus' face and body tightened, then his shoulders slackened as if something had given way. He sighed, apparently letting go of all doubts, then he leaned into Evelina.

"Of course not," he said, his voice flat and void of emotion. "Go on, Liz. I'll wait here."

Jonathan and Saga were less than fifty metres from us. When I reached them, their eyes were dazed, their shoulders shaky, as if they'd just stepped out of a maze. Saga hugged me.

"Shit," she said. "I swear I was going in the right direction. I mean, I've been here before and I knew which way you had gone. But still… I don't know."

"What?" I asked.

The dark, stiffening sensation crept back up the nape of my neck. Saga wrinkled her forehead, confused.

"I just couldn't figure it out," she said. "It was like my inner compass went crazy or something."

Jonathan swayed slightly and quickly rested himself on a crooked young birch. He let out a low burp.

"Sorry, sorry. I haven't got much sense of direction either."

"Just come with me," I sighed. "We'll go get Rasmus and Evelina, then we'll head back home."

"Now?" Saga frowned.

"Yes, now," I said. "The wind is catching on and I think we should just get out of here before we get stuck in a storm."

To my relief, they didn't question the lie. I didn't want to explain the real reason. Not yet. Not the echo. Not Evelina's eyes. Not the way her grinning lips stretched too wide. And certainly not the gut-deep certainty that she had something to do with Tove and whatever had happened that night.

The thought made my stomach churn again. I was leaving, and fast. Jonathan and Saga trailed after me without a word. Ferns and low blueberry bushes clawed at our legs. Usually, I loved that soft, green caress of the forest. Now, it felt like fingers, trying to drag us back, keeping us here forever.

Soon, we reached the edge of the cliff. Evelina was there, alone, leaning her back against the rustled fence. The wind tugged at her long blond hair, whipping it across her face.

Evelina gestured to the tree line, away from us.

"He had to do his business in the woods," she said. "He'll be right back."

She stretched her arms out towards Jonathan.

"Sweetheart," she squealed. "Come give me a hug. I'm freezing here. Did Liz tell you a storm is coming?"

"She wants to leave," Jonathan said, twinkling as he stumbled towards her. "But I want to stay and hug you!"

He threw himself into her arms. She wrapped them around him, slowly, almost tenderly. Like a mother cradling her long-lost child. Her hands slid up his back, fingers spreading wide.

That's when they changed.

First, her fingers whitened and stretched, like the joints suddenly lost control, pushing the bones outward, making them grow like twigs on a tree. Then her long, bright pink nails, glossy and perfect, curled upward and cracked. One by one they lifted from her fingertips and peeled off like brittle petals, scattering on the wind like something long dead. Beneath them something else emerged. Something far longer, far sharper. Claws. Not curled and elegant like on a cat, but crooked splintered things, like the thorns on a blackened tree. They jutted out from her hands, glinting in the faint evening glow.

Before I could warn him, she plunged them into the base of Jonathan's neck. There was a wet, tearing sound. A gasp, then blood. A red gush down the back of his pastel-blue polo.

Saga and I screamed, cries that tore out from the very bottom of our souls. The kind of scream that already knows: there is no escape. No salvation.

But Jonathan didn't scream. Evelina, or whatever that thing in front of us was, bent close to his ear. I saw its lips move, whispering something. He stood frozen, his arms limp at his sides while blood soaked through his shirt, the soft blue darkening to something almost black.

All at once, the creature let go. Jonathan swayed, just like he had in the woods. Then he straightened. Without a word, without hesitation, he grabbed the fence, planted one foot on the steel mesh, and climbed.

A split second later he was gone. Lost in the abyss.

The creature wearing Evelina's face turned towards The Rock of Whispers. Its head snapped back, as though answering a silent, sacred call.

"You want me to ask?" it said, its voice a deep vibration that crawled through the ground and into my bones. "Then I'll ask for you."

"Where are they?"

It was more a growl than speech, rising from the roots of the mountain, spreading like dark electricity through the air, humming in the ground beneath my feet.

The wind died. The forest held its breath.

My knees buckled and I sank down on my knees.

Then the echo came back, loud and crystal clear:

They are nowhere.

Nowhere. Nowhere. Nowhere.

Saga was trembling as I grabbed her hand and pulled her down next to me. Clung on to her.

The being turned back to us. Its eyes were all jet black now, deep and glossy as a midnight sky. Its hair had grown, falling in golden waves all the way to its knees. That smile, Evelina's signature grin, made sense at last. It had never belonged to a human face.

It stepped towards us. With each stride, its features softened. The claws retracted. The black eyes went back to clear blue. Only the hair remained unchanged.

I swallowed hard. Everything tasted like metal. Saga sobbed quietly in my arms.

"You killed Tove."

It wasn't a question. Now I understood what the echo had tried to tell me.

A faint shiver ran through the creature. Was it regret? Could it feel anything? I couldn't say.

"She is with the mountain now," Evelina—it—said gently, though the voice didn't belong to Evelina. Each word carried a dry, echoing weight, like they were drawn through ancient stone.

"But why?"

I didn't know why I asked. As if this thing could give answers. But something in me had to try.

The creature bowed its head and studied me, almost tenderly.

"She tried to alter the balance," it said in words that came from all around us, vibrating on our skin like a shallow earthquake. "She tried to bind the mountain. Reshape what should not be altered. The mountain does not forgive such trespass."

The balance.

The words sat heavy in the air, like ash after a fire. I had heard them before—from Tove, three years ago. Setting the balance right was all she talked about while she lit sage and laid out her carved runes. My stomach clenched.

"She knew," I whispered. "About you."

The being held out its hands to us.

"And now you know too," it said, back in Evelina's voice again, all polished and pleasant. "Come on. Let's go back to camp and have a drink. I don't know about you, but my throat's drying up."

It helped us to our feet. Saga still cried. The thing disguised as Evelina wiped her tears with the pad of its thumb. Completely human, except for one detail. No fingernails. Just soft, rounded flesh where its claws had been.

It led us through the woods. We followed. We couldn't not.

Back at the campfire clearing, a breeze lifted its long hair. It fluttered aside, revealing its upper back, just above the strap of its top. There was nothing there. No skin. No flesh. No bones.

Just a hole. A hollow black void.

At the edge of my mind, a faint memory brushed through me. A scent of darkness and death, a yearning from the very heart of the forest that felt all too familiar. Like one of Grandma's fairy tales. Only this tale was true, and with every step we were drawn deeper into its rhythm.

As if it felt my stare, the being stopped. It stood completely still. I could feel its breath wash over me, cold and heavy. Hear it rustle the leaves around us.

"I trust you will keep the balance," it said. The voice came rumbling through the air, making the ground tremble below our feet. "I know you will."

It proceeded towards the fire, the food, the scattered backpacks.

As we watched, the hole in its back closed and vanished without a trace. In moments, the creature held Evelina's shape again, flawless and familiar.

Saga wiped away her tears. It looked like a tremor passed through her as she drew in a breath, then sank to the ground, shaking. I don't think she saw when the creature glanced back at us.

I did. And what I saw froze me to the spot. Those glossy, Evelina-coloured eyes did not simply look our way. They examined us with a depthless pitch-black coldness. A coldness that folded itself around me, sinking beneath my skin, past muscle and marrow until it settled somewhere deep inside. It wasn't a warning. It was a claim.

Whatever peered through Evelina's eyes would not let us go.

Not now. Not ever.

HIT AND RUN

by Markus Sköld

JOHANNA IS SCRUBBING the blood off the front of the car. The right front headlight is broken, there's a big dent in the hood, and a spidery web-pattern of tiny cracks across the right side of the windshield where the stranger struck his head.

It's late. Almost two in the morning, and she needs to be up early to take the bus to work tomorrow. Tomorrow... later this morning's more like it, but she needs to clean this up. She can explain the damages to the car—maybe she hit a bin somebody'd left too far out into the street. Yes. A bin sounds plausible. She can't, however, explain the blood. So that has to disappear. It needs to be this way. For Saga. Anders wouldn't hesitate for a second to use this to get full custody of their daughter. She knows she's fucked up in the past, but since he asked for a divorce, she's been really good, really tried. And now this. It's like she couldn't just mess up a little bit, she had to go and fucking kill a man.

With the blood gone, Johanna rinses the dirt off the small

shovel she usually keeps in her car in case she ever needs to dig herself out of a snowdrift. She turns off the lights and goes into the house through the connecting door. Anders has decided they're going to sell the house, despite the fact that Johanna loves it. He's the one who wants to leave, why can't it be like in the American movies, where the man leaves and the woman gets to keep the big house and live a good life off her ex-husband's money?

She catches a glimpse of herself in the mirror. Hair in disarray, dirt all over her outfit, dirt on her face. She needs a shower.

While the warm water beats down on her shoulders she starts crying. Mud—and probably the stranger's blood—circle the drain. All evidence disappearing, like none of it ever happened.

Once she's out of the shower, she steps into the kitchen. Her gaze is immediately drawn to the wine fridge. She could really use a drink right now. The house is empty. Until she picks Saga up after football practice tomorrow, it's just her. And she just killed a man for fuck's sake. She grabs a bottle at random. A Gewürztraminer that she knows Anders wanted to save for a special occasion. She uncorks the bottle like it's second nature and pours herself a large glass.

As she wets her lips with the wine she can't help but see the stranger's face. It probably wasn't so, but now, in the strobing flashes of memory that are bombarding her mind, she's certain the stranger smiled at her in the beam of the headlights. Not a friendly smile, but the sickening smile of a disturbed individual. Somebody who'd been standing there, in the dark, waiting for her. Like he knew she was going to hit him. And for some reason, relished it.

Closing her eyes, she tries to rid herself of the image,

but it keeps growing stronger. She chugs the wine, gasping for air as she puts it down on the counter.

The clock on the wall above the door tells her it's now two thirty in the morning. Johanna draws a deep breath and steadies herself. She wishes she could call in sick tomorrow, but with the divorce and everything, she's taken too many sick days already. Any more would warrant a sit-down with HR. With Gunilla, the HR manager who enforces the rules like a prison warden and seems to have singled Johanna out as her next victim.

She pours herself another glass, reasoning it'll help her fall asleep faster. As she's walking upstairs to the bedroom, she drains the glass and leaves it on the floor at the top of the stairs. Maybe it's actually the wine, or maybe it's the adrenaline wearing off, but all of a sudden, she's very tired. With the towel still wrapped around her, she crashes into bed.

SHE'S BARELY LANDED when the alarm goes off. Eyes scrunched shut, she reaches for her mobile on the bedside table. Unable to reach it, she reluctantly opens one eye. The mobile isn't there. She can hear it, but it isn't where it usually is. Through an act of sheer willpower, she sits up, trying to remember where she put it. Her leaving the mobile on the bedside table has become such a ritual that it's basically muscle memory. She can't recall a single time when she hasn't left it there.

The alarm seems to be coming from the other side of the room, near the window. She stands and as she gets closer, she sees it, lying on the window sill. Like it's on display, like somebody wanted her to know that they had moved it.

The stranger.

She pushes the thought away. He was dead. She's sure of it. His blank eyes, the huge dent in the forehead. She feels queasy when thinking about the brain matter she scrubbed off the windshield. No, he's dead. Absolutely. No question about it.

But who moved the phone? Saga's supposed to be at her dad's until Johanna picks her up after football practice. Calling out her name, she heads for her room. The upstairs landing leads to five rooms: Anders's office, the master bedroom, the snug, the bathroom, and all the way at the end, Saga's room.

Her daughter's not there. The bed is made and all her things are in their proper place. Johanna usually can't help but make a mess, and Anders isn't much better. It's amazing how unlike them their daughter turned out to be. Sometimes, perhaps, children see their parents as a cautionary tale and develop habits that are completely counter to them.

Johanna checks the time and lets out a cascade of profanities. Out here the buses don't run as often as in the city. If she misses this one, she's gonna be late for the morning meeting.

A clean pair of trousers and a fun top, and she's ready. She considers heels for a moment but discards the idea and puts on tennis shoes instead. It's about a kilometre to the bus, and she has less than ten minutes to get there.

The bus is already at the stop, and Johanna waves her arms, hoping the driver is going to be merciful. He is, and she thanks him profusely while trying to catch her breath. Her hair is damp and she's sweating through her clean top.

The only other passenger is an elderly woman sitting in the forward section of the bus. Johanna grabs a seat in the middle. The old woman eyes her, shaking her head, like she's judging her. Like she knows what she's done. Johanna musters a smile and the hag looks away.

Johanna finds a pack of tissues in her handbag and tries to discreetly wipe away the sweat from her armpits and forehead. The bus jerks, making her struggle with the makeup. She puts the mirror close to her face and is just about to apply mascara when she spots something in the reflection and almost screams out loud. The stranger sits in the back of the bus, his cold glare on the back of her neck.

It's impossible. She must be imagining things. Slowly, she turns her head. It's the same man, she's sure of it. That face. The face that's burnt into her mind for the rest of her life. The one she saw in front of her the whole time she was scrubbing down the car.

He's staring right at her. A crooked smile on his face. But the huge dent on the side of his head is gone. All that remains is dried blood caked in the ruffled tufts of hair. His clothes are still soiled with dirt from the shallow grave she dug for him by the side of the road.

Johanna can't breathe. Panicking. On pure instinct she pushes the button for the bus to stop. The driver casts a short glance towards her in the rear-view mirror and shakes his head. The bus slows down and Johanna gets up to stand by the doors. She peeks nervously towards the stranger in the back of the bus. If he were to get up to follow her, she doesn't know what she would do. Is that why he's here? Does he recognise her? Maybe he did survive, somehow. But she felt his pulse, it was gone. And she knows how to check for vitals. She worked as a healthcare assistant for a few years, before she met Anders. The stranger can't have survived. By the time she had dug the grave, he was as cold as the night air.

Finally, after driving a small distance, the bus comes to a halt at the next bus stop. Johanna frantically pushes the button to open the doors, and as soon as they do, she's out. The stranger doesn't follow. In fact, when she looks up at the bus, he's not in his seat anymore. There's nobody there. She staggers over to the bench next to the bus stop. Shivering. Tears pooling in her eyes, in denial about what she just saw. Her guilty conscience conjuring things that aren't there. But it felt so real.

By the time the next bus comes around, she's already late for work. The driver takes an excruciatingly long time at each stop, making sure every single passenger has found a seat before allowing the vehicle to keep moving.

The morning staff meeting is already over when she finally arrives. Since the new regulations, you need an education to work as an HCA, but Christina—her old boss—managed to find her a position in administrations. The staff meeting is mostly for the doctors and nurses, but it's considered bad form to miss it, even for the administrative staff.

Johanna is just about to sit down at her desk when she hears Christina's voice.

"Can I see you for a minute?"

"Sure, no problem."

Johanna follows Christina into her office.

"Could you close the door, please?"

Johanna does as she's told and then takes a seat on one of the visitor chairs. Christina's desk is pushed up against the wall, which means the chair is at the end of the desk. It's an uncomfortable position to be scolded in. Somehow, it'd feel more natural to sit across the desk from the person yelling at you.

"I'm really sorry about this morning. My car… it needs to go to a shop, so I had to take the bus and—"

Christina puts her hand up to stop her.

"Listen, somebody's made a formal complaint about you."

Johanna's body goes numb.

"About me... who? What for?"

"I can't tell you who. But I've been told you've been intoxicated at work."

An acid bomb goes off in Johanna's chest. She may have been hungover a few times, but drinking at work...

"Never! Who says that?"

"Johanna, this is serious. I'm allowed to give you a warning, but you are still on probation. HR's recommendation was to let you go immediately."

"That fucking bitch..."

The words escape her before she can stop them.

"What?"

"She hates me. I don't know why she has it in for me."

"Gunilla is a professional. She applies the same rules to everyone."

Johanna scoffs.

"Look, Johanna. We worked together in the past, and I really thought I could depend on you, even though you can't be an HCA anymore. You're putting me in a bad position by allowing this sort of thing to go on the record."

"But I—"

"I don't want to get another one of these complaints. Is that clear?"

Johanna takes a deep breath. Nods.

"I understand."

"Alright. Then get back to work. I know Nora needs the staffing numbers for next quarter, if you could put that together for her."

Johanna goes back to her desk and opens up the spreadsheet, determined to find the numbers Nora was asking for, but she can't make heads or tails of any of it. All she can think about is what Christina said. That, and the looming shadow threatening everything: the stranger she buried a few metres into the forest. She pulls up a fresh browser window and types 'keep custody after manslaughter'.

The results are far from comforting.

A manslaughter conviction can have a significant impact on child custody, but it doesn't automatically result in the loss of parental rights. The court will prioritise the child's best interests when making custody decisions.

The child's best interests… Will they decide that it's better to award custody to the mother, with a slight drinking problem, whose employment is hanging by a thread? Or will they decide it's in Saga's best interests to live with her father? The stable, financially secure person who can provide for her. Johanna suddenly feels sick.

The staff toilets are at the other end of the office. She doesn't want to run. But she doesn't want to throw up in one of the bins either. Especially not after hearing that people think she's drinking at work. Holding her breath she makes a beeline to the toilets, trying to make it look like she's slightly late for a meeting.

There are three stalls. One of them is occupied, and she knows from experience that they're not very soundproof. The occasional wee is unavoidable, but anything besides that is out of the question. But the nausea's building. Johanna can't hold it in any longer. She slams the door shut, locks it, and kneels in front of the bowl. She hasn't eaten since yesterday, and as soon as the mostly liquid, bile-tasting sick has left her, she stands up and wipes tears from her eyes. She listens for any signs of the person in the next stall. Usually, you can't even move without the sound carrying over to your porcelain neighbour. But now, everything's quiet. Too quiet.

Johanna opens the stall door and tip-toes to the sinks. Seeing herself in the mirror confirms that she's a hot mess. The mascara has started to run, her hair is in disarray, and there are droplets of sweat on her forehead. She catches a glimpse of the next stall in the mirror. Still locked. Whoever's in there's really quiet. Maybe they're just taking a break from everything. Sitting silently scrolling on the phone. That means they've heard everything she just did. But they haven't yet seen her. Other people have, though. Half the office must've observed her hurry to the loo. The cat's out of the bag no matter what she does. She grabs a paper towel to try to fix the worst of the sweat and mascara.

Suddenly, the vacant lock flips over to white. Johanna draws a breath, bracing herself. But the door doesn't immediately open. Instead, the handle moves slightly, like whoever's inside is struggling to figure out how to work it. And in an instant an almost paralysing fear grabs hold of her.

It's the stranger.

No, that's impossible. She's still not sure if it was actually him she saw on the bus, or if it was her imagination.

No, it was him. You know it was.

If it was him. If he survived somehow, he could have been on the bus. It even makes sense in a twisted kind of way.

But he can't be here. Not in the office. You need a

key card to get in, and there's a receptionist who would almost certainly have noticed a dishevelled man with dried blood on his face. Not to mention how he'd manage to stroll through the office to the toilets unhindered.

Unless he's not human at all.

She jerks as the handle moves again. The door opens. Slowly. Johanna can't look away. She can't run either. It's like her brain is screaming at her to move, but her body won't comply.

The door swings open. It's dark inside the stall. She can't make out whether or not there's anybody in there. There must be. How else did the vacant lock flip?

"Hey."

Johanna recoils at the sudden sound. Heart racing, she discovers Nora, just entering the toilets. Her colleague stops and stares disapprovingly at her.

"What?"

"Nothing… I—"

"You're like… sweating…"

"No, I just—"

"Whatever. I need the loo." Nora heads for the middle stall, the one that by all accounts houses a dead man.

"Wait!"

Nora turns towards her, hand on hip, eyebrows raised. "Do you mind?"

"It's not that. Just listen—"

Nora sneers, turns around and in the same motion flips her hair over her shoulder and steps into the stall. She slams the door shut. Johanna can hear her muttering through the door.

"Crazy wino bitch."

* * *

By half past three she still hasn't managed to put together any of the numbers Nora needed from her. She can't stop thinking about the stranger.

Maybe she should just turn herself in. It was an accident after all. She wasn't drunk last night. He appeared out of nowhere. There really wasn't anything she could have done to avoid the tragedy. But the terrifying truth is that none of that matters. It's the bad decisions she made afterwards that are the problem. She still decided to hide his body and scrub her car clean. Who was he? Why was he in the middle of the road in the middle of the night? And why did he just stand there, staring at her, with that horrific smile on his face? Like some demented apparition.

She gathers her things and tries to avoid making eye contact with anyone as she heads for the door. Late to the morning meeting and now the first to leave. She'll get fired for sure.

The practice pitch is a twenty-minute bus ride away, and for the first time today Johanna is actually on time.

Saga is on the pitch, playing with the ball. Johanna waves at her from the sideline. Her daughter waves back, a big smile on her face. Johanna continues waving. Seeing Saga makes a lot of her anxiety melt away. It's a reminder of why she did what she did last night. The alternative would have been to not see her again. Awarding full custody to Anders. Maybe getting to meet her daughter every other weekend. Or worse: once a year on her birthday. What kind of visitation rights does a mother in prison have?

Saga passes the ball to one of her team mates. Seconds later, the coach blows his whistle and all the girls gather round.

"Johanna."

She tenses up when she hears Anders's voice behind her and turns around. Damn him, he's still handsome.

"Anders."

"I've scheduled an evaluation with the real estate agent for next week."

"Already? I haven't even started looking for a place yet."

And there's a murder weapon in the shape of a car in the garage.

Anders shakes his head and sighs deeply.

"I don't wanna drag this out any longer. You've had almost half a year."

"Three months, Anders. I've had three months to try to pick up the pieces of my life. Shattered because you couldn't be bothered to give us a chance. Half of which I used to get a job."

"It's four. Four and a half, you just chose to ignore everything for the first month."

Johanna bites her lip. It's true she didn't think he'd go through with it, that she could repair things, but Anders was serious. She's just about to say exactly that when she catches something out of the corner of her eye. Her eyes widen when she realises that it's the stranger. Standing at the far end of the pitch, not watching the girls playing football, but staring directly at her.

She can't breathe. He's still dressed the same way; she can make out the dirt on his suit from across the field. His pale complexion highlights the dried blood on the side of his face.

"I need to move on, Johanna. Can't you understand that? I want my life back. I don't want to fight, but if that's the way you want to play it... I'm warning you. You'll lose."

Johanna gasps for air and looks at the stranger across the pitch, who is still watching her.

"Hey, look at me when I'm talking to you!" Anders barks.

She snaps out of it. Looks at Anders, trying to hide the tears pooling in the pits of her eyes.

"My lawyer is champing at the bit to have a go at awarding me full custody. But I've held him back. Saga needs you. She needs her mum. But if I don't start to see some cooperation from you..."

He lets the sentence, with all its implications, fade away.

"Yes, of course."

"Good," he says, draws a deep breath and lowers his voice. "We can make this work, Johanna." It's his diplomacy voice. His salesman's voice. She's heard it a million times before, and over the years she's grown to hate it. So many times she's been compelled to agree, when actually she wanted to scream right in his face. "It's important for Saga to feel like we're still a family. That she belongs. You know?"

Johanna's jaw's aching from clenching her teeth. She nods and shoots another glance towards the stranger. Only he's not there anymore. Just another parent, who looks nothing like the stranger she killed and buried.

"I know..."

Anders nods, obviously pleased that he has won the argument once again.

"Okay. I gotta run."

"You're not gonna watch?"

"Wish I could. I already told Saga. She understands."

"But..."

"Bloody hell, Johanna. It's not like it's a fuckin' recital. It's just football practice. I'll pick her up after school next

Wednesday. Oh, and if you could get my old golf clubs from the cellar? I'm taking Lova golfing next weekend."

The name of his new girlfriend makes Johanna's skin crawl, but she manages to produce a smile as she answers.

"Sure."

After practice, Saga comes running. Johanna wraps her arms around her and kisses her on the cheeks, on the forehead.

"Mum, stop!"

"You don't know how glad I am to see you, munchkin. Come. We mustn't miss the bus."

Saga shoots her a sideways glance.

"The bus? Where's the car?"

"Mummy had a bit of an accident so the car needs to go to the shop."

"Are you okay?"

Johanna pulls her daughter close while they're walking to the bus stop.

"Of course I am, darling. Come on now. We only have a couple of minutes to catch that bus."

The bus is half full. Johanna studies each of the other passengers carefully before finding a seat for Saga and herself, as close to the exit as possible. The stranger isn't among them. Still, she can't fully focus on Saga's stories about school and whatever the teacher said, and how much fun she's had at Dad's, and when is he moving back into the house.

That last bit is where the knot in her stomach tightens.

"He's not, munchkin. You know how we talked about this. You're gonna have two homes now. One at Dad's and one at Mum's. It's gonna be great. You'll get two birthdays, two Christmases, two of everything."

Saga's face lights up.

"Two summer holidays?"

Johanna tickles her.

"Cheeky bugger! Only the one summer holiday, I'm afraid."

Johanna looks up at the next stop display.

"This is us. You want to push the button?"

They walk hand in hand from the bus stop back to the house. The house that Johanna has called her home for the last fifteen years or so, filled with memories of a future that wasn't meant to be. She cautiously glances at Saga, trying to gauge her reaction. She doesn't want to bring it up, in case she feels the same way. But it seems her daughter is fine with it all.

"I'm gonna watch TV," she announces as soon as they're inside.

"Alright, I'll join you in a minute."

Johanna hears Saga's feet tapping up the stairs to the snug as she goes down to the cellar to fetch Anders's golf clubs. He never wanted a telly in the ground floor drawing room. That was the place for entertaining, board games, and conversations, not mindlessly consuming 'artificial audiovisual stimulation', as he'd call it. But it's Saga's favourite room of the house.

AROUND HALF PAST nine, Johanna says it's time for bed, school night and all. Saga groans for a moment before she gives in and shuffles off to brush her teeth.

Once the bedtime story is done, Johanna drifts back down to the kitchen. She takes a long breath, her eyes inevitably drawn to the wine fridge. She promised herself she wouldn't, but Saga's already in bed. And it's not like she has a real drinking problem. She still manages to hold down a job. She's almost never late, except when she totals her car, killing a man. And she bloody well deserves a drink after a day like this. While she's mentally rationalising her actions, her body has already pulled a bottle from the fridge.

She pours herself a large glass, then downs most of it. It's like balm to a burn. A sense of relief and calm spreads throughout her body. She turns around, glances out the window, then stops, mid-turn, and drops the glass. It shatters. Wine and glass shoot across the floor.

The stranger is standing in the middle of the front garden. Looking at the house. Looking at her.

Johanna closes her eyes, trying to force the hallucination away, but when she opens her eyes, he's still there.

"No..."

Shaking her head, she closes her eyes again to make the stranger disappear. But this isn't like when she saw him on the bus, or by the football pitch. This time, he won't go away. She gasps when he begins walking towards the house. She's racking her brain, trying to remember if she locked the front door or not. The stranger is getting closer to the house. Slowly but surely.

Finally, the paralysis lifts. Johanna starts for the front door when a crippling pain shoots up through her leg as she steps on a piece of glass. She staggers to the kitchen counter, pulls her foot up, and sees blood welling up around a jagged shard of glass lodged deep in her sole. Her fingers tremble as she pulls it out. It's a strange sensation to feel the sharp edge cut into her flesh. A spurt of blood pumps out when it dislodges, and she throws it to the floor as she moves out of the kitchen. Careful not to place weight on the wound, she limps on the side and heel of her foot towards the front door.

Through the tall window by the side of the door, she sees the outline of the stranger approaching. He's close. Johanna ignores the pain and runs towards the door, turning the lock at the same time the door handle is pushed down. The stranger jiggles it a few more times and then steps in front of the side window, staring at her.

Her heart is trying to beat itself out of her chest. As suddenly as he moved in front of the window, he turns and walks away. She leans in, hoping to catch a glimpse of where he's gone, but he's nowhere to be seen.

What other entrances are there? The garage is locked. She made sure of it. That's where the car is. Then there's the utility entrance and the patio. They should be locked, but she can't say for certain. The stranger went right, which means the utility entrance is closest.

Johanna gets going, leaving bloody footprints with each step she takes. She reaches the main hallway as she partially hobbles, partially jumps on one leg. She's sweating, beats of her pulse echoing in her ears. Whimpering, she pushes the door to the mudroom open. Relieved to find the outside door closed and locked, she bolts back out, heading for the back living room. The one that opens up onto the patio.

The entire length of the living room is floor-to-ceiling windows, overlooking the back garden. The moment she sets foot in the room she discovers him. He's standing outside, waiting, just a few yards away, eyes fixed on her. That horrifying smile still on his face.

"What do you want!" she cries.

He doesn't respond, only tilts his head slightly to one side.

"I'm sorry! It was an accident!"

Still no response. She takes a step back from the door.

The bleeding sole of her foot sticks to the floor. The entire house is filled with bloodied footprints from her running from one end of the house to the other. She closes her eyes again, willing the stranger to disappear. He was dead when she drove away. A haunting suspicion begins to manifest. What if this is all in her head? Maybe she's starting to lose her mind. But when she opens her eyes again, he's still there. And for a brief moment, she is stricken with the realisation that this stranger, this thing, is here for one reason only. To torment her.

"Please go away..." Her voice is trembling. "Please leave me alone."

That's what starts him moving. He's striding deliberately towards the patio door, and that's when she notices that it's not locked.

She runs, every single movement sending waves of pain up through her foot. She reaches the patio door and just as she grabs the handle to lock it, the stranger pulls the door open, and Johanna along with it. With a shriek, she tumbles past the stranger and lands on the decked floor.

She gets up just in time. The stranger's coming straight for her now. No more mind games. Frantic, she looks around for something—anything—to defend herself with. She nearly trips over one of the potted plants. It's heavy, but with the adrenaline pumping, she manages to pick it up. She hurls it against the stranger, but it misses and hits the house instead. It breaks against the window with an angry thud, and a fractured pattern starts forming in the glass. Johanna gasps when the crack spreads, and seconds later, the entire plate of glass collapses, leaving an opening into the house.

She hears Saga's voice from upstairs.

"Mum...?"

Johanna dodges around the stranger and heads straight for the door.

Saga again. More panicked this time:

"Mum!"

Grabbing the handrail, Johanna half sprints, half pulls herself up the stairs. She runs down the landing and flings open Saga's bedroom door. Her bed is empty.

"Saga?"

Johanna's out of breath.

"Saga, where are you?"

In desperation, she pulls the sheets away, but Saga's not there. She drops down to the floor to check under the bed. Nothing. She opens the wardrobe and rummages through the clothes. Saga's nowhere to be found.

"Saga!?"

A creaking comes from the stairs. It's the sound the third step makes unless you put your foot down all the way to the side. It's the stranger.

Johanna bolts back out onto the landing and calls out again, but in a hushed voice.

"Saga!"

The snug. If Saga's not in her own room, that's where she will be. Only it's straight across from the stairs. Johanna slips into the bathroom and closes the door, leaving only a small crack so she can catch what the stranger does. The world narrows to the thin sliver of the doorway when she lays eyes on him. He just stands there for a moment, before he turns and walks towards Saga's room, following Johanna's bloodied footmarks down the hallway. She's still bleeding, a small amount of blood pooling under her foot. Anywhere she goes, he'll be able to track her, just by following the trail she leaves behind.

As quietly as she can, she opens the cupboard and

pulls out the first aid kit. The lock on the green plastic box clicks as she opens it. Her entire body tenses up. Did he hear that?

Spying out the door crack she sees him going into Saga's room and the terrifying thought that maybe Saga's still in there almost makes her run out after him. But she can't be. She looked everywhere. Instead, Johanna turns her attention to the first aid kit. There's gauze, iodine, scissors, but no goddamn plasters. Then she remembers the last time Saga needed one, which had meant lots of them for a while. She remembers her daughter bumping her knee and how she wasn't satisfied until her entire leg was filled with them. Bereft of plasters, Johanna instead goes for the gauze and starts unrolling it. She only has a few moments before the stranger realises there's nobody in Saga's room and comes back out to look for her again. Then she spots her pink, furry slippers in the corner. Abandoning the gauze, she slips them on her feet and returns to the door crack. He's not there. She opens the door and slinks across the landing to the snug.

"Mum!"

A weight is lifted from her shoulders when she hears Saga's voice. Her daughter appears from behind the sofa and runs towards her.

"I heard a big noise."

Johanna hushes her.

"I know, sweetie. But we need to be real quiet now." She takes her hand. "Follow me, okay?"

"Why? What is it?"

"I'll explain everything, just do as I say. Please."

Saga sobs and takes a firm grip of Johanna's hand. As they head across the landing to the stairs, Johanna spots the stranger just outside Saga's room, watching them.

"Come on, sweetie. We have to hurry." She pushes Saga ahead of her. "Get to the garage!"

She shoots a final glance at the stranger, who's still just standing outside Saga's room. Johanna glimpses the back of her daughter's pyjama top before she turns the corner and disappears from view. When Johanna reaches the bottom of the stairs, Saga is already halfway to the garage.

The next part happens as if in slow motion.

The stranger takes a quick step out from the doorway right behind Saga. Johanna screams. How did he get there so fast? It doesn't make sense.

"Run, Saga!"

The stranger's arm shoots out to grab her daughter, but he fails to get a hold of her pyjama top. Johanna notices Anders's golf clubs by the clothes hanger. The bag tips over when she pulls the driver out. Saga keeps running, obviously terrified. Johanna moves on instinct. She's only played golf once in her life, years before Saga was born. It was Anders who wanted her to tag along, to impress some potential customers. Back when he still found her attractive. She didn't do very well on the golf course back then, but there's no finesse needed for what she's about to do now.

She aims for the stranger's head. When the club strikes, it makes a satisfying, yet at the same time terrifying sound. The stranger staggers backwards. A dark viscous substance that may or may not be blood drips from the head of the club as she pulls it back to go for another swing. This time she aims lower, and the stranger's leg folds backwards when the head of the club connects with his knee. He topples to one side, raising his arm, as if to beg for mercy. But not one sound escapes his mouth. Not a whimper, no scream. He just stares at her with that same creepy smile that he's had since she first spotted him in the middle of the road.

Johanna takes another swing. The club strikes the stranger straight in the face, and finally, he's down. She raises the club again and lets it fall hard, cracking the stranger's skull open. The sound is reminiscent of a boiled egg smashing against a hardwood floor. She draws a stuttering breath, and drops the golf club on the floor, sobbing. Tears are flowing down her face, and she slumps to the floor because her legs can't seem to carry her anymore.

Saga.

She needs her, needs to make sure she's okay. With a feat of determination, Johanna gets back up on her feet and starts to follow her daughter into the garage, when a shiver forms somewhere near the base of her spine. She looks back to see the stranger's arm twitching.

It's impossible to breathe. Is there nothing that will stop him?

Another twitch. The leg this time. She can't stop staring at the broken mess that used to be the stranger's face. It's just spasms, she tries to tell herself. Just the last few neurons firing before the system shuts down for good. She's witnessed it happen at work a few times. A shriek escapes her when the stranger suddenly sits upright.

She stumbles backwards, away from the stranger. Her handbag sits on the small table in the hallway and she grabs it as she passes by, then she runs to the garage to find Saga.

Her daughter sits on the floor in front of the car, with a look of sheer terror on her face, breathing heavily.

"Saga, darling. Are you all right?"

"What's happening, Mum? Why did you make me go here?"

"We have to leave. He was trying to hurt you. I was protecting us."

"What's happened to the car?"

"I told you, Mum had a small accident."

"But the window is all broken."

"I know, honey, just get inside. You can sit in the front seat next to me."

Johanna gets in behind the wheel and pushes the garage door opener. As soon as it's open enough, she puts the car in gear and steps on the gas.

"Slow down, Mum!"

Johanna forces herself to ease her foot off the accelerator.

"Where are we going?"

"I don't know, sweetie."

"Are we going to Dad's?"

"No!" Johanna shakes her head. "I mean, no, we can't."

She goes silent as the car approaches the spot where she ran the stranger down. It was almost twenty-four hours ago, to the minute. She half expects to find him standing there again. Is mentally preparing to hit him again. For good this time. But there's no sign of anyone.

"We should go to a hotel," she says. "That'll be fun, right?"

Saga has her head turned down.

"Who is *he*? You said that *he* was trying to hurt us."

Johanna takes a moment before answering.

"I don't know. A stranger."

She parks the car outside the first roadside hotel she sees. The pair of them must be a sight. Saga in her pyjamas and Johanna in her pink, bloodied, fuzzy slippers. She kind of hopes it looks like they got out of a domestic disturbance situation. That way, she won't have to explain anything.

Turns out the receptionist—a girl no more than eighteen years old—doesn't even seem to notice.

The room on the third floor is small but clean. Saga goes directly to bed, but Johanna goes to stand in front of the window and look out over the carpark.

She hasn't even begun to think of what to do about the state of the house. The smashed window where she threw the flower pot. What is she gonna tell Anders? Is the stranger still there? Should she call the police?

Her train of thought is interrupted when she spots a figure, standing next to her car. It was bound to draw attention, with its dents and cracked wind shield, but then she realises: it's not just some random bystander.

It's the stranger.

Her heartbeat takes off like a coursing dog. She spins around and goes straight for Saga, now sleeping under the covers.

"Come on, honey, we gotta go again."

Saga moans, half asleep.

"No, I don't wanna."

"I'm sorry, sweetie, but we need to keep running."

MY CHRISTMAS HOLIDAY

by John Ajvide Lindqvist

Translated by Marlaine Delargy

Hi my name is Alice and I'm eight years old and I'm going to tell you about my Christmas holiday although I'm mostly going to tell you about Christmas Eve.

My Christmas Eve was weird and not much fun because my daddy died almost a year ago and Ray came along instead.

Ray is stupid and I don't want him to be Mummy's boyfriend.

I don't believe in Father Christmas because last year I realised Daddy was Father Christmas, he'd just put on a Santa suit and a mask.

I knew Daddy was Father Christmas because he was wearing one of those rings you wear when you're married, Mummy used to have one too but she doesn't have it any longer because she sold it when Ray needed money for his car.

I didn't tell Daddy that I knew he was Father Christmas because I thought it was fun to sit on his knee and lean against the cushion that he had under his jacket to give him a big tummy and he talked in a strange way, kind of *hylki pylki* like they do in Finland and it made me laugh.

So when Christmas Eve came along this year, I mean last year, I told Mummy I knew Father Christmas wouldn't come because I knew Daddy was Father Christmas and he was dead.

Then Mummy said that Father Christmas would definitely come and at first, I was a bit scared because I know Daddy is lying in the churchyard, all of him, because he didn't want to be burned, but then I realised Mummy meant that Ray was going to be Father Christmas and I said I didn't want Ray to be Father Christmas.

I didn't want Ray to be Father Christmas because he's nasty and he pinches me hard when Mummy isn't looking and I get bruises and he says that soon he's going to do things to me and if I tell anyone he'll kill me so I haven't even told Mummy.

I'd asked for a Nintendo DS and I knew that Mummy had bought a Nintendo DS because I'd happened to open the cupboard and I said to Mummy that I wanted my Nintendo DS now, I didn't want Ray to give it to me.

Then Mummy got cross and said that I wouldn't be getting a Nintendo DS at all if I didn't want it from Father Christmas and that Father Christmas would be upset if I wasn't pleased to see him.

Late in the evening Ray said he was going to chop some wood and he went outside and I knew he was only saying that so he could put on the Santa suit and the mask although he was very drunk and I hoped he would accidentally chop off his head while he was chopping wood even though he wasn't actually going to chop wood.

Then Mummy and I sat and waited in the kitchen and

Mummy asked if I wanted some sweets but I didn't want any sweets because I couldn't stop thinking about Ray touching me and putting me on his knee and I didn't want him to do that.

Ray was gone for a very long time and the strange thing was that it actually sounded like he was chopping wood even though he was only pretending.

Then there was a knock on the door and Mummy told me to go and open it but I didn't want to so she went instead and I heard her in the hallway saying stupid stuff like oh here comes Father Christmas isn't that nice although she knew it was only Ray, and by the way he stinks.

Then Father Christmas came into the kitchen and he smelled even worse than usual and he didn't say anything probably because he was so drunk and he couldn't remember what he was supposed to say and he almost fell over.

And then he reached out to me but only with one hand because he was holding the sack in his other hand, and it looked really heavy.

I didn't know what to think because his fingers were very fat, kind of like sausages, but on one finger he was wearing the same ring as Daddy used to wear, the kind of ring you wear when you're married although Mummy had sold hers and this ring almost disappeared because his fingers were so fat.

Last year the other reason I realised it was Daddy was because I recognised his eyes in spite of the mask, so I looked at Father Christmas but there was only blackness where the eyes were supposed to be but I wasn't scared because I was sure it was Daddy because he was wearing the same shoes too.

Then Mummy started screaming because she realised Father Christmas was Daddy and he put the sack down on the floor and a lot of stuff ran out, I guess it was blood and the whole rug was red and soaking wet.

And then Father Christmas opened the sack and showed Mummy what was inside and then she fainted and then I looked too and although I'd wanted a Nintendo DS it was still a good present in a way and now I'm not going to write any more because the lesson is over.

Besides, Grandma has promised that I can have my Nintendo DS when the police have finished whatever they're doing in our house.

Alice

CONTRIBUTOR BIOGRAPHIES

Nanna Árnadóttir is an Icelandic journalist, writer, and secondary English teacher with a background in news, culture, and storytelling. Her fiction writing includes the novel *Zombie Iceland*, and short stories such as 'Salt Baby' in the anthology *Trouble the Waters: Tales from the Deep Blue*. Her work as a journalist is published in venues such as *Vogue*, *The Guardian*, and *The Reykjavík Grapevine*.

She says about her story in this anthology: "My work is shaped by my interest in power dynamics. The inspiration behind the story 'You See Me, Don't You?' is that I observe how images from disasters capture my attention when I doomscroll through the news, but as a media consumer I can still just swipe on. It's as if the whole experience is designed to make it easy to look away from other people's pain. I think Nordic horror often explores the unseen costs of survival and isolation in a hostile landscape. My story imagines what happens when a picture on social media does *not* fade but instead traps life inside it. What if a photograph of you actually took something from you, and then also made you relive it?"

Madeleine Bäck is a Swedish author inspired by the mysteries of northern nature and the old folk tales of Gästrikland, where she grew up. She has written several horror books, mainly for children and young adults, blending the uncanny with the everyday. In Sweden she is best known for her folk horror trilogy *Vandrarna* (*The Wanderers*), set in the same shadowed universe as 'Echo', her short story in this anthology. Readers familiar with that world may spot an Easter egg or two woven into this tale. 'Echo' is her first story written in English.

Bäck says: "'Echo' is a visceral, slow-burn horror set on the mist-veiled heights of Kungsberget, where three friends return to seek answers about their missing friend. The mountain answers, but what rises to meet them is something as ancient as time and as hungry as darkness."

Boel Bermann is a praised Swedish author whose dystopian works focus on exploring human darkness. Her debut was the acclaimed novel *Den nya människan* (*The New Human*) in 2013. She has since published four novels, of which the latest is *TÖMD* (*EMPTIED*) from 2024, about a near future where emotions are bought and sold. She has also contributed short stories to several sci-fi and horror anthologies such as *Waiting for the Machines to Fall Asleep* (2015), *Stockholms undergång* (*The Downfall of Stockholm*), *Mörk Framtid* (*Dark Future*), and *13 svarta sagor om superskurkar* (*13 black tales about super villains*), to name a few. Bermann has also contributed to the popular Swedish podcast *Creepypodden* and participated in the SVT TV-series *År 1 Miljon*. Besides her authorship, Bermann currently works at a game company and has a background as a journalist. She's also a member of the writers collective Fruktan.se. She always closes the wardrobe before sleep to keep the monsters from escaping. Find out more about Bermann's work at her webpage: boelbermann.se or on Instagram: @boelbermann

Bermann says about her story in this anthology: "The idea for 'The Storm' came from the kind of super villains that claim to have the intention to save the world, but through their actions cause havoc, destruction, and pain. I combined a bureaucrat with good intentions with the fear of losing a loved one and the horrors of natural disasters and how unprepared our society is for the chaos that ensues."

Steinar Bragi (b. 1975), of Reykjavík, Iceland, is the author of several books of poetry and prose. Debuting as a twenty-three-year-old with the critically acclaimed poetry collection *Svarthol* (*Black Hole*), he later turned to prose with the novel *Konur* (*Women*), a claustrophobic abstraction of the price of being a woman in capitalist society. The book was later nominated for the Nordic Council Literature Prize. Bragi, a nascent master of contemporary horror and sci-fi, was again nominated for the Nordic Council Literature Prize in 2022 with his first science fiction novel, *The Truflunin* (*Disturbance*), which is in development for a TV-series on Amazon Prime. Bragi continues to illuminate the darkest corners of our collective psyche with Lovecraftian detail as he recovers from the Icelandic winter.

Bragi says of his story 'Little Boy': "The story in this collection is probably influenced by the absurdity of growing up in a tree-less, recently constructed Reykjavík suburb—a row of boxes stretching for an infinity across a desert, or so it felt like when I was ten. If that is not horror in itself, then the nightmare was taking walks in the evening and seeing the flashing TVs lighting up people's windows, box after box after box."

Tor Åge Bringsværd was a Norwegian author who wrote both for children and adults. Born in the town of Skien in 1937, he made his literary debut in 1967. He sadly passed away in August 2025, just days after confirming the translation of his story to this anthology. Bringsværd was a major name in Norwegian literature and he was the recipient of several awards as an author and playwright, including the Norwegian Critics Prize for Literature, the Ibsen Prize, and the Arts Council Norway Honorary Award. He was translated into over thirty languages (despite—as he used to say—his name having two impossible Norwegian letters that almost no one outside Norway knows how to pronounce). He lived with his wife in a small village in southern Norway, where a river occasionally flows through their garden. He told us that while there are few fish in the river, there are, on the other hand, ducks and beavers. Beneath a big apple tree at one end of the garden, Bringsværd spent most of the year writing in his own office cabin, complete with a weather pig (Nasse Nøff, a.k.a. Piglet) on the roof and a lively badger family beneath the floor. His life motto was: *coincidences are our friends* (but it could just as easily have been: *whoever keeps both feet on the ground is standing still*).

Aleksander Brun is a Norwegian author who, through his passion of storytelling, creates compelling narratives where everyday life slowly gives way to the strange and supernatural. Originally from Jostedal in the Sogn district, he now lives in Bergen with his wife and daughter. He made his literary debut in 2024 with *Under Huda* (*Under the Skin*), a collection of short and gooseflesh-inducing horror stories that explore the supernatural and the eerie that hide in the seemingly ordinary.

Brun sees the horror genre as a vast and thrilling landscape, enabling readers to explore fear and terror in a controlled environment. True horror, for him, occurs when something once familiar and safe becomes unknown and dangerous. For this anthology, he wrote the story 'Wrecked', which he says is rooted in a personal nightmare tied to reality: the fear of losing someone dear.

Danish author **Mikkel Harris Carlsen**, born in 1974, has written strange and eerie fiction for well over a decade. His second collection of short stories, *Midnatsmuse* (*Midnight's Muse*), from which the story in this anthology originates, was nominated for an award for best Danish horror fiction in 2015.

"This story contains many of my usual preoccupations," he says, "rented rooms, loss of self and integrity, an early to mid-twentieth century setting—writing a plot with a mobile phone in it makes me nauseous—and a sense of ambiguity and uncertainty. Is Mr Schaday, the creepy neighbour of the story, a menace to society or a saviour?"

Carlsen is the recipient of several grants and winner of the Niels Klim Award in 2014 for best science fiction short fiction with a story about the saving and destruction of the Mona Lisa during the end of the world. "In my stories it's usually the end of the world as we know it," the author says. As of late he seems to have succumbed to bibliophilia and writes exclusively novels about book collectors and antiquarians, although the eeriness persists.

* * *

Born in 1957, **Jon Ewo** has worked as both editor, consultant, publisher, and librarian. He is one of Norway's most productive authors and has, since his literary debut in 1986, published over 150 books, mostly within the genres of science fiction, fantasy, horror, and crime, but also nonfiction. Ewo writes for all ages, and his work has been published into nine languages. Ewo has been awarded both in Norway and abroad, including Norway's Ministry of Church and Culture's Literature Prize, the Dutch Zilver Zoen, and the Brage Prize. He's also been nominated for the H.C. Andersen Prize three times and shortlisted for the Astrid Lindgren Memorial Award Prize once. Read more at Ewo's webpage: https://jonewo.net

Ewo has collaborated with fellow authors Arne Svingen and Ingunn Aamodt on the popular horror series *Marg & Bein* (*Marrow & Bones*), with scary stories for middle schoolers, where Ewo so far has contributed with nine. Some of his latest novels for adults are *Hjertet har flere enn fire kamre* (*The Heart Has More Than Four Chambers*) from 2023 and *Sorg er en slu jævel* (*Grief is a Cunning Bastard*) from 2025.

Ewo explains about the background for his story in this anthology: "I once visited an old, shadowy cemetery and learned of the fate of those in the old days who were criminals or had committed suicide. Not welcome in God's fields, they were buried outside the cemetery. It was then that the idea came to me: maybe some people are just so evil that their spark of life may not be extinguished by death, but they live on, and they become strong and dangerous again."

* * *

AR Frederiksen is a Danish author whose short fiction has been accepted most recently by *Cosmic Horror Monthly*, *Shortwave,* and *Haven Spec.* Frederiksen volunteers as a first reader at multiple English-language magazines, reading everything from narrative poetry, short fiction, and flash fiction. Her short story, 'The Drowning Bones' in *Haven Spec* 2023, featured in the official Nebula Reading List. She lives in Denmark with her Minnesotan spouse and angry senior citizen of a chihuahua. Represented by FinePrint Literary Management, Frederiksen can be found online as @ARFrederiksen and at www.arfrederiksen.com

Her story in this anthology is one of the first stories in which Frederiksen realised that while horror is a universal language at heart, it hits the sweet spot when the minimalist traditions of Danish storytelling are combined with the more expressive English language, without anything being lost on either side in the process.

Marko Hautala is a Finnish writer whose novels and short stories feature a unique blend of psychological horror and realism. His work has been translated into eight languages. He has received the Tiiliskivi and Kalevi Jäntti awards and has been nominated for several other awards in his native country. Internationally, his novelette *Pale Toes*, was nominated for the Shirley Jackson Award in 2020.

His story in this anthology is based on a real Finnish call-in radio show from the late 1980s, hosted by the psychologist Pekka Sauri. Hautala says: "Writing the story felt exceptionally creepy and personal, to the point where I still feel a bit uncomfortable thinking about it. I used to listen to the call-in show depicted in the story, and some of the call-ins were quite unsettling. More importantly, that period coincides with a strange experience that still occasionally comes up in conversation with old friends. I won't go into the details, but if I were to believe in demonic possession, that incident would fit the description."

Margrét Helgadóttir is a Norwegian author and anthologist living in Oslo, Norway. Her short fiction appears in many magazines and anthologies, such as *Future Tense Fiction*, *Luna Station Quarterly*, *Girl at the End of the World*, and *Sunspot Jungle*, to name a few. Her debut book—*The Stars Seem So Far Away*—was a finalist in the British Fantasy Awards 2016 and is an apocalyptic road tale set in a far-future Arctic world. Helgadóttir is editor of the anthologies *Winter Tales* (2016) and *Nordic Visions: The Best of Nordic Speculative Fiction* (2023), and the anthology series *Fox Spirit Books of Monsters*, seven volumes published between 2014 and 2020. Three volumes were shortlisted in the British Fantasy Awards as Best Anthology (2016, 2017, and 2018), and Helgadóttir was also awarded with Starburst Magazine's inaugural Brave New Words Award in 2018 for her editorial work on *Pacific Monsters*. Find out more on her website: https://margrethelgadottir.wordpress.com

Rakel Helmsdal is a Faroese author and artist. She has published twenty-nine books (novels, collections of short stories and picture books), as well as short stories, poems, and plays. She describes herself primarily as a storyteller and chooses the medium—texts, plays, poems, pictures, sculptures—depending on what the story requires. She thinks the age of the audience is of little importance and says that most of her stories are just for humans—children, adults, old, and those in between—the only difference is that in stories for children you are not allowed to take away hope.

Several of her books have been translated into other languages. Her all-ages novel *Toran gongur* (*The Sound of Thunder*) was published in Norwegian and Estonian last year. Helmsdal has also been nominated several times for the prestigious prizes Nordic Council Children and Young People's Literature Prize and the Astrid Lindgren Memorial Award. Her novel *Hon, sum róði eftir ælaboganum* (*She Rowed After the Rainbow*) received the West Nordic Council Children and Young People's Literature Prize in 2016. In 2019 the London Symphony Orchestra performed Helmsdal's symphonic fairy-tale *Veiða vind* (*Catch the Wind*) at the Barbican.

Helmsdal's story in this anthology takes place in the same world as in her dystopian novel *Dreymsótt* (*Dream Death*) from 2024, a small, isolated community ravaged by a pandemic called Dream Death. In the novel she describes the horrors of abuse of power, violence, and extreme control, and the almost hopeless attempts at rebellion by some brave women. In the story 'When the Angels Came' a woman gradually realises that rebellion is the only way out of her hell.

Pasi Ilmari Jääskeläinen is a Finnish author who is renowned for breaking genre boundaries and dark humour. His debut novel *The Rabbit Back Literature Society* from 2013 (originally published in Finnish in 2006) is a mix of the realistic and fantastic. Jääskeläinen has twice won the Kuvastaja Fantasy Prize given by

Finland's Tolkien Society and he has been awarded four times the Atorox Award for Fantasy. Several of his works are translated into English, including the novella *Where the Trains Turn* for Tor.com, a World Fantasy Best Novella nominee.

Jääskeläinen says about his story in this anthology: "I originally wrote this story for an anthology of modern versions of classic short stories. I was given Edgar Allan Poe's 'The Masque of the Red Death' as a starting point. It's about a fraudulence of memory: what if I were, without realising it, a kind of a monster myself—guilty of some unforgivable act locked away beyond the reach of memory, only to have it return to haunt me...

"To earn my bread, I teach Finnish language and literature to high school students, but writing books is my passion. My stories, though rooted in realism, often contain elements of horror and ghosts that linger between the lines. As a child, I learned that vampires and zombies don't exist—but one can never be entirely sure about ghosts, especially not at midnight, when you're left alone in the dark, surrounded by strange sounds and shifting dark memories."

Hildur Knútsdóttir was born in Reykjavík, Iceland. She writes fiction for both adults and teenagers, as well as plays, screenplays, and short fiction. Knútsdóttir is known for her evocative fantastical fiction and spine-chilling horror. Her horror novella *The Night Guest* was chosen as one of the best thrillers of 2024 by *The New York Times*. Knútsdóttir and Mary Robinette Kowal were shortlisted to the 2025 World Fantasy Award for *The Night Guest* audiobook. Her work has received various nominations and awards, including The Dublin Literary Award, The Icelandic Women's Literary Prize, The Icelandic Literature Prize, The Reykjavík Children's Literature Prize for best original work, and The Icelandic Bookseller's Prize. Knútsdóttir's youth novel *Hrím* was nominated for the 2024 Nordic Council Children and Young People's Literature Prize. Her story in this anthology, 'The Shape of Stones', was a 2026 Locus Award Top Ten Finalist.

Gertrud-Marie Kreutzmann is a twenty-seven-year-old teacher and writer from Greenland. She grew up in Greenland's second-largest town, with a population of around six thousand inhabitants. After completing her teaching degree in 2025, she moved to a small community in Northeast Greenland with fewer than four hundred residents. Kreutzmann is a new writer but she has always had a passion for storytelling. The story in this anthology is her second short story accepted for publishing, both in the horror genre. She debuted with the short story 'Chase You', a psychological horror tale exploring the transition from childhood to adulthood. The story was featured in *Allatta! 4.0*, an anthology based on a writing contest for young adults in Greenland.

Her contribution to this anthology explores the presence of a *Qivittoq*, a hermit living in the Greenlandic wilderness. In Greenlandic folklore, qivittoqs can be both kind and cruel, and in this story, you meet one which is filled with anger towards people and society.

John Ajvide Lindqvist is a Swedish author with a background as both a magician and a stand-up-comedian.

Today he's a well-known author with several acclaimed novels and short stories, several within horror and fantasy. His debut novel was *Låt den rätte komma in* (*Let the Right One In*), in 2004, and his works include novel titles such as *Hanteringen av odöda* (*Handling the Undead*), *Människohamn* (*Harbour*), *Lilla stjärna* (*Little Star*), and also the short story collection *Pappersväggar* (*Let the Old Dreams Die*). 'Border', one of the short stories in this collection, was made into a feature film in 2019. Lindqvist was also a writer for the television series *Reuter & Skoog* (1999) and wrote the screenplays for Swedish Television's drama series *Kommissionen* (2005) and for the film *Let the Right One In*, based on his novel. His work has been awarded several times, especially in connection with the script for the film *Let the Right One In*, but also the Selma Lagerlöf Prize. His work has also been nominated to awards such as Tiptree, Hugo, BFA, and Stoker. Lindqvist is married to the author Mia Ajvide and lives in the archipelago of Roslagen, Sweden. Find out more on his website: www.johnajvidelindqvist.com

Sólrún Michelsen is a Faroese writer who writes both for children and adults. She has written numerous novels, short stories, fantasy, poems, and hymns. Several of the books have been translated into other languages. Michelsen has received several awards, including the Faroese Literature Prize in 2008. In 2004 she was nominated for the West Nordic Council's Children and Youth Literature Prize for the poem collection *Loppugras* (*Wolfgrass*). In 2015 she was nominated for the Nordic Council Literature Prize for the novel *Hinumegin er mars* (published in English in 2023 by Francis Boutle

Publishers, with the title *On the Other Side is March*). In 2026, she is a nominee for the Nordic Council Children and Young People's Literature Prize, for the book *Sjókæti (A–OY)*, illustrated by Annika Øyrabø.

Michelsen says she has always loved scary stories: "Even as a child with too much imagination. I like the ones that slowly creep up on you, or that you don't quite understand what's going on."

Pivinnguaq Mørch was born in Upernavik, North-West Greenland, in 1993. He holds a graduate degree in cultural and social history from the University of Greenland, and is currently teaching social studies and Kalaallisut, the Greenlandic language, at the Greenland Business School. Mørch is part of a new wave of young Greenlandic writers with thought-provoking and socially critical works. In 2013 he won the first Greenlandic Poetry Slam. In 2015, selected poems and stories by Mørch were published in the collection *Arpaatit qaqortut* (*The White Sneakers*), later shortlisted for the Nordic Council Literature Prize (2019). His short stories also feature in the anthologies *Ung i Grønland – ung i verden* (2013) and *Himlen over Kina* (2021). In honour of his father's (Hendrik Mørch) literary work, Mørch has also written several stories that reflect on his father's poems. These stories and poems are collected in the anthology *Kinaassuseq* (2018). Later works include the children's book *Qaammassuup oqaluttuaa* (*The Moon's Tale*) from 2020.

In Mørch's story in this anthology we meet a shaman and a tupilak. A tupilak is a creature in Inuit/Kalaallit mythology made up of animal parts, even human features. A shaman may create a tupilak for the sole purpose of killing someone they don't like. If the tupilak fails, it will eventually return to its creator and kill him. Mørch says that regret is a major theme, as the shaman ultimately regrets creating a tupilak, especially a tupilak with evil intentions.

Martin Schjönning (b. 1982) is a Danish author who lives in a haunted house by the forest, with his significant others and a menagerie of pets. After a few decades in fringe publishing and sex toy marketing, he now works in a bookshop and writes the occasional horror story. Schjönning debuted in 2011 with the short story 'Anonymt Bidrag' ('Anonymous Contribution') in the anthology *Velkommen til Dybet* (*Welcome to the Pit*), edited by Mathias Clasen. His work has since featured in several horror collections. Schjönning's first novella, *Deroute*, was published in 2015, followed by his first full-length novel, *Afsind* (*Out of Mind*), in 2016. His latest book, *En Stormnat* (*A Storm Night*), a Faustian gothic tale, was published in 2023.

'Neither Heaven nor Hell', his story in this anthology, is his first written work published outside of Denmark. Schjönning says: "We have a strong literary tradition of social realism in Denmark, and I believe it's essential for art to ask uncomfortable questions. I've written about ghosts and homelessness, vampires, and drug addiction, I'm working on a classical possession-story about cultural estrangement and animal cruelty. Righteous indignation is what drives me.

"In Danish folklore, the will-o-wisp—who we would call 'lygtemanden' (the lantern man)—is often the damned revenant of a 'skelflytter', a 'boundary-mover' who illicitly moved markers of ownership during the night to cheat neighbours out of their land. In a poor agrarian society like nineteenth-century Denmark, this was truly a cardinal sin. It seemed obvious to me, that the modern lygtemand is a corrupt landlord and property developer, being punished for his crimes, but also taking on the role of a tempter-punisher himself, luring new victims to their deaths, similar to how he enticed hapless tenants in life. My story is also about how nature, in its most primeval form, the bog, rightfully retaliates against humanity, and the self-inflicted curse of shame we all too often put on each other and particularly on ourselves if our sexuality or relationship form does not fit the society's norms."

Johanna Sinisalo is a Finnish author and screenwriter who has won among others the Finlandia Prize and the James Tiptree, Jr. Award. Sinisalo has been called "the queen of Finnish speculative fiction". Much of her work deals with societal topics, such as equality and environmental issues. Sinisalo's writing has been translated into around twenty languages. Four of her novels have been translated into English, all praised by readers and critics alike: the Tiptree-winner *Not Before Sundown* (U.S. edition *Troll – A Love Story*), *Birdbrain*, *The Blood of Angels*, and *The Core of the Sun*, which made the Tiptree Honor List. Sinisalo's novelette *Baby Doll* was shortlisted for the Theodore Sturgeon Memorial Award in 2008 and the Nebula in 2009. You can find several of Sinisalo's short stories in English in many anthologies such as *Year's Best Weird Fiction, Volume Four* (2017), and she has also edited

The Dedalus Book of Finnish Fantasy, an anthology of Finnish speculative fiction. As a screenwriter, Sinisalo's most known work is the original story for the 2012 cult SF comedy movie *Iron Sky*.

The author says about her story in this anthology: "I have always flirted with horror in my writing. I'm delighted if my readers feel disturbed in some way and start to see unknown qualities in everyday surroundings. For me, horror basically means losing control. Something scary happens, and you are not able to fight the threat with ordinary means. In my story 'The Joys of the Table' I have tried to play with the idea of how one never really knows who is witnessing and judging what they do in private."

Markus Sköld is a Swedish author fascinated by what hides in the dark, both outside and within us. He's a novelist, most recently of the terrifying haunted house story *Andeviskningar* (*Spirit Whispers*) from 2025. He also writes short stories and has worked as a narrative designer for video games. You can find out more about him at his website: markusskold.se

He says about his story in this anthology: "The initial idea for 'Hit and Run' came from the idea of someone scrubbing blood off their car. What if they got away with it? Nobody knows, except the one they killed… and was this person even human to begin with? Sometimes, not knowing what's real and what's not is the most terrifying thing of all."

CONTRIBUTORS' COPYRIGHT NOTICES